SECRETS OF SEA PINES

The Battle for Hilton Head Island's Treasure

Robert J. Perreault

Charleston, SC
www.PalmettoPublishing.com

First Edition

Hardcover ISBN: 979-8-8229-0559-7
Paperback ISBN: 979-8-8229-0560-3
eBook ISBN: 979-8-8229-0561-0

Also, by International Best-Selling Author:
Robert J. Perreault

Charles & Mary Gramer Series
Secrets of Sea Pines
Robber's Row
Spanish Wells

Lacie Webb Series
The Disney Riddles
Operation Disney
Hapless Souls

To my Mom.
We shared a love for mystery and thriller novels.
I believe she told me to write this book and helped me to do so.
I also think that she would have enjoyed reading it if she was still with us.
RIP Mar.

Disclaimer

1

1947

ATLANTA, GEORGIA

Atlanta in August was not the time or place that Joseph Gramer wanted to be. He lived in a small town called Hinesville, about one hundred miles away. Although the Georgia sun was just as intense in Hinesville, dozens of palmetto trees in his yard provided a blanket of shade for his home. His back porch overlooked a large lake. If the wind was right, he and his wife Pearl spent hours in the shade with a crisp breeze coming in from the water. If it got too hot, he simply jumped in.

Joseph was a successful man at fifty years old and dressed the part. His face was prematurely wrinkled from a lifetime of stress that made him look closer to sixty, but he still had an aura of vigor about him. He was tall, lean, and in perfect physical condition. There was just enough gray hair left on his head for the need of a comb.

Women found him attractive, and men respected him. After all, everyone in town knew that he had fought in two wars—The First and Second World Wars. To be in active duty for two wars and come home without a scratch was something to be commended, and commended he

1

was. He retired from the military as Lieutenant General and was soon elected mayor of Hinesville.

During his military career, he'd found the time to amass a small fortune in lumber. Thirty years ago, he'd started as a lumber hauler for a local company and had eventually opened his own lumber mill that he now ran with his son, Charles.

Again… Why did I have to come to Atlanta in August? Hinesville is so much better, he thought while wiping sweat from his brow. He was here for one reason and one reason only: his wife. Her fiftieth birthday was fast approaching, and he wanted to get her something extra special. Nothing at the local gift shop rose to the standards of "special enough" for his loving Pearl. He had spent weeks combing through catalogs and newspapers, searching for that one thing that would show her just how much he loved her. Finally, one day, while walking in downtown Hinesville, he stopped at a news rack to pick up a copy of the Atlanta Gazette. He liked to read this paper at least once a week to keep abreast of national and world news. The Hinesville paper was fine for local news and events, but Joseph found the need for a broader scope of coverage.

A couple of weeks back, while sitting on a park bench across from the local Presbyterian Church in Hinesville, he began his Saturday morning ritual. He sipped his black coffee from the Lighthouse Café and read his newspaper. It was his way of escaping from a long week of work and spending some quality time with himself. This day was one of those rare summer days in Georgia that everyone prayed for. There was an occasional white, fluffy cloud floating through the bright blue sky, little humidity, and a pleasant breeze. This did not go unnoticed. Joseph could sit there all day, but Pearl was waiting for him on their back porch with a glass of sweet tea and maybe a biscuit with her homemade jam. He wouldn't miss that for the world.

While browsing through the newspaper, he came across an advertisement for an upcoming auction in Atlanta. The only auctions he had ever attended were cattle auctions when he was growing up. He chuckled, thinking about how much he'd enjoyed listening to the auctioneer talk so quickly. He could not understand a word the man was saying, but the whole atmosphere had been so exciting. Part of him yearned for the naivety he'd had as a child. Life was good as an adult, but something about a child's innocence appealed to him.

This auction was to be held in August and contained items from New England's colonial period.

"Perfect," he said aloud to no one in particular. Pearl loved the colonial period. She would read book after book about the Boston Tea Party, Paul Revere, Plymouth Plantation, and other related topics. What interested her most of all were the Salem Witch Trials. She would read books and pamphlets about the subject and then share all her learnings with him. He found it spooky, so he did not share the same passion she had for the topic, but he was always willing to listen.

Maybe I can buy something at this auction of real value that she will treasure forever. To do so, he had to think of a way to keep it a secret. He could not just tell her he was going to Atlanta to buy her a gift. It needed to be a surprise. *Simple.* He would tell her he had to go to Atlanta for business, which he occasionally did and would come home with a thoughtful gift for his wife of almost thirty years.

****

As he walked the Atlanta streets, the humidity was unbearable. Droplets of sweat poured relentlessly down his face as he walked to the auction. It was like someone opened the floodgates to a dam. He wanted to take off his jacket, but there were two problems. One, it would be improper, and two, he could only imagine what his undershirt looked like. A short-sleeved shirt wouldn't even help on a day like this. He imagined his blue oxford shirt looked like he had just taken a dip in his backyard oasis.

After looking at his watch, the leather band seemingly glued to his wrist, Joseph realized that the auction started in only twenty minutes. Since he was a few blocks away from the auction house, a huge smile came across his face. He knew all the items to be auctioned off since a list of them had been mailed to his office. He had studied the items for a week, so he would be ready to bid on the ones he knew Pearl would love. That was one thing he'd learned from his military career: Be prepared.

While spending hours looking over the items, one particular stood out: a document written by Cotton Mather. Mather was a New England Puritan clergyman and writer in the sixteenth and seventeenth centuries who had been a prominent figure in the Salem Witch Trials. He wrote hundreds of pamphlets and books, but there was only one that Joseph wanted—*On Witchcraft*. It was a first edition from the library of a man from Plymouth, Massachusetts. It was to be auctioned today. If Joseph could bring this book home to his darling Pearl, he knew he would get sweet tea and biscuits every day until he died. He laughed to himself just thinking about it.

The auction house was on the first floor of a three-story brick townhouse on a street lined with gas light posts and cobblestone sidewalks. The first thing he thought of when he walked up the stairs of the building was that it reminded him of Boston, where he and Pearl vacationed a few years back to tour the historical sights. It was one of Pearl's favorite vacations ever. They'd walked the Freedom Trail, seen the Boston Tea Party, and toured Harvard Yard. She still talked about it to this day. As he entered the auction house, the fans blew the oven-like heat from one place to another. All they accomplished was to help dry the sweat from his face.

"Good afternoon," said a beautiful young lady with "Gretchen" handwritten on her name tag.

"Good afternoon, Gretchen," replied Joseph. "I'm here to register for today's auction."

"Simply fill out your name and address in this book, and I will provide you with an auction paddle. Once you are interested in an item, all you have to do is raise the paddle to bid," she explained with an overly eager smile.

He did as he was told and sat next to an old couple sitting in the front row. Dozens of people filled the tight rows of seats. The crowd and perceived demand for the auctioned items did not frighten Joseph since he'd already decided that he was taking home the Mather book regardless of what it cost him. After all, he had the money. He lived a frugal lifestyle and never splurged on anything for himself. Pearl was another story. He did not hesitate to spend whatever was necessary to make her happy, and today was just the day for that.

As the auction started, adrenaline surged through him more than anything. His pulse was racing, but he'd learned in the Army as a skilled rifle sniper that to complete a critical mission, one had to keep calm no matter the situation. Like a Hall of Fame baseball player at the plate with two outs in the ninth inning of a tied ballgame, nerves and excitement meant nothing to him. He had a job to do, and, by God, he would see it done.

He watched as the first dozen or so items went up for auction. Some of them did not sell. Others sold for reasonable amounts that he would be glad to pay for his intended purchase. When Cotton Mather's book came up, they started the bidding at ten dollars. Joseph quickly raised his paddle for the first offer. The old man sitting beside him raised his paddle when the bid went to twenty.

Once the old man bid, the others began to hesitate. This was no surprise to Joseph; the old man had bid on several items and won three of them already. It was obvious that the guy had money and was not afraid to spend it. Each time the old man won an item, Joseph congratulated him. The old man and his wife had been gracious in returning his gestures.

When the auctioneer asked for thirty, Joseph duly raised his paddle. This kept up in one of the tensest battles of the day until Joseph finally outbid the old man with a final bid of seventy-five dollars. He was thrilled with his win, even if it was off-putting that the old man did not congratulate him on it.

Not so gracious now. But who cares?

He'd just gotten Pearl the best fiftieth birthday present he could think of. It was time to collect his book and get out of this hellhole. Unfortunately, he had to sit and wait another hour or two until the auction was complete so he could pay and collect his prize. During that time, he sat and wondered what the look on her face would be like when she unwrapped her gift. That made the time go by much faster than he'd anticipated.

2

When Joseph arrived home to Hinesville, he went directly to his office at the lumber yard. He could not hide the book from his wife if she were at home when he arrived. The lumber yard buzzed that day as it did six days a week. Joseph's office was on the second floor of an industrial building. He had built it ten years earlier to support an increase in business. It was a ten thousand square foot, two-story metal building. The inside consisted of saws and seemingly endless conveyor belts moving the wood from station to station. The second floor consisted of a long, metal balcony that led to the executive offices, including his and his son Charles.

Joseph walked up the exposed steel stairwell to the second-floor balcony, where he overlooked his men at work. When he entered his office, he first called his son, who was in his office just a few doors down.

"Are you busy?" he asked his son with boyish enthusiasm. "I have something I want to show you."

Charles replied quickly, "I'll come at once."

As Charles made his way down the hallway, Joseph opened his leather briefcase and took out the book. His handsome twenty-six-year-old son knew what his father was up to since he was the only person Joseph had shared his plans regarding the auction.

The clean-shaven Charles entered the office and walked to the desk where he was sitting. "Let's see it," he said anxiously. On demand, his father handed him the book. Charles brushed his fine blond hair out of his eyes as he looked down at it. As he straightened the black tie that complimented his beige pants, white shirt, and sports coat, he thumbed the book's old and delicate spine.

"Wow, this really is from the 1600s," said Charles without taking his eyes off the book. "Mother is going to love this. I know how much she loves reading about the Salem Witch Trials." He started flipping through the pages, admiring the workmanship when he asked, "Did you read any of the pages during your trip back?"

His father replied, "No. I just kept it in my briefcase. This is the first time I have taken it out."

Turning page by page, Charles observed, "It's exquisite. I don't think I have ever seen anything so old."

As he was talking, Charles a folded paper flittered out. His first thought was that it was a bookmark. He laughed to himself, finding it funny that colonists may have used bookmarks too. Then again, even colonists weren't likely to read a book cover to cover, so he supposed the need for bookmarks in the 1600s was a real thing.

"Look at this," he declared. Charles took out the piece of paper carefully and showed it to Joseph. It was a piece of paper that had been stained yellow over the years and was equivalent in size to a receipt you'd get at the local drug or grocery store. It was frayed around the edges, which was not surprising, as it was likely over three hundred years old.

"What is it?" Joseph muttered. "Is it some kind of a bookmark?" He flipped it over to reveal some handwriting and showed it to Charles. It was hard to read because it was written in colonial-style cursive. It almost looked like calligraphy.

"What does it say?" inquired Charles.

His father replied, "It's difficult to read, but I think it's a receipt." It reads:

Plymouth, 1662

On the 16th day of February in the 1662 year of our Lord, Plymouth Savings Bank acknowledges that Samuel Goldsmith obtained and paid for security box number 17. Plymouth Savings Bank promises to hold the box and the items therewith for a period of five years or until the client wishes to retrieve said items. Signed, Steven Rands, bank manager.

Joseph placed the piece of paper on his desk and looked at his son. "What do you make of this?"

"It does appear to be a receipt of some sort. Maybe for a bank account?" Charles rotated the paper so he could read it as well. "Yes. It is definitely a receipt," he answered while squinting as if doing so would make it easier to read.

"Funny. This little piece of paper may be just as valuable as the book. I'm guessing whoever owned this book was unaware that it was in there." Charles could not take his eyes off it. The paper was now more intriguing than the book.

Charles looked up at his father. "Would you mind if I took this and did some research? I find this simply fascinating."

"What are you going to do with it?" Joseph asked.

"I'm not sure, but my first step will be to learn about Plymouth Savings Bank and see if I can find out anything about this Goldsmith fellow."

As they looked intently into each other's eyes, Joseph knew his son was plotting an adventure in his mind. Charles, from a noticeably early age, had been very inquisitive. He always wanted to know how something worked or why something happened. If his parents could not give him the answer he was looking for, he would inevitably find it out himself. As a result, the study of law was a perfect match for his personality.

Joseph grinned and snickered at his son, "Charles, the detective. Consider this a gift from me. The gift of knowledge, wisdom, and intrigue." He grinned. "Just be sure to keep me apprised of your findings." He then handed Charles the receipt, and he turned to leave the office. As he was about to close the door, his father asked, "Do you really think it will lead to anything?"

He turned and grinned. "Whether or not it does is irrelevant. I find more joy in the pursuit than the prize."

Charles closed the door behind him and hurried to his office. He already knew his first move.

3

1662

HILTON HEAD ISLAND, SOUTH CAROLINA

Two men traversed the maze of pine trees for hours until the tree cover parted and gave way to moonlight and stars. The Atlantic Ocean glinted in the distance. They continued their slow pace over terrain, which was unlike anything they were used to, tripping and stumbling over low-growing plants.

It was evening. The air remained thick with low country humidity. It had been eerily quiet throughout the men's journey. The only sound that interrupted the silence of the night was the crunch of broken branches under their feet and crashing waves on the beach in the distance.

Soaked with sweat and thoroughly exhausted, they had been walking through the dense forest for what felt like days. Such was the price for carrying a heavy chest full of gold, silver, and fine jewelry. Jingling with each step, the chest seemed to become heavier and heavier with the weight of the treasure. They were just yards away from their destination but needed to trudge a little further to find the perfect place to bury the treasure. As they approached a stream, the men lay the chest down to take a slight break.

"Captain," said the first mate. "Let us just bury it here. This is as good of a place as any."

Equally tired, the captain replied, pointing to the beach while trying to catch his breath, "We simply need to cross this stream. The burial spot is just ahead."

They had finally reached the southernmost part of the island. Neither man knew where they were going. They were not familiar with the layout of the land. How could they? They lived in Plymouth, Massachusetts, over one thousand miles away. They were part of the Massachusetts Bay Colony created by British Colonialists who had left England in search of religious freedom. The colony's leaders had commissioned Captain William Hilton, an experienced and well-respected mariner, to sail his ship south to explore other regions of the country that could be colonized.

As an incentive for finding a new colony, Hilton was given the treasure they were carrying. He could easily have left it at home, but someone might steal it. In recent months, Plymouth had been victim to thieves breaking into people's homes and taking valuables. It would not be a far stretch for criminals to realize that Hilton was paid handsomely for his bravery, so there was no way he would take the chance of it being gone when he returned.

Hilton was in his mid-forties. His long ponytail of light brown hair reached halfway down his back. He always tried to keep his facial hair in check, but since they had been at sea for over fourteen days, his beard was growing nicely. His career as a mariner had brought him up and down the eastern seaboard several times, but this was his toughest voyage yet. Two weeks earlier, he'd organized a crew of ten men for the voyage, including the man next to him, Samuel Goldsmith. Hilton had far more seafaring experience than the other men, but each of them was a proven mariner in his own right. Their journey had been arduous. Many times, the boat nearly capsized because of the rough seas. Only his skill and experience had kept his team alive and his treasure from sinking to the bottom of the ocean.

During the three days they were on the island he called "The Carolinas" after his deceased wife of eighteen years, they had seen no sign of life and found no evidence of any habitation even though the island was fruitful, full of vegetation, rivers, streams, and wildlife. It would be a perfect place to charter a new colony. He just needed to get his crew back home after burying the chest. The treasure would help him start a new life in The Carolinas when he returned with many other folks from Plymouth who would help him create a new colony in such a lovely place.

"Lift!" The two men struggled to raise the chest one last time. Hilton was much smaller than Goldsmith, so he grimaced from the weight of the treasure each time he lifted it. Goldsmith was the first to step into the stream. The lukewarm water covered his already soaked boot as he plunged his leg in shin deep.

"We're almost there," Hilton reassured him. "See those pine trees by the sea? That is where we shall bury the chest."

Goldsmith was entirely in the water when Hilton took his first step into the stream. When he did, a school of fish swam by with help from the stream's current. He wished he'd brought a net to catch some and bring them back to his crew for a feast later that day.

Unfortunately, something else also wanted to eat the fish, but instead, it turned its eyes to another prize. There was a small alligator swimming down current with only its eyes above water. Hilton never saw it coming. The alligator leaped out of the water, opened its mouth full of razor-sharp teeth, and latched onto Hilton's left arm. He screamed in agony as it

13

clinched down on his forearm. He dropped the chest, grabbed his left hand in the gator's mouth, and tried to shake it off him. Luckily for him, it was not a full-grown gator. If so, it would have performed a death roll sending him under the water with little chance of survival. He swung the small gator back and forth, but it would not release its grip. Without a doubt, his dream of starting a lucrative life on this beautiful island was about to be cut short by one of its meanest creatures.

The gator's one possible weakness became evident as the pain increased in proportion to the amount of blood lost. He dug his index finger into the beast's eye with his right hand. He gouged deep enough that he popped the eye out of the socket. As it dangled from bloody ligaments, the alligator released its grip and scampered away.

Hilton fell into the stream's bed and crawled up the bank to escape. His hopes of the beast being satisfied were overhasty. One eye stared back at him, ready to attack again. Just as the creature approached, Samuel Goldsmith came from behind and swung a large tree branch at the gator's snout. The branch broke in half and thudded with the contact. The beast scurried down the stream in obvious pain. The attack was over.

"Are you okay, Captain?" asked a shaken Goldsmith, who saw substantial amounts of blood pouring out of his arm.

Hilton staggered out of the stream holding his bloody arm while screaming in pain. He fell to the ground and, with a trembling voice, said, "I need an article of clothing to stem the bleeding. Please give me something."

Goldsmith ran to his friend and removed a scarf from his neck. He wrapped it around Hilton's bicep and tied it tightly. "The wound is severe, Captain. We must return to the ship immediately to properly care for it."

Hilton lay on the ground and pointed to the south, where the forest opened to reveal the Atlantic Ocean. In the distance, the hard-packed sand of the beach was unencumbered by the tree canopies overhead. The soothing sound of the waves crashing against the shore was inviting.

"I need to rest and keep pressure on my wound to lessen the bleeding. Drag the chest underneath those sea pines and bury it yonder," Hilton said through gritted teeth.

Hilton pointed to a group of ten large pine trees isolated from the others lining the beach. The small cluster was unique from the others that lined the coast. He could find this spot again when he returned. It would be the perfect hiding place.

It took a while for Goldsmith to drag the chest to its ultimate resting place. He dug a hole while Hilton watched, falling in and out of consciousness. When Goldsmith finished digging, he dropped the chest in the hole and filled it with dirt. When he covered up the hole, he returned to his friend, who had garnered enough strength to sit up.

"Will you be able to walk back to the ship, Captain?" Goldsmith asked with a concerned look on his face.

"I do not have a choice, Samuel," Hilton replied while struggling to stand up. "I must return home. Our colony back in Massachusetts will consider me a hero for finding a place like this: A place that will spare us from the cold winters that cause so many of us to die."

Goldsmith's chest swelled with pride over his friend's strength and will to survive. He put his hand on Hilton's good shoulder to motivate him and proclaimed, "They will be so joyful, Captain. If truth be told, I will propose they name this island after you. I suggest they call it Hilton's Island."

4

The hike back to the ship took much longer than getting to the island's south side. Hilton gradually lost energy as the scarf around his arm grew darker shades of red. When they reached the ship, the crew was getting ready for bed. A few of them noticed the condition of their captain, so they carried him to his quarters. Fortunately for Hilton, as he required on each of his voyages, at least one crew member had the medical experience to manage illness or injury. In no time at all, his bloody scarf was removed and replaced with a proper bandage.

The extent of his injury was severe enough to warrant the crew to return home to Massachusetts immediately. The plan was to stay a couple more days, continuing to explore the island, but the wound could get infected if Hilton did not get proper medical treatment soon. Talk of amputation of the arm and even death was whispered among the crew during the journey home.

The trip back was more dangerous than it had been searching for The Carolinas. The main reasons were that the captain was stricken to his quarters with his injury and that the further north they traveled, the rougher the seas got. Temperatures soon plummeted, forcing the crew to find warmer clothing and leaving Hilton shivering in his bed. Each day grew colder and colder. On the last evening before arriving in Plymouth, Hilton's condition worsened. Fever set in as infection spread through the wound into his bloodstream. He might not survive the night, but Hilton had such a sense of duty to his colony that survival was his only choice.

After returning home, Hilton's health continued to decline. The town's doctor tried to stave off the infection, but the damage had already been done.

The infection had gotten so bad that it was too late to amputate the arm. As a result, Hilton found himself bedridden, with his strength weakening daily. He was strong enough, however, to provide the colony's leaders with all the details of their trip. His discovery led them to decide that, in the spring, they would commission another crew to The Carolinas to start the new charter. They celebrated Hilton as a true hero.

After another few days of bedrest, he still couldn't break the fever. The infection and near-death experience now frightened the feeble man so much that he drafted his last will and testament. He was not a wealthy man, but the treasure bestowed upon him for finding The Carolinas would provide for his son Andrew, his only living relative since his wife had passed away a few years before. He had often considered remarrying, but his love for the sea had prevented him from doing so.

While sitting in his bed and drafting his will, he reckoned back to why The Carolinas charter would be so valuable. Surely, if not for the alligator attack, he and his fellow townsman would soon be hunting the ample supply of deer, tending to the lush gardens, and drinking from the clear streams that wove across the landscape. Instead, he spent his last days shivering in his bed overlooking Plymouth Bay, frozen from the harsh New England winter.

He was able to draft his will and also drew a map showing where he'd buried the treasure. Unfortunately, the next day he took a turn for the worse. Since returning, he had not gotten out of bed and struggled to even eat and drink. He was not the most intelligent man in the colony, but he didn't have to be intelligent to sense death was approaching. With his last bit of strength, Hilton called his seventeen-year-old son Andrew into the room together with his dear friend Samuel Goldsmith.

After saying his last words to Goldsmith, he asked him to leave the room so he could speak to his son in private.

"Andrew," his voice trembled. "In the top drawer of my desk is my last will and testament. Amongst other things, I have left you an item of immense importance. On my voyage to The Carolinas, I buried a chest full of gold and silver near a pristine beach on the most beautiful island. When the colony embarks on its next journey to the new charter, join the crew and start a new life on that island. The chest will provide the riches you deserve, and the island will grant you the resources to live a prosperous life."

While Hilton labored to give his son details regarding the buried treasure and the riches to be bestowed upon him once he found it, Goldsmith lingered in the other room with the door cracked, listening to every word. His blood boiled at Hilton's intentions for the treasure.

While Goldsmith helped his friend carry the treasure across the island that fateful night, he assumed he would share the wealth with him when they returned to the island. It wasn't fair for Hilton to keep it for himself. After all, he was his first mate, and it was commonplace for the ship captain to share his earnings with his closest men.

Goldsmith wasn't just his first mate, however. He was his best friend, and someone William Hilton had just betrayed. After all, he shivered like him during the wintry nights of the voyage. When they ran out of food, they both went hungry. Hilton wasn't the only one who prayed and feared for their safe passage home. The entire crew risked their lives for the voyage.

He whispered to himself, "Something has to be done. A treasure chest full of gold and silver does not deserve to be given to Hilton's undeserving son. It belongs to me."

Hilton was growing tired, but his voice remained calm when he shared with his son, "It is time for me to sleep. Leave me now and retrieve my will. Secure it in the safest of places as it will provide you with the coordinates of where the treasure is buried and a map to help guide your way. Remember, riches make even the best men do things that commoners would never dream of. Trust no one. For what I am giving you is a new life."

Andrew kissed his father on the forehead and sadly left the room. He had already lost his mother. This might be the last time he saw his father alive. Still, he couldn't help the energy from galvanizing his limbs over his new lot in life. His father always provided well for him and taught him to be a self-sufficient fisherman, but this gift was more than he could ever have imagined.

Hilton's son went to his desk as directed. Unfortunately, he found nothing in the top drawer when he opened it. He then foraged through the other drawers, but there was nothing besides some pamphlets and books. He went back into the bedroom to ask his father for guidance. Maybe he had forgotten where he'd placed the will.

Unfortunately, he was too late. William Hilton had taken his last breath.

That was also right about when Samuel Goldsmith unforgivingly raced out of Hilton's house with his friend's will and a treasure map tucked into his coat pocket.

5

William Hilton's funeral was well attended by the residents of Plymouth. They held it in a small church overlooking Plymouth Bay. The place was sentimental to Hilton since he and his wife had been married there eighteen years prior. It was a simple white building made of wood. There was no stained glass found in large European cathedrals, but large windows wrapped around each side. They packed the two aisles of pews with people sitting shoulder to shoulder. It was not big enough to fit everyone who wanted to attend the service, so many stood outside in the cold to pay their respects. There was not a single person in any of the local shops that day. All came to mourn the heralded mariner.

Shortly after saying goodbye to his dear friend, Goldsmith walked down Ocean Street with his grown son, Lawrence, to meet with the local banker. It had been a little over a week since he'd stolen Hilton's will and, during that time, Andrew Hilton had been asking everyone in town if they had seen it. No one had, but Goldsmith it was enough to make Goldsmith's hair on the back of his neck stand up. He didn't know the punishment for stealing another man's last will and testament, but the local constable would not take the theft lightly.

He needed a safe place to hide it. Recently, he'd heard that the local bank had begun storing valuable items for customers at a minimal cost. It would be a perfect place to store the will. Even though Plymouth was a God-fearing town, it had become a victim of burglaries. Folks had reported lost items in their homes.

A concerned Goldsmith met with George Rands, the manager of Plymouth Savings Bank.

"Good morning, Mr. Goldsmith. I am sorry to hear about the loss of your friend William," Rands said carefully. "Mr. Hilton was a fine customer of mine. I also considered him a friend."

Goldsmith paused; his expression pensive. "Thank you, Mr. Rands. Let me introduce my son Lawrence." They shook hands. "William and I traveled the world in the spirit of God and for the good of our colony. I pray God rests his soul and that he is together with his wife in heaven."

After their mutual greetings, they walked side-by-side into a large office, where Rands closed the door behind them. He took a seat behind a large, ornate desk. Goldsmith and his son sat in the two chairs across from him. Goldsmith had not given the bank manager a chance to ask the reason for his meeting, so he burst out with, "I understand your bank is now storing items for your customers."

Rands replied, nodding his head with excitement, "Yes. We call them safe deposit boxes. For a small fee, we provide you with a metal box built by the local blacksmith. Put whatever you want inside it, and we will store it in our safe with our gold and money."

"What would be the fee for such a service?" Goldsmith asked in a monotone voice.

"It's nominal," answered Rands. "We do not intend for the service to be profitable. It is more of a way to branch out and provide other services to our customers. As you know, there are rumors of another bank opening in our colony. Therefore, we must do all we can to preserve our clientele.

"Marvelous. I wish to pay for five years of storage and place the item in the box immediately," Goldsmith demanded.

With that, they proceeded to the basement. As they walked down the granite stairs, with each step, the air grew colder and colder. February in Massachusetts was bitterly cold, but he had never before felt the cold of an underground, unheated basement. He saw Rands' breath as he apologized for the chill.

"We don't feel the need to heat the safe during the winter months," he said. "After all, we only come here once or twice daily."

The bank's safe was not what Goldsmith had expected. He had seen another safe at a friend's house, but it was no bigger than a loaf of bread. He presumed that a bank safe would be larger but not this big. It was an actual room. The door to the safe was an actual door, like one at his house, but they did not make it from wood. It was metal, and the safe walls were also metal.

Rands gloated, "The miracles of modern science, don't you think? A room made of metal. It is impervious to flood or fire and is impossible to break into. Needless to say, your items will be safe with us."

The bank manager did not allow Goldsmith in the safe for obvious reasons. He waited as Rands exited the safe, holding a metal box. Rands handed it to him.

"Could you please give us some privacy, Mr. Rands?" asked Goldsmith.

The bank manager closed the door to the safe and returned to his office. Goldsmith took Hilton's will out of his coat pocket and placed it in the box. He closed it, turned to his son, and said, "Lawrence, what I have placed in this box will change our lives forever. If something ever happens to me, I need you to promise that you will retrieve the items at once."

"What is in the box, Father?" asked Lawrence.

Goldsmith lied to his son. "It is MY last will and testament and a map. On my last journey to the south, I buried a treasure on an island. The contents will provide our family with prosperity for generations. Promise me. It is our family legacy."

Lawrence nodded his head in confidence. "I promise you, sir. I will make our family proud."

They returned to the bank manager's office and handed the box to Mr. Rands.

"I will provide you with a receipt that you can use to retrieve your items when the time comes," said Rands. A few minutes later, Samuel and Lawrence Goldsmith left the bank with a paper receipt that read:

On the 16th day of February in the 1662 year of our Lord, Plymouth Savings Bank acknowledges that Samuel Goldsmith obtained and paid for security box number 17. Plymouth Savings Bank promises to hold the box and the items therewith for a period of five years or until the client wishes to retrieve said items. Signed, Steven Rands, bank manager.

As they parted ways on the sidewalk, Goldsmith told his son that he would hide the receipt somewhere in his house and tell Lawrence where it was hidden the next time they met. They shook hands, and Goldsmith returned to his home. While sitting at his desk, thinking, *the idea of storing items in a bank is marvelous, but it has one fatal flaw: the receipt. How will I ever retrieve the will if I lose the receipt?*

He'd furnished his study with everything a gentleman would need in 1662: a large desk, bookcase, map, sitting chair, and a window overlooking the Atlantic Ocean. He now needed to find a place to hide the receipt where it would be safe from those scoundrels entering people's homes in the middle of the night and taking items for their own. After contemplating, he found the perfect spot. Just recently, he had purchased a book from the renowned writer and clergyman Cotton Mather.

Mather was a socially and politically influential Puritan minister, author, and pamphleteer from the Old North Church in Boston. Mather's beliefs and philosophies were admirable, especially his continued effort to rid the town of Salem of the witches and demons that had possessed their women. Mather journeyed to Plymouth once or twice a year to preach and sell his pamphlets and books to his followers. On his last visit, Goldsmith had purchased *On Witchcraft*, a book justifying Mather's role in the Salem Witch Trials.

What better place to put the receipt? He placed the receipt for the safe deposit box between the pages of his beloved book and returned it to its place with the dozens of others in his bookcase. He finally felt relieved. It had been a long day, and his heart still stung over the loss of his friend. It was time for him to lie down to rest and pray for the soul of William Hilton. During his prayer, he also asked God to forgive him for stealing his friend's will.

Goldsmith lived on the outskirts of town. His home was a small cottage made of brick with a granite foundation. It was the perfect size for him.

He did not hear the two men enter his home as he dozed off to sleep in the second-floor bedroom. On this night, entering the house was easy for the intruders. He had forgotten to lock his front door from the stress of the day. This occasionally happened, especially if he'd imbibed some alcohol with a friend or two at the local pub.

If he'd locked the door, Goldsmith would have easily heard the men break in since he was barely asleep when they did. Instead, they walked right through the front door and, rather than look for valuables like most burglars do, went straight up the stairs to the bedroom. Goldsmith awoke when he heard the door creak as the men entered the room.

Goldsmith sat up frantically and lit the lantern at the side of his bed. Once lit, he barely saw the two men standing at the door. As he sat up, his first thought was that his musket was at the bottom of the stairs, so he had no weapon to defend himself.

"I don't know what you want," he said, his voice quivering with fear. "I am a simple man. There is nothing in my home that is valuable."

Still blinking from his drowsiness, he tried to make out the identities of the two men. He then recognized the smaller man's voice when he barked, "Tell me where the last will and testament is!"

"Andrew?" Goldsmith asked while sitting up. "Andrew Hilton? Is that you?"

"Just give me my father's will, and there will be no trouble, old man. I know you have it. You were the last person in his study other than me. I vow to spare your life if you hand it over now." Young Hilton's voice was deep and gruff.

Goldsmith hesitated before speaking. He needed time to think. Turning his back to the men, he got out of bed and walked towards the fireplace. "Your Father's will is not in my possession. I find your accusation false and insulting. He was a dear friend of mine and a fellow patriot. I would never do such a thing as you accuse me of."

The fireplace was crackling, providing an orange glow that permeated the room. Goldsmith picked up the stoker, an iron rod with a handle and a sharp pointed hook at the end that was used to move the logs around in the fire. *Tonight, I will use it as a weapon.*

As he finished stoking the fire, he grasped the stoker tightly. He planned to threaten the boys and make them leave. Holding the stoker like a sword, he turned around swinging while trying to say, "You have to learn...."

Before he could finish his threat and turn around completely, the other man in the room, who was significantly larger than Andrew, approached Goldsmith with a raised musket and slammed its butt over Goldsmith's head. The thrust of the blow caused him to fall forward, staggering through the bedroom door and landing atop the stairs. Blood trickled from his forehead as he tried to keep conscious after the fall. He had been in fights before, so he was familiar with what a blow to the head felt like, but he had never been hit this hard. The pain was enough to make him nauseated. With what little sense he had left, he hoped this might be the end of the encounter, and they would leave empty-handed.

Trying to recover from the blow, he rolled over and tried to get up. When he did, he lost his balance and tumbled down the stairs. The two men laughed as they watched him slam awkwardly into each stair. When he finally reached the first floor, blood was pouring from his head and other spots on his aching body. When he looked up through the scarlet mask flowing down his face, the two men were walking down the stairs.

He pushed strands of blood-soaked hair from his face as he cried, "I do not have the will! Why would I take his will? It has no value to me."

"You know about the treasure, old man," Hilton replied. "He gave that treasure to my family and me. I must follow through with his wishes."

The larger gentleman added, "We can do this the hard way or the easy way: You tell us where it is, and you wake up tomorrow with a headache and a cut on your forehead or… you don't wake up."

Goldsmith already knew his fate, so he muttered, "If these shall be my last words, then so be it. I do not have possession of the will. You are gravely mistaken. If you do me any further harm, may God forgive you."

Hilton walked to Goldsmith, who had dropped the stoker and lantern after his fall, so he was no longer a threat. He knelt beside him. Still dazed, Goldsmith tried to stand. Young Hilton laughed at his attempts to get up. He was a punch-drunk boxer in the final round of a prize fight. His mind told him to stand, but his legs and the rest of his battered body would not allow it.

Feeling mildly impressed by Goldsmith's strength and perseverance, Andrew shook his head and said, "As much as you are an honorable man and a friend of my Father, God rest his soul, I do not believe you, Mr. Goldsmith. I believe it's in this house."

Those words might be the last Goldsmith would ever hear. Although dazed, he knew there was little chance for survival. In a last-ditch effort, he gathered as much strength as possible and threw a punch at the man kneeling over him. If he hit him in the perfect spot on his face, he might have knocked him out with one blow, then tried to subdue the larger man alone. The idea was futile, but he didn't see any other option.

Hilton easily saw the weak, slow, wide-ranging fist coming toward his face, so he simply moved to the right as Goldsmith flailed wildly and found himself face-first again on the floor.

His time was up. *Is this my penance for stealing the will? If so, God did not wait long to punish me. That is for sure.* Goldsmith said one last prayer for his soul and the soul of his dear, departed friend, and then asked forgiveness for the sin that he had committed.

The two men stood over him and shook their heads in disbelief. Goldsmith felt the first kick to his head by the larger man. The other fifty kicks to the head, torso, groin, and legs were unnecessary. He was dead after the first blow.

Andrew and his partner spent the rest of the night ransacking Goldsmith's home in search of the will. After several hours, it was clear that the will was not in the house. They looked everywhere. They destroyed his desk, ripped the bookshelf from the wall, and checked for loose floorboards. They did everything they could. Everything but look through the pages of the actual books.

Lying on the floor of Goldsmith's study was a copy of *On Witchcraft* with a safe deposit receipt inside its pages. The men stepped over the book and a dozen others while leaving the house into the dark, chilly night. The weight of killing a man who may not have had the will weighed heavy of Andrew's shoulders, but he was right. He *had to* be right: Goldsmith was the only person who could have taken it.

****

After not hearing from his father for a few days, Lawrence Goldsmith visited his home to check on him. He found him dead on the kitchen floor when he entered the unlocked door. The pools of blood had started to quagmire around the body of a man he presumed to be his father but could not be sure. His face was so savagely beaten that he could not conclusively prove it was him. He had to look away and cover his nose with a handkerchief. The stench of death resonated throughout the home. He became nauseous from the smell and could no longer look at the mangled body. He knew what he had to do. Before he notified the authorities, he searched throughout the ransacked house, looking for the safe deposit receipt. In a matter of minutes, it was obvious that whoever did this to his father was looking for something. They did not appear to steal anything. His watch was at his bedside. His wallet was in his den.

The only logical explanation for this crime was that someone knew about the treasure and was there to get the will and map. Unfortunately, an exhaustive search of the house did not produce the coveted receipt. If only he had looked in the Cotton Mather book on the floor of his father's den, the Goldsmith legacy might not have been lost forever.

****

After a month and no sign of Samuel Goldsmith, the coroner determined that the mangled body must be him, so they put him to rest next to his dear friend William Hilton.

The town was terrified by the gruesome murder. Town leaders soon required that residents not leave their homes after dark and that they sleep with their lanterns on to prevent another intrusion.

Meanwhile, the town mourned the two lost souls while also fearing that none remained to guide them back to the warm, safe place they called "The Carolinas."

6

1947

HINESVILLE, GEORGIA

Charles Gramer had a challenging time finishing his work at the lumber yard that day. He liked the practice of law and enjoyed working for his family's company, but he always fantasized about being one of those detectives he saw in the movies. His favorite actor was Humphrey Bogart, and his favorite movie was *The Maltese Falcon*. He often dreamed of going to the big city and opening his own detective agency. He envisioned a beautiful lady entering his humble office late at night in desperate need of help. Charles would then comfort her with confidence and charisma before finding what she'd lost or protecting her from some sort of evil. In the end, he would always solve the case. It was a pleasant dream. Someday, he hoped, it might even become his reality.

After work, Charles drove home to his downtown apartment. He lived in a large brick building comprised of eight apartments, two on each of its four stories. His apartment was on the second floor. He had a delightful view of the park across the street from his living room. He told people how much he enjoyed the idea and how it relaxed him to watch the children play on a bright spring day, but he got home from work so late every night that he had little time or energy to enjoy it.

He kicked off his shoes, took off his coat, loosened his tie, and plunked down on a recliner. Since it was Friday night, he allowed himself to indulge in a bourbon before dinner. After a stinging sip of Kentucky's finest, he reached for a notebook and pencil. It was time to figure out a way to learn what that three-hundred-year-old receipt was for.

His first thought was of Samuel Goldsmith. He would need to find out who he was and why he'd kept a bank receipt in a Cotton Mather book. Scenarios bounced around his head. If the receipt were of importance to him, he would have stored it in a safe place. *Did they have safes back in the 1600s?* If they did, Goldsmith would have stored it in one.

His next thought intrigued him. If the receipt was still in the book, then no one had ever claimed the items in Box 17. If someone had placed the receipt in a safe or a desk, then upon his death, a family member would inevitably have found it and returned to the bank to collect whatever was in the box. It appeared this had not happened in Goldsmith's case. Now he was excited. *There must be something of enormous value involved.* The ice rattled in his glass as he took another sip of his bourbon.

Once the bourbon had been polished off, Charles went to the phone and called the only person he knew who would know about colonial records: his mother. He just needed to make sure he did not ruin the surprise.

After a few rings, she answered the phone. "Good evening, Mother. It's Charles. I hope I'm not disturbing dinner?"

"No, son. Not at all," she replied in the soft, kind voice that Charles had loved since childhood. "Your father is not home from work yet. He was in Atlanta yesterday on a business trip, so I am sure he is catching up with work at the lumber yard."

After a little small talk, he slyly asked, trying not to hint at the gift she would soon be receiving, "How would one go about finding out information on a Pilgrim? You know, from the Mayflower."

She was taken aback by the question. Most of her son's phone calls revolved around some recipe he was making or advice on a girl he was courting. "That's a strange question," she replied, amused. "Would you mind me asking why you are interested in such a topic?"

Like walking a tightrope, he fibbed, "I'm reading a book about colonization, and the name Gramer appeared in it. I wondered if our family might be related to them."

Pearl was pleased that her son was taking a similar liking to her passion for early American history, so she was eager to provide as much insight as possible. She explained, "In the early years of the New England Colonies, birth, marriage, and death records were kept by the Secretaries of each colony. I would guess that the County Commissioner now keeps these records, or they are annexed at the Massachusetts State Archives."

A zing of thrill pranced through Charles' body. He hoped it wouldn't be as easy as going to the local library or university, where they would have some sort of book he could read. He also figured it would not be that simple. Honestly, he'd always known that his adventure would inevitably lead to Massachusetts.

He thanked her for the insight, finished the phone call, and sat back in his recliner. Now that he knew where to start with finding out about Goldsmith, he next had to turn to Plymouth Savings Bank.

This would be easier, he thought, because he'd studied bank regulations in law school. For example, the FDIC kept detailed records of banks. It was just a matter of discovering what had happened to this particular one. His best guess was that he would have to go to Massachusetts for that, anyway. He was sure that records of defunct banks were held in Boston somewhere.

Pouring another bourbon, Charles thought, *August is a wonderful time to visit Boston… maybe I can see a game at Fenway Park. Better start packing!*

7

1847

BOSTON, MASSACHUSETTS

The Long Depression of the 1800s caused a fiscal crisis the young United States had never seen. Families went hungry. Stores lacked food and supplies, while banks were closing.

The Plymouth Savings Bank had operated successfully for almost three hundred years, but today was to be its last. Customers no longer trusted the institution, so they withdrew their savings while others defaulted on the loans they'd been given.

William McCarthy was the bank manager. He was in his mid-fifties. He had blond hair, so it wasn't clear if he was going gray or not, and most of it was still in his possession. He was neither tall nor fat. He'd aged well, retaining the look of confidence and assurance that a typical bank manager had. One job that he had to do in preparation for closing the bank was to contact each customer who had a safe deposit box. He had been doing this over the past few months and reached almost everyone. It was a long and arduous assignment. He did it without complaint, hoping to get hired for the same position at another bank after his own closed down.

Precisely at 9 a.m., two men in expertly tailored suits and top hats entered the bank. McCarthy reached out a hand and greeted them as pleasantly as he could, considering the circumstances.

"Hello, gentlemen. My name is William McCarthy. I am the bank manager."

"Greetings, Sir. I am Federal Agent G. Nelson Stetser, and this is my colleague, James McCann. We are here to confirm that all accounts are closed and to retrieve any items or funds that have gone unclaimed."

For a moment, an unspoken tension lingered between the men, then McCarthy responded, "We have a few accounts that remain open and a few safe deposit boxes that have not been accounted for, but other than that, we are fully vacated."

As they walked into the vault, McCarthy felt a bit defensive that not all his customers had liquidated their accounts. McCann eased his mind a bit when he assured him, "Well done, Mr. McCarthy. It is impossible to liquidate every account. We find that there are always a few accounts that have been abandoned long, long ago. Sometimes it is the account of someone who forgot to tell a family member that they had an account or safe deposit box." These words soothed McCarthy's conscience and allowed him to continue with this day that he had been dreading ever since the bank's owner told him they would be closing.

For what seemed like hours, the three men meticulously went through the bank's accounts. One by one, the agents confirmed which accounts were closed and liquidated. Once they'd finished with the accounts, they moved on to the safe deposit boxes. The agents and McCann opened each metal box that the bank records showed had already been emptied. This task was monotonous but understood that it had to be done.

38

As the agents continued their mundane project, McCarthy asked them what he thought was a poignant question. "So, what happens to the accounts and items in the safe deposit boxes that are abandoned?"

Stetser explained, "We deliver all the items to Boston, where agents will store them in a conservatory and categorize the amounts in each account and the account holder's name. This allows us to quickly find an account if a person, most likely an heir, attempts to retrieve the money."

While this made sense, it was not the answer McCarthy was hoping for. Apparently, he did not ask the question correctly. The safety deposit boxes were of more interest. What did his customers put in these boxes? Jewels, gold, heirlooms, paintings? Even though he held a prestigious job in his community, McCarthy did not have the wealth necessary to need a safe deposit box. Financially, he was extremely comfortable and supported his family well, but he lived a simple life. Saving his money was better than spending it wistfully on ornate objects.

McCarthy cleared his throat, glancing at Stetser as he asked, "Let me rephrase my question. What happens to the items in the safe deposit boxes? I have always been curious about what's inside them and even more about those few boxes that went unclaimed. After all, who would spend the effort and money to get a box and place such an important item in it, yet never retrieve it?"

The agents found the answers to the bank manager's questions to be intuitive. Stetser found the conversation made the time go by faster because he was more interested in reading over the bank's accounts than opening and closing metal boxes.

In response, McCann turned to McCarthy and pointed out, "Excellent question, Mr. McCarthy. When we return the unopened boxes to Boston, agents will open the boxes by force while staying mindful of the possibility of any delicate items contained therein. They determine what they will do with the items based on what they are."

McCann continued, "For example, often there is money in the box. If so, that's easy. Like the other bank accounts, they deliver the money to the Federal Reserve. Other items like jewelry and gold are held in a secure and remote location where they'll sit in another metal box, waiting to be claimed by their rightful owner."

"Interesting. So, what happens if the items remain unclaimed, which I suspect some do?" asked McCarthy.

Stetser jumped to answer, "After ten years, they'll sell the items at auction on the steps of the Custom House on State Street in Boston. It happens on the first Monday of September each year. I have attended the auction a few times. Many people show up, and it's quite exciting. It is common to see one hundred people on the steps of the Custom House watching in anticipation. At the same time, the auctioneer stands at the front door revealing auction items one by one and encouraging the bidding process."

Agent McCann chimed in with yet more insight, "There is one exception to the process, however, if there are documents found in the boxes. People often store important documents in safe deposit boxes that have little monetary value but have other significant value to the owner."

Agent Stetser continued the back and forth, "For example, the most common document stored is a property deed. In that case, we deliver the deed to the newly established Registry of Deeds, where they safely store and categorize the document."

"I've heard about the new Registry," McCarthy replied quickly so as not to interrupt the influx of knowledge the agents had bestowed upon him. "I find it impressive that the government seeks to account for all the property owners in the Commonwealth. It seems to be an impossible task."

"Nonetheless," said Stetser, "it will be accomplished."

McCarthy had one more question that had been eating at him all morning, but he was hesitant to ask, it might be too inquisitive. What if his questions had made him a nuisance while the agents were conducting their work? Regardless, he had to know the answer. It had been bugging him for months.

He walked to box number seventeen and placed it on a large desk in the middle of the vault. He looked at both gentlemen, whose eyes narrowed curious about what might come next.

"The items in this box have been here for over two hundred years. Actually, they are in a metal box inside this box. The bank built a new vault about fifty years ago when it was renovated. At that time, all the customers transferred their items to the newer, more secure boxes in the new vault except for one customer."

He continued wondering out loud, "I was told that the bank manager at that time had tried for months to contact the customer or the heirs to no avail. Ultimately, he simply took the old box and placed it in a new one. To this day, no one has claimed it. From the day I started working here, I've always wondered what was in this box."

McCann and Stetser seemed intrigued by the question, the box, and the story. McCann seemed a bit bewildered. He had only been on the job for a little over a year and had never encountered such a situation. Agent Stetser, on the other hand, was a seasoned veteran and prided himself on knowing every aspect of his job. He was never afraid to ask questions to colleagues or superiors. The more he knew, the better chance he had of being promoted from field agent to manager in one of those large, plush offices where his superiors spent their days.

In a stern yet almost overconfident tone, Stetser said while staring right at him, "When we come across boxes this old, one of our staff archivists accounts for them and determines what to do with the items. We treat most old boxes the same way we treat the others. They usually contain money and gold, so we send them to the Reserve. But there is one exception," he continued, "and that has to do with paper. Paper that is two hundred years old needs to be stored properly to preserve it. We don't have the ability to safely store ancient paperwork, so we deliver those items to Yale University, where they archive them with all their other priceless, ancient documents."

"Very interesting," replied McCarthy. "So, if there are papers in the box, I can visit Yale to view them?" By the look on Agent Stetser's face, he seemed annoyed by the extent of the manager's questioning.

With a slight laugh, he responded, "That would be impossible. See, Yale archives the sealed items for one hundred years. No one can view the documents until they unseal them. In this case, that would be in 1947. I suspect you will not be present to view the document at that time."

Ignoring Stetser's sarcasm, McCarthy asked the final question on his mind. "What documents are generally sent to Yale? Books?"

Agent Stetser took a deep breath and exhaled. His patience was wearing thin. "No. They auction books because they have a monetary value. The most common documents they archive for us are... last will and testaments."

Agent Stetser's answer was ignored. McCarthy fantasized about jewels, gold, and silver in the box. How anticlimactic would it be if the only thing left in the infamous safe deposit box, he'd wondered about all this time was just some old guy's will?

8

1947

HINESVILLE, GEORGIA

The following day, Charles was up at the crack of dawn. It was going to be another hot and humid day in Georgia. The weather would be unbearable for some, but for native southerners like the Gramers, the heat was just another part of their day. Charles told friends at Yale that anyone who says they love the Georgia heat is lying. Every single person in the south welcomes the coolness of the fall. If they say otherwise, they are just not telling the truth.

Charles dressed accordingly for this August Saturday. He wore a pair of tan khakis and a white V-neck to hide his sweat. He'd learned early on that a light-colored shirt other than white would turn a darker shade from the perspiration by noontime. For a person of his stature in his town, that look would not go over well.

He finished his toast and hard-boiled egg, eager to start his adventure. He strolled through Hinesville's downtown, past brick-faced boutiques, and the barbershop on the corner. Victorian homes with the doctor's and attorney's shingles sat shaded by ancient oaks.

In the cool of the morning, the twenty-minute stroll didn't last long enough to make him melt onto the sidewalk. He passed a row of benches near the front door of the train station with a few early travelers waiting. The shade inside the one-story building dropped the temperature a few degrees, and Charles was excited to approach the ticket window.

Charles went to the ticket booth to see if a train was leaving for Boston soon. An old, gray-haired gentleman was behind the glass and eager to help. One thing that Charles loved about the south was the people's sense of hospitality. Everyone was willing to help their neighbor. He hadn't felt the same about New England while at Yale.

The older man looked through his schedule and noted that the next train to Boston would be the following day at 10 a.m. He also told him the ride would last twenty hours and cost five dollars. Charles bought a one-way ticket and left the station with a spring in his step. Tomorrow, he would begin his journey to find out what lay inside that mysterious safe deposit box.

On his walk home, he stopped at the local coffee shop to order a cup of black coffee. The shop was a mainstay in the community. In fact, his parents used to frequent this place when they were dating. Over the years, it had become a Hinesville monument. The old booths and scratched-up counter did not deter the townsfolk from spending their hard-earned money there. The food was bland, and the coffee was cold, but the restaurant's informality had its own charm.

When he got his coffee, he left the shop, crossed the street, and went to the bench where his father was sitting. Charles knew his Saturday routine. He'd planned his visit to the train station with the knowledge that his father would be sitting on the same park bench as always, just reading his paper and sipping his coffee.

"Is this seat taken?" he joked as he sat beside him.

Joseph chuckled. "I am meeting a lady here in a few minutes to run off to Havana together, but I suppose I can spare a few minutes for my favorite son."

Joseph had always had a good sense of humor, so his joke was of no surprise. He always had something funny and clever to say. It was an admirable trait for a man with such high stature in his community. Maybe that was one reason people liked him so much.

"So, guess what I just did?" asked Charles.

His father's reaction was immediate. "You bought a train ticket to Boston."

Shocked by the accuracy of his answer, Charles conceded with a sigh, "How on Earth did you know that?"

Joseph looked at him with a knowing grin. "I live with your mother, genius. She shared with me the conversation you had with her last night. I know you well enough. I suppose you're here to tell me that you'll be taking a few days off from the lumber yard."

That made sense to Charles. His excitement had skewed his judgment a bit. He would have to make sure that would not happen again. If he were to solve this mystery, he would need all his wits about him.

"You know me better than myself sometimes." Charles shook his head in amusement. "I shouldn't be more than a few days."

With that, Charles shook his father's hand and left the bench so Joseph could rendezvous with his pretend girlfriend and Charles could pack for his long train ride to Boston.

9

Charles Gramer usually went to church with his parents on Sunday mornings. It was a ritual that his family had established when the children were little. It hadn't thrilled Charles at a young age, but as he got older, the time with his family was more enjoyable. Traditionally, the family would attend mass together. Then Pearl would cook up a feast at her home, after which Charles and Joseph, Jr. would inevitably bring leftovers home for their lunches the following week. Charles was often the envy of the lumber yard cafeteria when he opened a meatloaf sandwich with a slab of onion or a roasted pork sandwich with coleslaw on a toasted roll.

Joseph and Pearl understood Charles' absence this Sunday and were not surprised because Joseph had shared yesterday's conversation with Pearl the night before. Still, it did not feel the same whenever one child was absent from their family's Sunday tradition.

While the Gramer family entered the hundred-plus-year-old church in downtown Hinesville where they'd baptized each of their children and where Joseph and Pearl had been married so many years ago, Charles was stepping onto the train to Boston.

His train ticket told him to find Compartment 14. As he walked through the dining car, he noticed that it was only a few cars away on the left side of the train. It would be nice if the compartment were empty so he could continue mapping his journey. As he opened the door, he was both disappointed and happy. The compartment was not empty. A beautiful woman was sitting to the right. She wore a tight white dress that dropped just below her knees. He could not tell for sure because she was sitting down.

Nonetheless, the dress was well-fitting and complimented her toned physique. She had red hair. Charles had a thing for women with red hair. He'd dated a redhead at the University of Georgia his sophomore year and had been hooked ever since. When he fantasized about women, which wasn't often, he did so with the image of a woman who looked remarkably similar to the one sitting right in front of him.

Compartment 14 was slightly bigger than a typical restaurant booth without a table. It fit four people, but anyone would agree that it would be pretty tight if four people occupied it for a twenty-hour trip. Besides the two cushioned benches facing each other, it also had storage above them and a large window on the outer wall. The latter would be necessary for the first part of the trip, as the temperature had already reached eighty degrees, and it was not even ten in the morning.

When the woman heard the door open, she looked up from the book she was reading, made eye contact with Charles, and then he thought, *Wow, that's the smile of an angel.*

"Good morning, ma'am," said Charles. "It appears that we will spend the next twenty hours or so together. It's a pleasure to make your acquaintance." *Play it cool, Charlie. Play it cool.*

"Good morning," she replied. "My name is Mary. Mary Wheaten." Her voice was gentle yet confident. Charles could tell instantly that she was both educated and intelligent, while her smile showed her to be sweet.

"Hello. I am Charles Gramer. It's nice to meet you." His voice cracked just a bit.

She raised her eyebrows quizzically. "Are you related to Joseph Gramer from Hinesville?"

"That depends," he answered with a smirk. "My father is Joseph Gramer, and my older brother is Joseph Gramer, Jr. Take your pick."

Mary gave Charles a purposefully awkward look. "I went to school with your brother Joseph. I remember him as an outstanding athlete. He and I both ran track in high school. He won the county long jump his senior year. Why do I remember that? I have no idea."

She was impressive. "Yes. He won the long jump. I attended that track meet. Funny. I remember that day well, but not well enough, I suppose. I definitely would have remembered seeing you there."

She blushed at the sly compliment as he sat across from her.

Mary returned to reading her book when Charles sat down.

After getting settled, he casually glanced at her. *Please God, do not have any other passengers come into this compartment. I want every minute I can get alone with this beautiful woman.* In reality, he knew there was likely going to be another passenger joining them. It was uncommon for a woman and man who did not know each other to share a compartment. They would typically book another woman in it, or the woman would stay in a "Ladies Only Compartment."

With that, he lifted his suitcase into the storage area above his bench, hoping he had not offended Mary with his underhanded compliment. It was not in his nature to be so direct, but it just came out of nowhere. To pass the proverbial olive branch just in case, he asked, "Would you like help with your luggage? I'd gladly stow it away for you."

She again looked up from her book. "That would be appreciated, Charles. Especially if there will be another passenger joining us." As Charles lifted her bags into the storage area above her, he looked at his watch. *9:55 a.m.—Only five minutes until we leave. Let's get going!*

The train's whistle blew at 10:07 a.m. Charles knew exactly the time as he was sweating every minute, both literally and figuratively. He occasionally had to wipe the sweat off his upper lip because of the Georgian humidity. The figurative sweat came from the possibility of his sitting across from this beautiful woman for twenty hours with no one to disturb them.

To his surprise, his wish was granted. As the train pulled away from the station, Mary and Charles were the only two passengers in Compartment 14. Together they glanced at each other and said simultaneously, "Have a great trip." They both wholeheartedly chuckled at the coincidence. The hilarity continued when they both blurted simultaneously again, "Jinx!" Both their eyes widened, and their jaws dropped with the coincidence.

Charles wondered (and hoped) that Mary was only a fraction as interested in him as he was in her after such a fleeting time. He had only known this woman for a few minutes, but he had to admit that he had never felt this way about anyone before. He welcomed the feeling. He was ready for love.

"Ms. Wheaten," Charles said as he swallowed, "I'm concerned that you might find it uncomfortable to be alone with a man in this compartment. As you may know, it is not common. I am more than willing to find another place to sit for the trip if you want me to."

Mary considered his offer and was pleased with his chivalry. "I can take care of myself, Mr. Gramer. I'm a good judge of character. You appear to be a fine young man. Plus, I have taken several self-defense classes. Trust me. You don't want to mess with me."

Charles' voice trailed off as he replied, "Duly noted, Ms. Wheaten. I promise to keep my hands to myself and be the proper gentleman my mama raised me to be."

The two continued to chat on and off for the first couple of hours of their trip. The rest of the time was spent mainly with Mary reading her book and Charles aimlessly staring out the window. Her beauty and his desire made it hard for him to concentrate on the landscape or anything else for that matter. What he found most fascinating in the past couple of hours was that he had scarcely thought about the three-hundred-year-old piece of paper resting safely in his briefcase. It had taken up most of his thoughts the past few days, but this woman had put a spell on him. He couldn't think of anything but her.

A little after noon and about fifteen minutes after Charles had finished reading the newspaper from cover to cover, he mustered up the courage to ask, "Would you like to join me in the dining car for lunch?"

Again, Mary looked up from her book, placed a marker on the page she was reading, and dramatically slammed it shut. "I thought you would never ask."

Charles was excited but relieved at the same time. As he stood, he offered his hand to Mary to politely help her up from her seat. Then, for no reason whatsoever, he said in a poor English accent, "Then together we shall dine, my fair lady. Take my hand, and I shall guide you to your carriage."

She giggled as she stood, replying in an equally bad English accent, "Such a fine gentleman. The lady is charmed and eager to accompany you."

Charles opened the compartment door for her and let her lead the way to the dining car. He had two reasons for letting her lead. The first was obvious: Chivalry was not dead. His father had taught him well. He always told him to treat a woman like someone would treat their mother, with love and respect.

The other reason he let Mary lead the way to the dining car was not so honorable. He simply had been dying to see her figure when she stood up. She was beautiful while seated, but her body from behind almost knocked him to the floor. Her shoulders tapered down to her narrow waist, which sat atop a well-defined bottom. Her legs: He could tell she ran track in high school. They were perfect. They were lean and muscular but not too much so. If a guy saw her walking down the street, her legs could cause a car accident.

Charles was so enamored by Mary from behind that he failed to see a small stair in the hallway. As a result, he indirectly got what he'd been hoping for; an opportunity to touch her legs. As he tripped and fell forward, distracted by the shape and figure of the woman in front of him, he had no choice but to grab Mary's legs to break his fall. She jumped forward in surprise and screeched, "What the -"

As he clumsily got up from the ground, he apologized profusely, "I'm so sorry. I meant no disrespect. I tripped over that stair and accidentally fell into you. I'm so sorry."

Still recovering from the shock, Mary looked into his eyes and saw his sincerity and remorse. He looked like a wounded puppy. He had only acted as a perfect gentleman during their brief journey, so she forgave him.

To lighten the mood, she pointed to his chest with her left hand while raising a fist and threatened, "Try that again, and you'll have more for lunch than just a hamburger. You'll get a knuckle sandwich."

For a dramatic pause, she cinched her eyes and pressed her lips after saying it. Then, after a few moments of seeing the fear in his eyes, she showed Charles her sick sense of humor that her sisters found annoying.

She laughed. "Just kidding. It was an accident. Don't worry about it. Let's go eat lunch."

Charles pretended to wipe sweat from his brow. He purposefully took a deep breath and exhaled. "Whew. That was mean... but funny. It appears I deserved that."

She smirked, turned, and led them to the dining car for their first of many lunches together.

10

Lunch for Charles was a ham and cheese sandwich. Mary tried the Italian wedding soup. They spent most of their time comparing folks they knew from Hinesville. Mary was two years ahead of Charles in school, so she was acquainted with many of his brother Joseph's friends. By the time Charles ordered his second sweet tea, he'd learned that Mary had grown up just a few blocks from his childhood home. They were surprised that they had not met before. Chances would have it that, at some point, they would have crossed paths at the local swimming hole, neighborhood picnics, or bible study. Nonetheless, they were both giddy to have finally met.

After lunch, they returned to their compartment. Mary returned to her book for a bit while Charles inadvertently fell asleep to the soothing sound of the train chugging along. When he awoke an hour later, Mary poked fun at him. "Good morning sleepy head. Boy—Are you a snorer!"

"You're kidding, right?" he asked reluctantly. "I didn't snore, did I?"

"Oh, you snored all right. In fact, you were snoring so loud that the maître d stopped by to mention that travelers complained the noise was ruining their lunch."

"Haha. Hilarious. By the way, you never told me what you do. Are you married? Do you work? I'm guessing you're a stand-up comedian, like Bob Hope."

"I'm an accountant at the local paper mill. You know, the one on the west side of town. I started working there right after college. It's a temporary gig until I go on tour with the USO. What do you do for work?"

"I run my father's lumber company, Gramer Lumber. I've worked there periodically since I was young but took time off to study at the University of Georgia, and I just finished my law degree at Yale," Charles gloated, hoping to impress her.

"Is that why you're traveling north?" she asked. "To visit Yale?"

"Funny enough, no. Do you want to hear a cool story?"

Charles told her how his father bought Cotton Mather's book at an auction for his mother and how Charles had found the mysterious receipt between its pages. Mary was interested in the story but far more interested in his passion for it. He had an energy about him that was appealing. She asked several poignant questions at the right times, which made the conversation go on for hours. By the time he'd finished his retelling, she knew his plan and what he thought he might find at the end of his journey. When Charles told her that his first stop would be the Massachusetts Archives in Boston, her eyes lit up.

"That building is on Washington Street in Government Center. I know it well. I went to Boston University, so I know the city inside and out. During my four years of studying, I made it a point to learn every part of Boston. Each weekend, I would just walk and walk and walk. One day, I would climb the cobblestone streets in Beacon Hill. The next, you could find me in the bleachers at Fenway Park." She had started to ramble, so she cut herself off.

Charles was fascinated with her passion for Boston but also with the fact that she had a college degree. "I am extremely impressed. Boston University is a fine academic institution. I bet not too many of your female friends share the success that you've achieved," he acclaimed and continued, "Most of the girls from my class either learned how to type and became secretaries or married their high school sweetheart and started a family. Few went to college."

"My family believes in higher education. My mother told me early on that I would attend college, so I always knew I would go. Plus, I was not ready to settle down after high school. I believe people should see the world and live life before they marry."

Charles had never met a woman that shared the same values and passion for life as he did. At first, her beauty had attracted him, but then her sense of humor had knocked her up a peg. Now that he knew she was a college graduate from Boston University, no less, she'd just officially become the most interesting woman he had ever met.

"So, what's the reason for your visit to Boston?" Charles asked.

"I'm attending my fifth-year college reunion next Saturday. I thought I would arrive early to enjoy the city and visit with some friends who still live in the area."

Finding that she was going to be in Boston for a week and did not have any specific plans, Charles made his move. "Maybe if you are free tomorrow, we could meet for another lunch? I'm going to be at the Archives when it opens. Do you know of a nice restaurant or café in the area?" he asked, waiting anxiously.

"Faneuil Hall and Quincy Market are just a few blocks away," she replied confidently. "You can get anything you want at Quincy Market. There are dozens of vendors selling seafood, hot dogs, clam chowder, pizza, you name it. I used to go there all the time for lunch."

"So, it's a date?" he asked, eyebrows raised.

"It's a date," she agreed. "Besides, I too am interested in visiting the Archives. Would you like some company?"

"That would be swell. I could use another scholar to assist me. Since you are an accountant, I think you might find this particularly interesting," he said suspensefully.

Charles then reached for his briefcase and placed it in his lap. He opened the briefcase and removed a manila envelope.

"This is what sparked my interest in this little adventure I have created," he said as he gently removed the ancient piece of paper from the folder and handed it to her.

Mary softly held the receipt with both hands since she could tell how old and fragile it was. She had seen nothing like it before. The handwriting was exquisite. It had always embarrassed her that, during her formative years, her handwriting had been so bad. Maybe that was why she'd been good at math. She didn't like to write. Numbers spoke to her more compellingly than words.

"So, you think this is a bank receipt of some sort?" she asked. "It appears to be. I studied finance my senior year at BU. I remember learning that they did not use bank deposit books until the early nineteen hundreds. Before that, they simply gave you a receipt whenever you deposited money."

She handed the slip back to Charles, who returned it to the envelope, closed the briefcase, and returned it to its original position at his feet. Charles nodded in agreement with her assumption while growing distracted by the dulcet fragrance emanating from her body.

"I hope the Massachusetts Archivist can tell me what happened to Plymouth Savings Bank and any possible unclaimed accounts they might have possessed. Let's meet at the front of the building at nine o'clock," he suggested.

He then looked at his watch and saw they had been talking for over two hours. It was now just after six. *It's time for dinner. Let's see if my luck will continue.*

"Would you like to join me for dinner? I promise I will not grope you in the hallway again. I hear they are serving pot roast. I will be extremely pleased if it is half as good as my mother's."

"You drive a hard bargain, Mr. Gramer," she jokingly replied. "No groping and pot roast? How could a girl resist?"

Dinner, like the rest of the day, was filled with quirky remarks, funny stories, and questions about each other. The more he spoke, the more Mary found him fascinating. The more she spoke, the more deeply Charles fell for her. At about eight o'clock, they returned to their compartment with their bellies full of pot roast, pecan pie, and vanilla ice cream. They'd both enjoyed the food and the company. It thrilled Charles beyond belief when they entered the compartment, and Mary took the seat that Charles had invited her to take a few hours before... next to him.

They continued to talk for about another hour. Each of them was exhausted from the enormous meal they'd just eaten and the rumbling of the train. As Mary dozed off to sleep, she slouched to her left and rested her head on his shoulder. Charles didn't dare move an inch, just sat there exultantly until he too drifted off to sleep.

Mary woke first, right before sunrise, and noticed that she was leaning on Charles. It mortified her to think she'd done such a thing. *A lady does not rest her head on a gentleman whom she'd just met*, she thought. What would he think of her? No respecting man would consider such a thing as proper. She just hoped he had not noticed. Perhaps she'd leaned over during the middle of the night after they'd both already fallen asleep.

Charles did not wake up for about another hour. This gave her plenty of time to fix her hair and makeup with the compact she traveled within her makeup bag. She also went to the bathroom to brush her teeth. If he'd noticed their sleeping arrangement after all, at least she'd look refreshed and have fresh breath when she apologized.

When Charles woke, his first sight was of Mary sitting across from him cross-legged and reading the newspaper. She appeared to have been up for quite a while. He felt a little embarrassed when he looked at his watch, yawned, stretched, and realized what time it was.

"It is not the Ritz Carlton, but I slept like a rock in our cozy little compartment," he said to her. "How did you sleep? What time did you get up?"

"I rose right before dawn. I saw the sun rise over an enormous field of lilies. It was spectacular. I was going to wake you, but you were snoring again," she quipped.

He wondered if she'd slept all night with her head resting on his shoulder but did not find it proper to ask. *Had she done it intentionally or not?* He suspected the latter since she seemed like the type of woman who would have been disgusted by the notion so early in their "relationship." So, he just kept it to himself. Maybe they would talk about it at another time when they were more comfortable with each other. He hoped and prayed.

"You will not let this snoring thing go, will you?" he asked while shaking his head. "Please allow me to excuse myself, so I can visit the restroom to shave, change, and brush my teeth. We should be in Boston soon, so I want to ready myself for such an exciting day ahead."

He left the compartment and closed the door behind him. While walking down the hall, the conductor notified the passengers via the loudspeaker that they would arrive at South Station within minutes. The hair on the back of Charles' neck pricked up at the thought of walking into the presumably centuries-old government building with Mary by his side.

11

The train's whistle blew at about 8:30 a.m. as it pulled into South Station. Mary always marveled at the iconic building overlooking the Atlantic Ocean. She loved the curved façade with two-story columns that harkened back to when it had been the busiest railroad station in America. Like many of its predecessors, such as Penn Station in New York, travelers unfamiliar with the building could easily get lost in the vast atrium, with hundreds of crowded travelers making their way to their destinations. Thankfully for Charles, Mary knew her way around it.

She was being picked up by a friend she was staying with who lived in Boston's affluent Back Bay neighborhood. Charles took a taxi to his hotel. He was staying at The Parker House Hotel. According to Mary, it was within walking distance to the Archives, plus it had the best dinner rolls in the world. They looked forward to having afternoon tea there during their stay. Mary thought it was a "must do" on his trip, especially since he was already staying there.

They said their goodbyes as they exited the train and confirmed they would meet at the Archives building at 9 a.m. If things changed, it was comforting to know that Mary could always call the hotel to reach him if necessary.

It took about twenty minutes for Charles' taxi to arrive at his hotel due to traffic. It would have taken him less time to get there if he'd walked because the hotel was only about a mile from South Station. He would have done so if not for his luggage.

Something instantly impressed Charles with the Parker House Hotel as he entered the oldest continuously running hotel in the country. The Italian-style stone and brick as he walked up the white marble stairs surrounded by arched windows led to a marble foyer where he was greeted by a well-dressed gentleman standing behind the reception desk.

After Charles had checked into the hotel, the bellman directed him towards the Archives building. Charles eagerly stepped out into the summer's day. He had spent a few summers in New England while attending Yale, so he was familiar with the climate. Like Georgia, New England could get very humid in July and August, especially August. Today was perfect, however. The morning air was still brisk during his walk, but soon the sun would grow stronger and settle into a comfortable mid-seventies' day. *Perfect weather for my attire*, he thought as he walked down the cobblestone street in khakis, a white shirt, and a blue blazer.

Mary was waiting for him when he walked up the granite stairs of the impressive building. It looked like a courthouse where the press would barrage attorneys on the top stair after winning a big trial. As he walked up the stairs, a plaque on the building's façade indicated that it had been built in 1917.

Mary had changed since leaving the train. She wore a green summer dress that accentuated her fit figure. According to the trends of the day, the dress had puffed shoulders, cinched atop the waist, and came down to her knees. She wore stylish but practical black wedge shoes that gave her some height but were safer than pumps or high heels when walking along the cobblestone streets. She'd learned that the hard way during her days at Boston University.

"You're late," joked Mary, pointing to an imaginary watch on her left arm. "I have places to go and people to see, you know. I can't afford to lose any time. I'm a particularly important person, you know."

Knowing he was five minutes early, Charles again appreciated her sense of humor. He was quickly learning that it was one of many qualities that attracted him to her.

He raised his shoulders and eyebrows innocently and tried to find a witty comeback, "I'm sorry. I was on the phone with the President of the United States. He needed my advice regarding some details about how we should end the war. It's just another day being Charles Gramer."

They both laughed as they entered the building. The directory showed that several state agencies shared the enormous space and that the State Archives were on the third floor. They walked up the ornate staircase, where they found a double door with "Massachusetts State Archives" carved on a plaque. They were both overly excited to start their journey of discovery together but were just as disappointed when the gentleman behind the counter could not help them. They had no records of banks in the Archives. They only stored physical items.

His name tag read: "Roger Daly"

"Mr. Daly, if there was an item or money abandoned at a now presumably defunct bank, might you have records of it here?" asked Charles.

"If the bank failed, the FDIC or a bank that assumed the failed bank's business may have the account or safe deposit box contents. After a while, the FDIC or the bank must transfer unclaimed property to the state. The process is called escheatment, which is the transfer of unclaimed funds or property to a state government," Daly offered.

Mary nodded her head in agreement. The theory of escheatment was coming back to her. She remembered a class she'd taken her sophomore year that had introduced her to the subject. Specifically, she recalled getting an answer right on a multiple-choice test because she'd connected the "cheat" part of escheatment to lost property. *It is funny how the mind works sometimes.*

Mr. Daly continued, "I'm afraid you're at the wrong agency. I suggest visiting the State Treasurer's office. They retain bank records and control the state's unclaimed property division. If you're looking for a failed bank and items from a possibly abandoned safe deposit box, that is the place you should be."

Mary joined in the conversation. "Do you know where the state treasurer's office is, Mr. Daly?"

"I sure do. It's right across the street," he replied with a grin while pointing a finger.

They thanked Mr. Daly for his help and guidance and left the building. They were staring at another government building across the street in less than a few minutes. The Treasury had a neoclassical design similar to the nation's treasury in Washington, D.C., but not as grandiose. *Still,* thought Charles, *it would definitely stick out in Hinesville.*

They found the treasurer's office pretty quickly. A reception desk welcomed them when they entered the large agency's headquarters. An older lady with horn-rimmed glasses sat at the desk and asked if she could help them. From her tone of voice and the scowl on her face, it appeared to both Charles and Mary that she really did not want to help them but was just going through the motions.

When Charles explained what they needed, she told them to sit on a bench to her right and wait for an employee that could help them. They thanked her with their southern drawl and charm, hoping to brighten her day, but that was unlikely to happen.

After a few minutes, a gentleman in a black suit approached them, introduced himself as Richard Dalton, and invited them to join him at his desk, which was within earshot of the receptionist. The space consisted of ten desks aligned in rows of two, each occupied by a man in a dark suit. There were a couple of office doors lining the far wall that presumably were for management. They sat in two chairs across from the seemingly polite gentleman and introduced themselves.

"We are interested in the Plymouth Savings Bank that was in operation in the 1600s and, more specifically, if the bank failed, what happened to its abandoned property?" asked Charles.

After Charles explained the reason for their visit, Mr. Dalton sat up and tilted his head a bit. "I can help you with that, Mr. Gramer."

"What is the first step?"

Mr. Dalton explained, "Finding what happened to Plymouth Savings Bank is easy. I will probably be able to get the answer for you as you sit and wait. It will take more time to uncover the whereabouts of an abandoned safe deposit box."

With that, Mr. Dalton got up from his desk and walked to a wall lined with filing cabinets. It didn't take him long to remove a folder and return to his desk. He opened the file, put on a pair of glasses, and began reading the contents. Only a few pieces of paper were in the folder, so determining what happened to the bank would not take long.

"The Plymouth Savings Bank failed in 1847. If I remember correctly, there was quite an economic depression during that time. They were one of many banks to fail," he explained. "It doesn't appear that another bank took them over. It was also almost one hundred years before they formed the FDIC, so any abandoned items would surely be in possession of the state treasurer."

His heart was pounding. He sat up and leaned over with curiosity. "Great. Now how can we find the contents of a safe deposit box?" he asked.

Dalton replied, "I will need some time to research this for you. Can you show me the receipt so I can better help you?"

Charles opened his briefcase, removed the manilla envelope, and delicately handed the paper to Mr. Dalton. He read it carefully and jotted down some notes. He could clearly see that the owner of the box was Mr. Goldsmith and that it was Box 17. Now all he had to do was find Box 17 from Plymouth Savings Bank, which had been defunct since 1847. That might be difficult.

Dalton told them that the research would take much more time than finding the bank's information. He suggested they go to lunch and return later that afternoon to see what he had uncovered.

"Great. We just arrived in town. I just checked in at the Parker House, and Mary is staying with a friend in the Back Bay. Neither of us has had time to eat yet today," explained Charles.

Mary could practically smell the clam chowder in Quincy Market. "I'm dying to visit Quincy Market and introduce you to New England clam chowder. I can't believe you went to Yale and never tried it. Let's go."

The blue sky welcomed the couple back to the cobblestone streets of Boston as they walked hand in hand with Boston Harbor in view. Mary's mind was racing. The thought of clam chowder and the possibility of finding the contents of the safe deposit box overwhelmed her. Charles was simply smitten by the thought of holding her hand.

12

Lunch at Quincy Market was unlike anything Charles had ever before experienced. Mary guided him into the immense granite building that had to have been one hundred yards long. Inside was a twenty-foot-wide hallway with food vendors on both sides. The sight of it was overwhelming, but the smells were knee-buckling. At one moment, the smell of pizza from the North End permeated the room. Then a minute later, freshly baked cannoli took its place. This went on and on with every step.

They finally decided on a local vendor that sold seafood. Mary had described clam chowder earlier in the day, so Charles was eager to try it. They each got a large bowl and walked to an atrium at the center of the building with dozens of large tables where customers could eat. They sat at an empty table alongside a picturesque window. Outside, a street performer doing magic for dozens of appreciative tourists entertained them.

"So, what's the next step on this magical mystery ride?" asked Mary while blowing on the piping hot chowder.

Charles replied, "First, I'm going to have to learn how to make Boston clam chowder. It is unlike anything I have ever tasted. I'm surprised in my four years at Yale that I never tried it. Then again, I spent most of my time in the library or at the local diner where I mainly ate hamburgers and french fries."

Taking another sip of chowder, he continued, "But I digress. It all depends on what Mr. Dalton finds. My biggest fear is that they auctioned the items in the safe deposit box years ago. If that's the case, then we part ways after lunch. You will enjoy your reunion, and I will return to Georgia."

Neither wanted that conclusion, but it was the most likely scenario. To remain optimistic, Mary raised her bottle of Coca-Cola for a toast.

"Here's to continuing your adventure and discovering what Samuel Goldsmith found so important and valuable as to store it in a bank over two hundred years ago."

They clinked their bottles, leered at each other, and returned to their lunch. After about an hour, they left the building and proceeded to the waterfront, where they sat on a bench and talked for a while. They were quickly learning that each had a good sense of humor, was dedicated to their family, and had a solid foundation in their Presbyterian faith.

At about 3 p.m., they headed back to the Treasury to see if Mr. Dalton had unearthed anything of importance. The uphill walk back was much needed as they'd both consumed about eight hundred calories of clams, butter, and heavy cream. The Treasury closed at four-thirty, so they figured they had enough time to sift through anything they might find.

When they entered the Treasury office, Mr. Dalton waved eagerly at them like they were long-lost friends. They rushed to his desk, shook hands, and sat back down in the same seats as before. Mr. Dalton had not taken a lunch break yet, which was surprising for a government employee. He asked about their lunch and talked about how much he liked clam chowder too. He also recommended they eat at the Union Oyster House, just a few blocks away. Charles had never tried oysters before, so he was intrigued. Plus, it was a great excuse to ask Mary on another date.

After a minute or so of small talk and pleasantries, Charles asked, "Did you find anything about the safe deposit box?"

Mr. Dalton took hold of an envelope and waved it in front of them. "I did indeed," he replied. He took a single piece of paper out of the envelope and continued. "It appears that Mr. Goldsmith did not store anything of any significant value in the box."

Charles and Mary stared at each other with puzzled looks and thought, *why would someone store something of little value in a safe deposit box?*

"Come again?" Charles asked quizzically.

"The only item that was in the box was a document. It was a last will and testament," replied Dalton.

Charles nodded as if to say he understood. Mary interjected, "It makes sense that a person would place a document of such importance with a bank. He must have been a wealthy and important man to have such needs. After my studies at Boston University, I worked at a bank and noticed that many customers did the same thing with such important documents. If you don't have a safe in your home, storing such items in a bank is very prudent."

Mr. Dalton raised his eyebrows and nodded his head in approval of her assessment, then threw a wrench into the situation.

"The most interesting thing about this," he expounded with eyebrows still raised and a smirk, "is that the will is not Mr. Goldsmith's. It belonged to someone else."

"Someone else?" they asked in unison.

"Someone else," he answered. "A gentleman by the name of William E. Hilton."

Befuddled by the discovery, Charles thought aloud, "Why would someone store another man's last will and testament in a safe deposit box? His own will was not in the box? And no other items? Just the will of another man?"

Mr. Dalton was just as confused as the two across his desk. He had no answers for Charles' wonderment, but he did have an answer for Mary's next question.

"So, where is the document now?"

"Well, it appears the Treasury took possession of the box in 1847 when the bank went under. Whoever opened the box determined that the document had no monetary value, so it was inappropriate for it to be auctioned off. In cases like this, we would usually keep the item in our possession and itemize it in the unclaimed property division. They didn't do so with this, however."

"Why not?" asked Charles.

"It says here in the notes that the will was ancient. It had been stored with the bank for over two hundred years. I suspect that is why it went unclaimed. When Mr. Goldsmith passed away, I assume he had his own will in order, so no one would suspect he would have had a safe deposit box with another person's will inside," explained Dalton.

"I'll go back to my original question," Mary said, matter-of-factly. "Where is the will now?"

Mr. Dalton responded, "The archivist apparently determined that the will was so old and in such fragile condition, the treasury could not safely store it in our warehouse with all the other unclaimed items. In such a case, we deliver such delicate items to an organization that can properly care for them. In this case, the file shows they delivered Mr. Hilton's last will and testament to the Avalon Project at the Lillian Goldman Law Library... at Yale Law School."

It has to be fate, Charles thought. *William Hilton's will is being held at Yale University Law School's Library: My adopted second home for four years.*

Charles scratched his head. In just one day, they'd discovered what was in the safe deposit box and where the items were. It would likely take several days to uncover such details. Maybe it was luck. Maybe it was fate. Either way, their adventure would continue.

"Thank you, Mr. Dalton," Mary chimed in. "Let's get going, Charles!"

When they walked out of the office, Charles attempted to cheer up the lady behind the front desk who begrudgingly welcomed them earlier that morning. "Have a wonderful day, ma'am."

She barely looked up to acknowledge his politeness. Instead, after they closed the door, she grabbed a piece of paper with a phone number on it. She dialed the number. When the person answered on the other line, she said in a classic Boston accent, "Someone else just came in looking for the safe deposit box."

The gruff voice on the other line responded with a simple command, "Find out who they are... immediately."

13

As they left the Treasury, Charles and Mary had a pep in their step thanks to their newfound knowledge. They exited through the large double doors of the building and took a seat next to each other on the top steps of the large granite staircase. The building was in Beacon Hill. They sat in silence, facing east and appreciating the magnificent view of Boston Harbor.

Mary was the first to break the silence. "I presume the next step is to visit your alma mater?"

"New Haven is a little over one hundred miles from here. The next thing I need to do is return to the train station and purchase a ticket for tomorrow. It's about a five-hour train ride. When I was at Yale, I came up to Boston a few times to watch the Red Sox play. It is a pretty easy commute."

"Would you like me to come with you?" asked Mary with a hint of hesitation. If she made the trip to Yale, she could return to Boston in plenty of time for her reunion, but at the same time, it may have been too assertive. After all, they had only known each other less than forty-eight hours, and she was inviting herself on a trip to Connecticut.

Charles stopped himself from jumping up and down.

"I would be thrilled to have you accompany me to Yale," he said in that stupid British accent he'd used on the train when asking her to join him for their first lunch.

Why the stupid accent, Charles? It must be nerves.

Mary shook her head back and forth in joking disapproval of his worn-out repartee. "I'll call you at the hotel later today to iron out tomorrow's travel plans. I'm meeting with a sorority sister later for dinner, so I'll phone you before then."

Charles hung his head knowing he would be dining alone that evening. He had grown fond of and accustomed to spending time with Mary. Yet, in the back of his mind, he knew they couldn't spend every waking minute together. After all, he was searching for a safe deposit box while she was here for her college reunion. He resigned himself to realize that any time he spent with her this week was a blessing.

They said goodbye with subtle pleasantries and shared their excitement at the next stage of their journey. Charles walked back to his hotel in a bit of a daze. He nearly ran into a half-dozen Bostonians on his trip back. His head was full of too much anticipation and joy. The one thing he kept asking himself was whether he felt this way because of the will or because of Mary. Either way, his absent-mindedness was dangerous to his fellow pedestrians until he reached the Parker House.

When he reached the hotel, the same doorman who'd welcomed him earlier in the day greeted him by name.

"Good afternoon Mr. Gramer. Welcome back to the Parker House. Will you be joining us for afternoon tea?"

"Not today," replied Charles. "I hoped you could fetch me a taxi. I need to return to South Station."

The doorman seemed a bit perplexed by the request but granted his wish. Charles was at the train station within twenty minutes. He purchased two roundtrip tickets to New Haven, leaving the following day at 8 a.m. He asked the driver to keep the car running while he bought the tickets. The driver was not opposed to the idea since he got a round-trip fare out of the deal.

When Charles returned to the hotel, he toyed with the idea of having afternoon tea as suggested by the doorman. After a minute of contemplation, he decided to wait and share the experience with Mary. This was no easy task, however. The aroma of the famous freshly baked Parker House rolls wafted through the hotel lobby. He had obviously had dinner rolls before. His mother made them almost every Sunday dinner. These rolls were different, however. He climbed the stairs to his room on the second floor, hoping the temptation would subside with the ever-lessening aroma. By the time he got back to his room, he had refocused his mind on Hilton's will and his alma mater.

After a desperately needed afternoon nap, Charles awoke when his telephone rang. He didn't know what time it was but assumed it was around 5 p.m. since the sun was just going down and Mary told him she would call before she left for dinner. They spoke briefly on the phone. He gave her the details for tomorrow's train reservation and agreed to meet at the station at about 7:30.

He showered and read the newspaper, which was given to him compliments of the hotel. As always, he went directly to the sports page. The Red Sox were playing the Philadelphia A's that evening, so he decided to catch a few innings. He didn't plan to watch the entire game since he had to rise early the following day but visiting Fenway Park even for a few innings was a special treat for him.

As he walked out of the hotel, the door attendant hailed the same taxi from earlier in the day. Charles was so anxious for the game that, while he left, he didn't notice a man sitting in the lobby who got up abruptly when he saw him.

The stranger hailed a cab as well. When he got in the car, he immediately said to the driver, "Follow that taxi."

Charles and the driver had a pleasant conversation on the way to the game. It took about a half-hour to arrive at Kenmore Square, where Fenway Park was located.

One thing that Charles liked about Fenway Park was how accessible it was. Kenmore Square was in the city's heart, so one could walk to a game, take a trolley, or hail a taxi as he did. He had been in the area several times to attend games, but he realized it had been during a weekend each time. After all, he was a law student, so he had little time to travel during his studies.

While waiting in traffic, Charles glared out of the car's backseat window. The area surrounding Fenway Park had a different vibe at night compared to a weekend day. There seemed to be more stragglers this evening as opposed to a weekend day. His hands began to shake. An hour before, Kenmore Square had been jam-packed with thousands of fans entering Fenway Park. Families, co-workers, and friends all crowded the streets, eager to enter the park. Since the game had already started, those joyful fans had been replaced by the homeless and other shady characters trying to sell tickets illegally to those who had not yet purchased one. He had heard about "scalping" tickets and knew it was illegal. He had read in the New York Times that they'd recently arrested a Navy cadet for scalping football tickets. The cadet actually served some jail time for the crime. Charles had never found the need to purchase a ticket in this manner before since the box office always had seats available.

There were cars bumper to bumper in traffic on Beacon Street, so Charles had the driver drop him off about two blocks from the park's entrance. With so much traffic, it would be quicker if he walked. He thanked the driver and paid his fare as he walked up Causeway Street to the ticket counter. He was relieved to see two people in front of him since the game had already started. He kicked the ground knowing that he'd already missed the singing of the national anthem and did not hear the umpire yell, "play ball!" That feeling did not last long when the smell of popcorn and hot dogs filled his nose with joy. He was hungry since he'd chosen not to eat dinner at the hotel, knowing he would have a Fenway Frank… or maybe two.

His mouth was watering at the thought of a hot dog with mustard and onions when the two customers in front of him turned around. "The game is sold out," said one of them. "There are no more tickets."

Charles' shoulders dropped when he heard the news. He was looking forward to the game. As he contemplated his next move, he was startled by a tap on his shoulder from behind. He turned around to come face to face with a teenage boy who looked to be about fifteen years old. He was thin and about two or three inches shorter than Charles. The clothes he wore looked like they hadn't been washed in days.

The boy brought his face closer to Charles until his mouth was inches from Charles' ear. "Hey mister," he whispered. "I have extra tickets to the game, $1.50, and you get to sit right behind the plate."

Charles knew the transaction the vagabond was proposing was illegal, but he had never sat anywhere other than the right-field bleachers before.

If he sat behind home plate, he could hear the crack of the bat, the snap of the catcher's mitt, and the umpire yelling "strike three!" His luck was riding pretty high in the past couple of days between meeting Mary and finding out about William Hilton's will, so he took the chance.

Charles reached into his pocket for the money when the teenager grabbed his hand and whispered, "Not here, man. You're gonna get us both in trouble. Follow me. There's a spot around the corner."

The young man led Charles about a block down the street and turned into a dark alley. "Come on," he said. "There's a streetlight just around the corner. I think of this spot as my office. We can do the deal here in privacy."

Charles reluctantly followed him a few more feet, where enough light allowed him to see the ticket. It had the Red Sox logo at the top, their opponent, today's date, and read Lodge Box 20. Row 10, Seat 2. *It is the real deal,* he thought. This was not how he'd envisioned getting into Fenway Park this evening, but it would have to do.

"$1.50 huh?" Charles asked. "Tell you what. I'll give you $1.25. Since it's already the second inning."

Charles reached into his coat pocket to remove his wallet before the young man could counter his offer. He felt a burst of energy at the thought of such an illicit negotiation in a back alley in downtown Boston. He had never done such a thing but was not afraid of a little risk.

While opening his wallet, a tall man in a black trench coat carrying a wooden baseball bat approached him from behind. He sauntered towards them while Charles handed the money to his counterpart. The man lifted the bat above his head and swung. Charles did not see the bat as it crashed against the back of his head. The blow knocked him out immediately. The impact made him fall forward. His nose was the first thing to hit the pavement, but he didn't feel it. He was unconscious by the time he hit the ground. Charles lay lifeless on the dirty pavement as the man grabbed his wallet, gold watch, his Yale school ring, and even the shoes off his feet.

"I lived up to my part of the deal, Mr. Goldsmith. Where's my money?" asked the teenager, unfazed by the brutal attack.

Samuel Goldsmith, named after his ancient relative from the 1600s, pulled out a wad of cash from his coat pocket and handed it to the kid. "Forget my name and pretend you never met me. Do you understand?"

The kid didn't answer. He simply turned and ran down the alley into the night's air.

Goldsmith followed the hoodlum with a steady paced walk. Just as his shadow drifted from the brightness of the streetlight into the darkness of the night, a police officer walked past the alley and saw the body lying on the ground. This was the officer's regular beat, so he had experience with this alley. He had witnessed many muggings during his years on the beat, but unfortunately, he had not successfully captured many of the suspects. He was a bit overweight, which showed by his waist size and chubby, red face. So rather than search for the suspect, he ran to the alley.

When the officer turned the corner, his worst fear had come true. He took out his flashlight to get a better idea of the scene and saw a man lying face-down on the pavement, surrounded by a pool of crimson blood pouring from his head.

14

Mary awoke early the following day on her friend Patricia's apartment couch. She and Mary had been roommates for all four years at Boston University. When they'd met freshman year, they'd instantly become friends. They had similar personalities, hobbies, and an equal drive to succeed. They were nearly inseparable for many reasons, but mostly because they were two of the few females in the university's business department.

The two had gone out for an early dinner the night before. Patricia let Mary choose the place since she was visiting. After talking about new cafes or restaurants that had opened since she'd graduated, they decided to eat at a small café on the corner of Charles Street. It had been one of their favorite spots during their undergraduate years.

Dinner was filled with laughter, reminiscing, and Patricia trying to convince Mary to return to Boston. She bragged about her connections in the banking field to let Mary know she could easily find a job. Plus, she mentioned the number of eligible bachelors in the city too. Mary couldn't help but be tempted. She loved Boston. If not for her close relationship with her family back in Georgia, she would most certainly have stayed in the city after graduation.

She also loved Patricia's apartment. It was a third-floor walkup on Beacon Street close to the State House. It encompassed one-half of the third floor, but not in a conventional way. It had large, antique floor-to-ceiling windows in the unit's front and back. The living room where she slept had incredible views of the Public Garden. Each morning she would open the curtains and gaze at the green grass. She was envious of the view and location of her friend's apartment but wondered if she could live in such a small space. She'd grown accustomed to her larger apartment in Hinesville.

The couch she slept on was a pull-out. She had a great night's sleep and was energized for her trip to New Haven. Patricia was in the shower when she left, so they said goodbye through the closed bathroom door. She stopped into the coffee shop on the first floor of Patricia's brownstone to order a coffee to go. She wasn't hungry for breakfast yet. Plus, she assumed that she and Charles would have lunch on the train in a couple of hours. Maybe she would stop by Quincy Market on the way to the station to pick up some clam chowder. Charles would love a surprise like that.

Mary hailed a taxi and was at South Station with time to spare. The large, ornate clock in the middle of the board showing the arrivals and departures read 7:15 a.m. The station was bustling on this Tuesday morning. Most men wore black suits and fedoras, while the few women wore stylish pantsuits. It was going to be another nice August day in Boston, so very few wore coats. Charles wouldn't likely be hard to find amongst the sea of businessmen because she suspected he would not be wearing a suit. Then again, he was returning to his alma mater, so maybe he intended to "dress to impress."

After reading the departure board, she walked towards platform three where the New Haven train would be leaving in thirty minutes. She noticed people getting on the train but knew that Charles would not be one of them. He would most certainly wait for her before boarding. The night before, they had not discussed where they would meet at the station, but they were both intelligent people. It was safe to say that he would not be waiting for her at platform seven, where the train to Worcester was departing.

Mary stood patiently on the platform with her makeup bag sitting by her side and purse slung over her shoulder. Charles was ten minutes late. *It is probably traffic,* she thought. She expected to see him hustling over to her at any moment. Moments turned into minutes, and minutes seemed like hours when the train conductor announced the last boarding call for the train to New Haven.

"All aboard for the train to New Haven. All aboard!" yelled the conductor. The words caused a pit in Mary's stomach.

Where is Charles? Did he oversleep? There is no way he would have changed his mind about visiting the Yale University Library. Maybe he'd left without her?

Mary sat on a bench in the terminal with her head hung low. She sat for almost an hour while running through every conversation she and Charles had had in the past day, trying to determine if there was something that she'd said or done that might have offended him. She had nothing. Their last conversation on the phone had been as pleasant as the many others they'd had the day before. It had ended with him wishing her a great night with her friend and a pleasant night's sleep.

After a while, it was apparent he wasn't coming. Instead of taking a taxi back to Patricia's place, Mary decided to walk. It was still early enough that the summer sun was not at its peak, and the humidity had not appeared yet. The walk would also give her more time to think. Most of her thoughts were of Charles. Her first thought was that if there had been a change of plans, he had no way of reaching her since she'd never given him Patricia's telephone number. That made sense to her.

Maybe he had to return to Hinesville for a family emergency? Perhaps it was business?

Then, as she was walking up State Street in the financial district, which was only about another twenty-minute walk to Patricia's, she had an idea: She would stop by the Parker House Hotel to see if Charles was still a registered guest. She turned left on Washington Street, then a quick right on School Street, where the hotel was located. She knew all the shortcuts in the city and was proud of that fact. She walked with a swagger and didn't mind showing it off.

She knew where the hotel was since she'd had afternoon tea there often during college. Every Christmas break, she would return to Georgia with a box of their famous dinner rolls for her family. They always enjoyed the treat and appreciated the gesture. She would do the same thing when she returned from her reunion next week.

She entered the hotel lobby that shared an entrance with the dining room. She waited in line while the receptionist cared for a couple of other guests. When it was her turn, she approached the desk and asked if he could please ring Charles Gramer's room for her. The young man behind the desk wore a slim blue uniform with gold buttons and a Pershing hat with gold trim. He obliged and called Mr. Gramer's room.

"I'm sorry ma'am," he said after about ten rings. "He does not appear to be answering."

Mary stuttered, "Could you tell me if he has checked out today or is still a registered guest?"

Scrolling through the pages of a thick leather book and running his fingers down to the bottom of the page, he replied, "He is still registered, ma'am. Would you like me to leave a message for him?"

"Please," she replied. "Tell him to call Mary at 2N-4L. I'll be there all day waiting for his call."

When she left the hotel, she was too confused and scared to notice the tall man standing a few feet away, jotting down her phone number in a small notebook.

Initially, she thought of taking the scenic route through the lush gardens of Boston Common but decided against it in fear of missing his call. With each step she took, the strange man followed not far behind.

She returned to an empty apartment where she sat waiting for Charles to call.

The phone rang about an hour later. She answered it on the first ring. "Hello?" she gulped.

"Is this Mary?" probed a man with a deep voice.

"This is Mary Wheaten. Is this the Parker House?"

The man responded with a concerned tone. "No. This is the Boston Police Department. I'm afraid your friend Charles has been in an accident. Can you come down to the station?"

"Certainly! I'll be right there. Is he ok?"

The man did not answer her question. "Please come to the station on Berkeley Street as soon as possible." Then the line went dead as the man, in a telephone booth across the street, hung up the phone.

Mary gathered her purse and left a note for Patricia. When she opened the door to leave the apartment, she was confronted by a man in a black trench coat. He smiled and let her pass as she walked for the stairs. Before she could take the first step, the man pushed her from behind. Mary tumbled down the stairs landing hard on the floor below.

The man calmly walked down the stairs and stepped over her ridiculing, "You think you can get my family's treasure? Think again."

15

Beth Israel Hospital's emergency room was relatively quiet that night. Usually, it was full of people with broken bones, children crying, and people sleeping in chairs while waiting for an update on a loved one. That night, it was empty except for an elderly man reading a magazine. The waiting room smelled of antiseptic cleaner rather than the standard weekend smells of vomit from a drunk college student or the body odor of a homeless man suffering from possible frostbite. The ER doctors and nurses expected a lull on weekdays. The weekends were when they got busier, probably because people were a little more reckless when they did not have to go to work the next morning.

The surgeon on duty was ready when an ambulance brought in a man with head trauma. The patient looked like someone had thrown him through a wall. His nose was severely broken. There were large gauze swabs stuffed in both nostrils to stop the bleeding. Both of the man's eyelids had already turned black and swollen. The EMT had wrapped his head with gauze, but even that was barely slowing the blood flow from the back of his head. An IV was in his left arm and another needle in his right, striving to replace the blood he was losing from his wounds.

While wheeling the stretcher through the hospital's double doors, the EMT barked out to the medical staff, "We have a male, approximately twenty-five years old, found unconscious, with sustained head and facial injuries."

They carefully transferred Charles from the stretcher to the hospital bed, with the doctors taking serious precautions, unaware of the extent of his injuries.

"His vitals are critically low. The patient has lost much blood," the EMT continued.

The doctor removed the once-white gauze, which had turned crimson from the wound. He found a large laceration on the back of his head, which needed to be addressed immediately.

"Does anyone know what happened to him?" asked the attending doctor.

A concerned police officer covered with blood was standing outside the hospital room but close enough to hear the question. "I found him lying in an alley near Fenway. I suspect he was attacked from behind and hit with a blunt object."

"Thank you, officer. That is helpful," the doctor replied. "Before we can do X-rays, we must close the wound to the head. Have radiation ready in fifteen minutes, after which I'll stitch him up and stop the bleeding."

In a soft Irish brogue, the officer asked, "Is he gonna make it, doc?"

"I think he will survive, but I am concerned with the extent of the head injury. Depending on how serious it is, I'm afraid he may be paralyzed, lose his memory, or have severe brain damage."

After the X-rays, it was determined that the head injury was rather extensive and that there was internal bleeding from the brain. To ease the swelling, surgery was necessary to stop the bleeding. As a result, they placed Charles in an induced coma. This was commonly done to prevent the patient from waking up too early and enduring the pain. Doctors feared that any physical or mental trauma could cause permanent damage to the brain.

Beth Israel Hospital was one of the best in the world, so it was no surprise that the surgery went well. Charles was placed in the ICU, where he was closely monitored. He was found with no identification, so the hospital staff decided to call him "John" until they could determine his true identity. The police officer who'd found him stopped by periodically to check on his status and, at one point, did a fingerprint test on him, hoping he might be in their database. They didn't have any luck.

After a few days, his vitals stabilized, and his prognosis became increasingly optimistic despite still being in the induced coma. What surprised the staff the most, however, was that no one visited "John." No one came to identify him, even with a newspaper article published by the Boston Globe describing the incident. All the hospital staff could do was wait until he was strong enough to remove him from the induced coma and hope he'd wake up and remember who he was. As the days went on, the reality of this became grim.

16

Patricia opened the door to her apartment building to see her friend Mary lying face down on the cement floor. She rolled her over and shook her unconscious friend.

"Mary. Wake up! Mary. Wake up!"

Mary blinked her eyes, trying to regain consciousness. She looked up at her friend and asked, "What happened? Where am I?"

Patricia responded, "You're lying on the floor of my apartment building's entry. You must have fallen down the stairs or something. We need to get you to the hospital."

"I'm all right. I just need a minute to clear my head," said Mary, as her wits returned.

"Nonsense!" exclaimed Patricia. "I'm going to hail a taxi and get you to Beth Israel just to ensure you are okay."

The two friends were in a cab racing to the hospital within minutes. They entered the doors to the emergency room full of patients waiting to be helped. Mary signed in at the reception desk and was told it would take about an hour to be seen. She was frustrated and told Patricia that they should just go home and get some rest, but her friend resisted. Mary was soon convinced to wait in order to determine that she didn't have a concussion or some other internal injury.

"So, what happened, Mary?" Patricia finally asked.

Mary had been asking herself the same thing. "I went to meet Charles at South Station, but he never arrived. I went to the Parker House to find him, but he was not there either." She was now thinking out loud.

"Then I walked back to your apartment and waited… then I got a phone call telling me to come to the police department. He told me that something had happened to Charles."

Patricia was confused. "The police called my apartment to tell you something happened to Charles?"

"Yes. He told me to go to the Berkeley Street station," a now confused Mary replied.

Patricia cross-examined her like a defense attorney. "Mary… how would the Boston Police Department have my phone number and know that you were at my apartment?"

Mary lifted her head and turned to her friend, bewildered.

Patricia then gave her closing argument. "I'm afraid to tell you, whoever called you was not the police. I think the caller has something to do with Charles not showing up at the train station. In addition, I think he had something to do with why we're here."

"Now that I think of it… When I left your apartment, a man stood in the hallway next to your door. Do you think—?"

"I think he pushed you down the stairs," replied Patricia.

The tense conversation was broken when a nurse shouted, "Mary Wheaten. Mary Wheaten." Mary raised her hand. "Please come with me."

Mary got up from her seat and followed the nurse into a room where a young doctor examined her. After they ran a few tests and checked her vitals, he determined that she did not have a concussion but noticed a few bruises on her shoulders and knees and a pretty big bump on her head. He gave her some aspirin and told her to rest for the next few days.

She thanked the doctor while wondering how she could 'rest' the next few days. *That's not gonna happen*, she thought. Charles was in trouble, so she needed to find him.

As she was leaving the exam room, behind her was a team of doctors, one of whom yelled, "Prep operation room four! Patient John needs immediate care."

If only Mary had turned around, she would have seen Charles being wheeled into surgery.

17

By the time Saturday arrived, it had been four days since Mary had last heard from Charles. Her reunion was at the Park Plaza Hotel's banquet room, just a short walk from Patricia's apartment. Mary's week was spent worrying about Charles. By the time Thursday came around, she knew that something was wrong. She called the Parker House each morning, asking reception to ring Charles' room. Each time, there was still no answer. She would visit the hotel each afternoon to see if he was still a registered guest. "He still is" was always the answer they gave. No one had seen him come or go all week.

Something is very wrong, she thought as she walked back to Patricia's every day.

After visiting the hotel one more time on Saturday, Patricia convinced Mary to go to their reunion. They both got there thirty minutes late in an attempt to look important. They enjoyed the company of their classmates and learned where everyone was living and what they were doing. In reality, Mary was just going through the motions. The reunion, in her mind, was ruined because of Charles' predicament. She just looked forward to getting to the train station the next day and returning home to Hinesville.

The next morning, Patricia was friendly enough to drop Mary off at the train station and, on the way, double park while she made one last visit to the Parker House. Again, there were no updates. The receptionist and door attendant wished her a fond farewell and a safe trip, both suspecting that something was afoul.

The train ride back to Georgia was not nearly as exciting as the trip to Boston. Mary shared a compartment with a young couple who had a baby that cried for the entire trip. After hours of the child's wailing, Mary sat in the dining car at the table where she and Charles had shared their first meal. She tried to finish the book she'd been reading when they first met, but the pages turned slowly as she lacked the concentration to focus on the plot. Eventually, she simply stared out the window, focusing on the farms, wildlife, and cloud formations. Not soon after, she sipped on her now-cold green tea, just counting the hours until she returned home.

The train arrived at Hinesville's station a little after 9 a.m. on Monday. Stepping down from the platform, Mary was reminded of how hot and humid Georgia could be in August. She longed to be back in Boston, roaming the streets with Charles, but the south would always be her home.

A porter helped carry her luggage to her car, parked in the station parking lot. He asked how her trip went.

"It was enjoyable. Boston is one of my favorite cities. Have you ever been?" she asked to be polite.

He replied, "No, ma'am, but I have always wanted to see the Red Sox play at Fenway Park."

"I was hoping to do the same this week with a friend, but it didn't work out, unfortunately," she shared. Then something flashed across her mind. "I'm sorry, sir, but I must go immediately. I am late for an appointment."

With that, she got into her hot car and instantly rolled down the windows to breathe some life into its steaming interior. She turned the ignition and drove swiftly out of the parking lot and onto Main Street. She drove down County Line Road for about fifteen minutes until she arrived at her destination: Gramer Lumber Company.

18

Mary parked her car with others next to what appeared to be the main building of the operation. It was a large, two-story metal building built for purpose, not style. At the front left side of the building was a glass door that read "Main Office."

When she opened the door, a little metal bell jangled over her head, but she was probably the only one who heard it because of a constant humming in the building. It was impossible to tell where it was coming from, but it was probably from one of the giant machines on the ground floor.

There was a receptionist's desk near the entrance manned by a lady sitting behind it on the telephone. She waved for Mary to approach her and then pointed at the phone, which was her way of saying that she would be with her when the call was over.

After putting down the receiver, the receptionist asked, "Can I help you?"

Mary introduced herself and asked, "I'm here to see Mr. Gramer. Charles Gramer. Is he in?"

"Mr. Gramer is away on business," she replied. Mary knew the receptionist was covering for his so-called vacation.

Ok. So, Charles still hasn't returned home. Now what?

"Is Joseph Gramer available? I'm a friend of Charles and went to school with Joseph, Jr. I just have a question to ask him. It is not business related."

The receptionist pushed a button on an intercom that went directly to Mr. Gramer's office. Mary heard the introduction and, in a distant voice from the box on her desk, heard Mr. Gramer welcome her to his office.

"Please go up the stairs. His office is the last one on the left."

When Mary reached the top of the iron stairs, she walked along the balcony toward his office. It felt more like a catwalk to her, as the floor was also made of iron rods. When she reached his office, she knocked on his door out of politeness even though it was open.

"Come in, Ms. Wheaten. Please take a seat," Mr. Gramer said while pointing to the leather chairs across from his desk. "What can I do for you?"

Mary played with her hair. Mr. Gramer resembled Charles. It was easy to tell he was an important man, but he had a warm, welcoming feeling about him.

"I'm sorry to bother you, Mr. Gramer. I know you are a busy man. I don't want to take up much of your time." She paused. "I'm here about your son, Charles."

Mr. Gramer's head tilted slightly to the left. "Charles? What about him?"

Mary told him all about the past week: the train ride, the Massachusetts Archives, the Treasury, William Hilton's will, Yale University Library, the attack on her... and the disappearance of his son.

"Have you heard from your son since he left for Boston?" she asked.

A worried look came over his face. "No. I have not. You were attacked? He never checked out of the hotel? You checked twice a day with the front desk? It appears you are worried about him and that you care for him," he added.

The statement snuck up on her a bit. She did not want to admit her feelings to his father but felt she had no other choice. "I have only known your son for a brief time, sir, but I have grown fond of him in that short time. I think he feels the same about me. He wouldn't have cut off all communication with me so suddenly. I am worried. I think something happened to him. I'm sure it relates to my attack, and I'm here to ask for your help."

Mr. Gramer got up from his chair and started pacing behind Mary. She didn't turn around to acknowledge him. What she'd told him was sinking in, and he felt the same way as she did: His son was in trouble.

After a minute of silence, he returned to his desk and directed, "Come with me. We have a telegraph machine downstairs. I suggest we send a telegram to the hotel where he was staying to confirm that he is still registered there and that no one has seen him since you were last there. If so, I will then telegram the Boston Police Department and report a missing person."

Once they sent the telegram to the Parker House, Mary and Joseph waited patiently for a response. After about an hour, the tape machine started moving. The telegram operator read the message and passed along the unwelcome news that all was status quo at the hotel.

Mr. Gramer asked the operator to find the number for the police department and dictated to him a message:

PRA89 43 GOVT=BOS BOSTON, MA 27 456P
BOSTON POLICE DEPARTMENT
BERKELEY STREET, BOSTON, MA

REPORTING A MISSING PERSON. CHARLES GRAMER WAS LAST SEEN ON TWELVE AUGUST AT QUINCY MARKET AND LAST HEARD FROM ON THE SAME DAY VIA TELEPHONE AT APPROX. 5:00 P.M. HE IS 26 YEARS OF AGE, 6 FEET, WITH BLONDE HAIR. HE IS REGISTERED AT THE PARKER HOUSE HOTEL. A REWARD OF $200 IS OFFERED.

CHARLES GRAMER, HINESVILLE, GA

His employee and receptionist gasped when they heard the message. Mary heard the receptionist say a quiet prayer for Charles.

19

It had been over a week since they'd admitted Charles to the ICU. His condition was improving, but not enough to remove him from the induced coma. His facial wounds were healing enough that the medical staff finally understood what he truly looked like. Patient "John" had become a mystery to the staff at the hospital. None of them could remember a patient being admitted this long without someone coming to identify them.

Each day, the police officer who helped Charles that frightful night stopped by to see if there was any progress on his condition or his identity. Each day he left the hospital a little more optimistic that he would survive but more frustrated that he remained alone. Based on the quality of the clothes he'd been wearing; he could tell he was a man of stature and wealth.

"Someone must be wondering where he was," he continually told himself.

****

At Tuesday's morning briefing at the Back Bay police precinct, the captain shared with his officers the telegram that had arrived the day before. On the chalkboard, he wrote the missing person's name, description, and details. Each officer took careful notes while he explained the circumstances.

Everyone except Officer David Flaherty, who just sat there and stared at the chalkboard. Flaherty was a fourteen-year veteran of the force who was popular with his fellow officers. He was short and stocky with an often-sunburned face from of too many days on his fishing boat.

When the briefing was complete, Officer Flaherty approached his captain and asserted, "I think I may know who the missing person is." He explained the call he'd gotten the previous Monday evening, the unidentified victim, and his visits to the hospital. The captain told him to make this his number one priority and to keep him apprised of his findings. Flaherty ran to his squad car to begin his investigation.

He entered the Parker House Hotel a few minutes later, thanks to the flashing lights he used, even though this wasn't an emergency. He often laughed at how civilians did not realize how often officers used their lights for convenience rather than necessity.

The receptionist at the front desk was taken aback when Officer Flaherty waved his badge in front of him but was not surprised when he mentioned Charles Gramer's name. The receptionist explained the visits from Mary and the mutual concern they shared for Mr. Gramer's wellbeing.

Flaherty asked for and received a key to Charles' room and went up to it, accompanied by the hotel manager. When entering the room, nothing seemed amiss. It looked like a typical room of a business traveler. His empty suitcase was sitting on the floor. His clothes were neatly folded in the dresser drawers, and a suit was hanging in the closet. The bed was made, and he'd organized his toiletries on the bathroom sink.

This did not seem like the room of someone who'd left in a hurry or was forced to leave. The only clue he found in the room that held any semblance of importance was his briefcase. It lay on the bed, unopened and locked. This was an obvious sign that Mr. Gramer left the hotel room on Monday for pleasure, not business.

The evidence found at the hotel was not earth-shattering but helpful. Flaherty's next stop would be a place that had recently become familiar to him: Beth Israel Hospital.

When he entered the ICU, the attending nurse welcomed him as she had a few other days he visited. He asked if he could meet with the physician responsible for patient "John." A doctor appeared at the nurses' station within a few minutes and introduced himself as Dr. Singh. The Indian doctor greeted Officer Flaherty with a firm handshake and asked, in a thick dialect, how he could be of assistance.

"We might have a lead on your unidentified patient. We suspect he might be a gentleman from Georgia. His father has been in contact with us via telegram. I would like to help identify his son without him taking a one-day train ride up to Boston," the officer explained.

The doctor replied, "How can I be of assistance?"

"When you examined him, did you find any noticeable birthmarks, scars, or anything his family might recognize?" Flaherty asked.

Doctor Singh squinted his eyes, crinkled his nose, and drew a deep breath. After a few moments, he shook his head and was about to speak when a nurse interjected.

"I have bathed patient 'John' each night for a week," she said. "I know something that could help identify him."

Officer Flaherty turned to her and took out his notepad.

"He has a large scar on his right shoulder. It appears that he may have had shoulder surgery at some point," she explained.

Flaherty jotted down his findings, thanked them both, then turned for the door. *I might have cracked the case of patient "John." Is a promotion to detective in my future?*

20

"**M**r. Gramer," said the receptionist over the intercom. "There is a telegram coming in for you."

Joseph ran from his desk down to the ground floor and read the telegram from the Boston Police Department. An unidentified, unconscious man in his mid-twenties was lying in a hospital bed with a large scar on his right shoulder. Joseph's mouth dropped, and his eyes widened. He directed his employee to return the telegram, identifying the patient and making them aware that he would be in Boston as soon as possible.

There was a tear in his eye as he ran out of the lumber yard and jumped into his car. His son was hurt and in trouble. He had no choice but to get Pearl, pack a bag, and get on the first train to Boston.

Not surprisingly, Pearl was shocked at the news. It took a few minutes for Joseph to calm her down enough to make sense of the situation. Once she was in a mental state where she could think straight, she packed their suitcases with essential clothing and a bottle of sleeping pills she felt she was going to need.

Joseph went to the den. He had a phone call to make.

"Ms. Wheaten," he said over the telephone. "This is Joseph Gramer. We met at the lumber yard yesterday."

It surprised Mary to hear his voice. "Good afternoon, Mr. Gramer. What can I do for you?"

"I may have some news about my son. It appears he may have been in an accident. We think he's in a Boston hospital: unconscious. That is why he has not contacted anyone in the past week."

The news didn't necessarily shock Mary. She knew something had happened to Charles when they lost contact. An accident explained his disappearance, but in her gut, she knew it was not an accident.

Mr. Gramer continued, "My wife and I are getting on a train to Boston tomorrow morning. I will keep you apprised of the situation."

Mary did not hesitate when she replied, "That will not be necessary, Mr. Gramer. I will be on the same train. I need to see your son and ensure he is all right."

It surprised Joseph that she was willing to travel so far again for someone she had just met, but he agreed.

"Very well, Ms. Wheaten. My wife and I will see you at the train station tomorrow at 11 a.m.," he said, then hung up the phone.

****

The train ride felt longer than twenty hours for the Gramers and Mary. Each had butterflies in their stomach. It seemed like every minute was an hour, and every hour felt like a day. Joseph and Pearl were kind enough to pay for Mary's ticket and let her join them in their compartment.

At the start of the trip, Mary explained to them how they'd met and their findings at the Treasury. She also shared how excited Charles had been to find the contents of the security deposit box and his upcoming trip to Yale. She chose not to share her thoughts on, what she believed, were attacks on each of them. It wasn't the time to do so. After all, they don't even know if it is Charles in the hospital yet.

Pearl quickly grew fond of Mary. They found that they shared the same family values, but at the same time, Pearl was impressed with her drive and passion for education. She found her intelligent and witty. Pearl had not liked many of the girls Charles brought home over the years, so she hoped she might see Mary again when the dust cleared.

After a restless night, the train whistle blew at 8 a.m. as South Station quickly appeared. Mary guided them through the busy terminal and showed them where they could hail a taxi to Beth Israel Hospital.

The cab ride took about fifteen minutes. There were very few words spoken in the car. The ride was filled with blank stares and worried looks. When they arrived, Joseph paid the cab driver, thanked him, and the three of them, suitcases in hand, hurried to the front door of the hospital. They rushed to the main reception desk and asked where the intensive care unit was. After a five-minute walk, they finally arrived at the ICU.

Joseph approached the nurses' station and boomed, "I'm here to see my son. Where is he?"

"Excuse me, sir," answered the attending nurse. "Who is your son?"

"His name is Charles Gramer," he replied in a concerned tone. "But I think you know him as Patient John."

The nurse's eyes grew larger than golf balls. She jumped from her seat and exclaimed, "Oh my! Come with me, Sir. Come with me."

As they hurried down the hall, the nurse, who seemed older than the Gramers, continued to talk. "We have all been so worried about John—I mean Charles. We were afraid that no one would identify him. I want you to know that he has been in all our prayers since he arrived."

Joseph was about to thank the nurse for her heartfelt intentions until she opened the hospital room door. He saw his son lying unconscious in a hospital bed with tubes coming out of his nose and mouth and IVs in both his arms. He then noticed his wife wobble; it was lucky for her that he did. It gave him enough time to catch Pearl as she passed out from the sight of her injured son.

21

Joseph and Mary lay the limp Pearl on the empty hospital bed next to her son's. Joseph waved his hands above her, hoping to provide some air. The nurse gently slapped her face to wake her up. After a few seconds, she regained consciousness. They sat her up slowly and gave her a cup of water to drink. Pearl resisted, claiming she wanted to be by her son's side, but the nurse would not allow it until she drank the water.

Once properly hydrated, Pearl rushed to Charles, kneeled beside him, and took his hand in hers. She repeatedly asked, "What has happened to my dear boy?"

Joseph stood over her and cried at the sight of his son. He remembered seeing him unconscious after his shoulder surgery in high school, but he did not remember the fear he felt now. It was sheer terror. The thought of losing one of his boys brought chills down his spine.

Whatever the cost, I will not let my son die.

While the Gramers wept at their son's bedside, Mary did the same from a chair nearby. The nurse who'd brought them to the room had left to get the attending physician. A buzz had already spread throughout the hospital at the news that Patient "John" had finally been identified. Staff walked past his room to confirm the happy rumor.

After a few minutes, Dr. Singh entered the room and introduced himself to the Gramers and Mary. He explained what they suspected had happened to Charles and how his injuries had prompted them to place him in an induced coma.

Joseph spoke for the first time after hearing the doctor's explanation. "Placing my son in a coma seems to be dangerous. Isn't that excessive?"

The doctor replied, "Traumatic head injuries often result in significant brain swelling. The swelling puts pressure on the brain, which reduces blood flow and oxygen and can damage brain tissue. To avoid this, we induce a coma to allow the brain to rest."

"How long will you keep him in this state?" asked Pearl. "Can you wake him up at any time?"

Dr. Singh had expected this question. It was the most common that a loved one typically had when facing this type of scenario. "We plan to bring your son out of the coma in forty-eight hours. The swelling has reduced significantly since his admittance, and his wounds are healing well."

A collective sigh of relief filled the room at the doctor's prognosis. It was the first sign of hope that any of them had since hearing the news of Charles' condition. The next question came from Mary, who was still sitting in the chair. She had tried to stand earlier but felt too weak and feared she would faint like Pearl. "When you remove him from the coma, how long will it take him to regain consciousness?"

The doctor turned to Mary and replied, "Good question, Miss. Unfortunately, there is no precise answer. I'm afraid there is no guarantee he will wake up at all. He was unconscious when he arrived, so we don't know what happened to him. As a result, we can't be sure of the extent of his injuries."

The optimism that everyone had just felt left the room faster than a burglar leaving the crime scene. The thought of Charles not waking up had never entered their minds.

The doctor left the room, assuring them that he would be back later in the day to check on him and that the nursing staff would closely watch him throughout the day. They thanked him for his assistance and assured him they would be by his side day and night.

Pearl broke down hysterically in Joseph's arms after the doctor left. Mary gasped at the thought of how scared and sad she felt about a man she had met not so long ago. She could only imagine how his mother was feeling. It was a pain that no one should have to endure.

After Pearl regained her composure, she walked across the room and hugged Mary. "Thank you for being here for my son," she whispered in Mary's ear. "Your presence will help him heal. He will be glad you are here when he wakes up."

Mary cried after hearing Pearl's kind words and asked, "May I go over and see him?"

"Of course, dear," she replied to the trembling young woman in her arms.

Mary gingerly walked across the room, sat beside Charles, and held his hand, similar to how his mother did earlier. She gave his hand a soft kiss and whispered to him, "Our journey is not over yet, Charles. We still need to find William Hilton's will, and I must bring you to tea at the Parker House. Please come back to us." Then she said, in her bad English accent, "I've missed you so, young chap."

Joseph and Pearl looked at each other affectionately upon hearing the accent. They then glanced back at Mary and their son and wondered, *Are these two in love?*

22

Mary and the Gramers took turns staying by Charles' bedside for the next couple of days. They typically did four-hour shifts, but whoever stayed overnight would stay longer because they would inevitably fall asleep. When not at the hospital, they found themselves sitting in their hotel room waiting for a call saying that Charles had woken up. There was no desire for sightseeing amongst them. They were each too worried to enjoy the beautiful city they found themselves in.

Every few hours, a doctor or nurse would come in the room to check on him. Each time they explained that his condition was improving slightly. Finally, Dr. Singh entered one morning and reviewed his vital signs.

He spoke directly to Pearl in a passionate tone. "His condition has improved enough over the past two weeks that it is time to remove him from the induced coma."

A collective sigh fell across the room. Joseph whimpered while hugging his wife. "What's the next step, doctor?"

"On Friday morning, the anesthesiologist will gradually withdraw the drugs from his system while I will carefully monitor his brain activity and other vital signs." He continued, "It might take up to seventy-two hours for him to wake up, but I am confident that he will at some point."

The next two days were long and arduous for the Gramers and Mary. The thought of Charles waking up kept them up at night and forced them to look at the clock constantly. When Friday finally arrived, Dr. Singh explained that they were not allowed to be present when Charles was removed from the coma.

They sat in the waiting room for a little over an hour until Dr. Singh approached them and announced, "He is out of the coma and breathing on his own. His vital signs are all stable. He did great. I think that he will be fine. He just needs to wake up now."

The Gramers got up from their seats and hugged each other in relief. Mary remained in her chair, with her hands on her face, head dropped in her lap, and crying tears of joy. Pearl quickly walked over and put her arm around Mary to comfort her and share in the joy.

The doctor explained that Charles was resting comfortably in his room, and they could now visit him. He suggested they continue holding vigil by his bedside so that when he wakes up, he would have a loved one there to explain where he was and what had happened.

When they entered the room, they were relieved to see the breathing tubes removed from his nose and mouth. He was still hooked up with IVs because they were necessary to feed him and keep him nourished.

"I don't know about you two," said Joseph. "But I'm not leaving my boy's side. No more four-hour shifts for me. I'm going to stay in this room until he wakes up."

Pearl and Mary both agreed. They would all remain in the room until he woke up. They knew it would be uncomfortable, but the thought of not being there when he woke was worse. They each took turns going to the cafeteria for the next two days to eat their meals. None of them spent more than a half hour at a time away from the room. The only reason someone would leave was out of sheer necessity: bathroom, shower, and eating.

On Monday afternoon, they were sitting around a table that a nurse had brought into the room days before. They placed it in the corner of the room and had three chairs so they could eat, do crossword puzzles, and play cards. The gin rummy matches over the past few days were getting rather intense. Mary joked that if Mr. Gramer lost more games to her, he might have to take a small business loan out to repay her for her winnings. Just like Charles, Joseph was growing fond of Mary's sense of humor.

After a particularly grueling card game, Pearl finally yelled out, "Gin!" to the dismay of Joseph and Mary. They all laughed as Pearl danced in her seat.

"What's all the commotion over there?" a weak voice asked from across the room.

The three turned in unison. Charles was awake! Joseph and Pearl rushed to his bedside. They each grabbed a hand. Mary barreled out of the room to get the doctor.

"Charles. It is Mother and Father. We're here. Everything is all right," assured Pearl while holding and kissing his hand.

Charles was trying to focus his eyes and shaking his head a little. "I have a headache and am so thirsty. Is there anything to drink?"

At that moment, Dr. Singh and a nurse came into the room with Mary. The doctor asked Joseph and Pearl to move away from the bed while he examined him. He shone a flashlight in his eyes and placed a stethoscope over his chest.

Again, Charles asked for a glass of water. "Doc, my throat is so dry. Is there any way I can get some water?" he pleaded in a raspy voice.

Dr. Singh directed the nurse to get water for his patient. In less than a minute, Charles was sucking from a straw like a soldier gulping water from a canteen on a hot battlefield. It took about ten minutes for Charles to gain his bearings, refocus his eyes, and get his voice back. He was still weak but slowly sounded like the Charles they all knew.

After his parents explained what had happened to him and that he had been in a coma for over two weeks, Charles looked across the room at Mary. "Who is that?"

Pearl whispered, "That is Mary: your friend that helped us find you."

Charles continued to stare at Mary who now looked vulnerable. She raised her eyebrows as if to say, *don't you remember me?*

He raised his hand and waved her to come closer so he could get a better view of her. He couldn't help but notice her long red hair while he gazed into her big green eyes.

As she ambled towards him, his father explained, "If it wasn't for Mary, I don't think we ever would have found you. She visited me at the lumber yard and told me something was wrong."

Charles never took his eyes off her. As she approached the bed, he reached for her hand and said with his bad British accent, "I suppose I owe the lady a large gratitude for what she has done."

Mary's eyes widened as her tears of sorrow turned to those of joy. "You remember me?" she asked, recognizing that lousy accent.

A smirk came across his face. "How could I forget you? You are the last thing I remember and the first thing I thought of when I woke up."

Relieved yet a bit annoyed, Mary playfully punched him on the shoulder. She leaned over and whispered in her bad British accent, "I'm not sure I deserved that, but just feel better chap. Then you can take me to Yale University as promised... to find Sir William Hilton's will."

23

The doctors told Charles that he would have to remain in the hospital another week so they could monitor his vital signs and make sure that he had made a full recovery. They removed him from the ICU and placed him in a standard room that was private and more spacious.

The Gramers reluctantly returned to Hinesville once his condition was stable, and he was continuing to gain strength. Charles promised his parents that he would return home after he visited Yale. Pearl fought the idea fearing whoever attacked him would do so again. She was convinced to let him stay when he explained that the assailant likely presumed he was dead or still in a coma, so he had no reason to conceive he would be a threat.

Each day, Charles ate three square meals and often took walks throughout the hospital wards to gain strength in his legs. He also did several crossword puzzles each day to sharpen his mind. He felt like his old self when he was ready to be released. He had his wits about him and the strength to continue his journey.

Mary arranged to pick up Charles at the hospital the morning of his release. She had purchased train tickets to New Haven the day before. The release was uneventful, which allowed them to reach South Station in plenty of time to catch the 10:20 a.m. train.

The five-hour train ride was comprised of speculation about what happened that night outside of Fenway Park and who attacked Mary. They were convinced the incidents were not random, but they couldn't reason why someone would want to hurt them. The only thing they had in common was that they were both from Hinesville, and they were interested in William Hilton. Regardless, they felt they should watch their backs and be as conspicuous as possible.

"I can't kick the feeling that someone hurt you, and it was likely because of me," said Charles.

"But why is William Hilton's will important enough to try and kill both of us?" replied Mary. "You could never have imagined anything like this could have happened. It's not your fault."

Charles continued, "True. But it's not so much about the will and adventure anymore for me. It's about finding out who did this to us and getting justice."

"I suspect when we read the will, it will provide some sort of clue as to who the attacker is and why we were attacked," Mary concluded.

They pulled into Union Station in downtown New Haven a little after three-thirty. Crowds rushed through the station. The sound of wing-tip shoes tapping against the marble floor made a constant echoing beat. It was not as big as Boston's South Station but resembled it. It was a large brick building. The walls were surrounded by floor-to-ceiling windows that let the afternoon sunshine through. It smelled of body odor and stale food. That may have had to do with what appeared to be several homeless people sleeping on benches.

Charles was familiar with the station from law school so knew they could quickly get a taxi to campus. The ride took only ten minutes. When they got out of the car, Mary was instantly impressed by the architecture of Yale's old buildings. She did a three-sixty spin with her head looking up at the seemingly endless steeples of the academic buildings. It differed from Boston University, which mainly consisted of high-rises on Commonwealth Avenue.

Being that it was August, the campus was relatively quiet. Students would not be arriving for the fall semester for a few more weeks, so it felt like they had the place to themselves.

It was a short walk to the Lillian Goldman Law Library. Charles knew just where it was since he'd spent most of his time studying in the large, five-story building. Like most others on campus, the library employed a collegiate gothic style. He'd learned a while ago that they'd modeled it after the King's College Chapel at the University of Cambridge in England.

When they entered the library, the main reading room welcomed them. It was surrounded by bookshelves on three walls that held hundreds, if not thousands, of books. Above the bookcases were twenty-foot-high windows that allowed the law students a glimpse of the sun on the off chance that they raised their heads from the book they were reading.

Charles led them to the main desk at the front of the room and asked the librarian where they could find documents preserved by the Avalon Project. The librarian directed them to a large wooden staircase that led to the basement. She told them that that's where they preserved all the ancient documents.

Charles and Mary quickly walked down the stairs where, at the bottom, they saw a large, ornate door with a modern plaque identifying it as the Avalon Project. They entered the room and were greeted by a young lady who was presumably a law student working there as an intern.

"We are looking for a document from the 1600s that we were told was given to you by the Massachusetts Treasury Department," Charles explained. "It was held at a failed bank, and the document went unclaimed. We were told it was given to you because you have the proper means of preserving such delicate items."

The young lady seemed eager to help. She had a comforting look about herself. It was a look that showed she cared more about academics than about hairstyle. She stood up from her seat and walked up to the counter where they stood.

She responded, "You're right. The Avalon Project specializes in ancient, even medieval documents. First things first: Do you have any idea when we came into possession of the document, or can you provide some sort of description?"

Mary decided to join in the excitement by answering, "We know that it is the last will and testament of a man named William Hilton. I would suspect that you obtained the document around 1847."

"I know that document!" she exclaimed as she eagerly walked around the customer service counter. "It's the one with the map. I actually had someone view it yesterday... The actual day we unsealed it." Mary and Charles looked bewildered.

She continued without missing a beat, "It has been archived for over one hundred years. You see, when we receive certain documents, we archive them and seal them. No one is allowed to view the document for one hundred years. In the case of Mr. Hilton, it was unsealed yesterday."

This twist certainly puzzled Charles and Mary. Neither had any idea that documents were archived, and by chance, they had arrived one day after it was unsealed. The coincidence was remarkable.

Eyebrows raised in confusion, Charles asked, "Wait a minute! There is a will AND a map… and someone else viewed them yesterday. Is that what you are saying?"

Charles had often fantasized about what might be included in William Hilton's will but wondered why there would also be a map. This adventure that he'd created had now become more interesting but also more dangerous. Ideas flashed through his head at warp speed.

The young lady broke his chain of thought when she responded, "That's correct. A man visited yesterday, right when the library opened. I remember because I had to get permission from my manager to unseal the documents. I can take you to view them right now. They're in a room down the hall."

Without saying a word, the three walked into a locked, airtight room no bigger than a child's bedroom. After unlocking the door, the young lady went directly to the back left-hand corner and opened a drawer. She removed a plastic bag with what appeared to be William Hilton's last will and testament—and a map. She placed the bag on a large wooden table. Mary and Charles were told to wear gloves and face masks before viewing and handling the documents. Once the room was sterile, she handed him the items.

Charles opened the plastic bag and removed the contents. In his hand was a single sheet of paper the approximate size of legal paper attorneys use. When he looked at the document, he asked the young lady, "I see the will. Where is the map?"

She spun around, surprised by the question. "Both documents are in the black plastic bag."

"That is where you're wrong. The will is here. The map is not," Charles said as he held up the will in one hand while raising the palm of his other hand to the sky. "No map."

She rushed over to the table to see for herself. "Yesterday, there were two documents in the sealed bag. How is there only one?" she asked, thinking aloud.

Mary responded to her redundant question, "It seems the gentleman who was here yesterday probably stole said map."

"And there is one thing that I know for sure," Charles chimed in, trying to finish her thought. "If we find that man, we find the map."

24

"Four tickets to Charleston, South Carolina," demanded the man holding a briefcase and smoking a cigarette. He paid the fare and walked to the platform where the train was set to leave in fifteen minutes. All four seats in his compartment were purchased together to ensure ultimate privacy. The six-foot, four-inch athletic specimen latched the top button of his black suit as he boarded the train.

When he reached his compartment, he placed his briefcase on his lap and opened it. It had two items: a 1600s treasure map and a 32-caliber handgun.

His family's destiny would soon be fulfilled.

****

The librarian gave them time alone with the document while she frantically ran out of the room searching for a supervisor. Charles delicately laid the document on the table so both of them could read it:

In the Name of God, Amen.

The twenty-seventh day of September, Anno Domini one thousand six hundred sixty and two, I William Hilton of Plymouth in the County of

Plymouth, Mariner, being in good health of body and of sound and perfect memory (praised be God) do make and ordain this my last will and testament.

In manner and form following first, I commit my Soul to God that gave it trusting and steadfastly believing to be saved through the merits of Jesus Christ, my blessed Savior.

And my body to the earth from whence it came to be decently buried in such place as to my Executor shall deem convenient.

And as concerning the worldly estate which it hath pleased God to lend me, I dispose of the same in manner following:

I give and bequeath to my children all of the lawful money to be paid at their respective ages of one and twenty years.

I give and bequeath all my household goods and furniture to my children.

I direct my only son Andrew to sail to the Carolinas, where I placed a buried treasure. Travel by sea for fourteen days whereupon you will see an island. At the southernmost tip of the island, starting at a group of ten large sea pine trees, walk to the north and then to the east, and there you will find the treasure. I walked at least five hundred paces to get to that spot, but I was not more than five hundred paces as the crow flew from the large sea pine trees. I am sure that I walked farther in the northerly direction than in the easterly direction. With the large sea pine tree at the origin and the positive yy - axis pointing to the north, graph the possible location of the treasure for which you will be rewarded by a life-pleasing God that is deserved.

I leave to my executor the sum of ten pounds which I order to be laid out for the decent discharge of my funeral.

All the rest of my goods chattels real and personal estate not hereby disposed I give and bequeath to my son Andrew Hilton whom I constitute and appoint Executor of this my last will and testament, and I appoint Mr. Richard Groves and William Turcot both of Plymouth in the said County of Plymouth Overseers of the same and give them five shillings apiece.

In witness whereof, I the said William Hilton have hereunto set my hand and sealed the day and year first above written.

William Hilton Signed Sealed and published in the presence of Richard Groves, Timothy Hanson, and William Turcot

After reading the will twice, they both stood in silence for a few minutes. It was challenging to read because of the old English writing style, but they both clearly understood why there was a map in the safe deposit box besides the will. It all started making sense now. William Hilton buried a treasure in either North or South Carolina.

Where did he bury the treasure? How much would it be worth today? Why would he bury a treasure?

Now they understood why some guy named Samuel Goldsmith had another man's last will and testament and had felt the need to hide it in a bank safe deposit box.

The next line of self-questioning was much more difficult to decipher.

How did someone else know about the will? How did they know it was being unsealed yesterday? Did they know about the treasure map? Did they steal the treasure map?

"So, your adventure has led us to this," said Mary. "A buried treasure somewhere in the Carolinas. I bet there are fifty islands in both states, so finding it would be nearly impossible. Add to that the fact that someone else knows about the treasure and is so eager to find it they stole a priceless document from the archives of Yale University Law School."

Charles was thinking the same thing. "How could someone else know that William Hilton's will was stored here one hundred years ago and knew the exact day they would unseal it?"

Mary opened her purse and pulled out a small notebook and pen. "Here," she directed, giving both to Charles. "Write down the passage about where he left the treasure. We will obviously need this information in the future if we intend to continue with what we can now officially call a treasure hunt."

Charles complied and wrote the passage word for word.

While he was writing, a thought came to him. "I know where he buried the treasure."

"How can you know where it is buried?" Mary asked.

"It is simple. He buried it on an island in the Carolinas. What's the name of the person who wrote the will?"

"William Hilton," answered Mary, her mind racing. "William Hilton... Hilton Head Island. They named the island after him!"

"Bingo. Buy that girl a Coke," Charles said while pointing and winking at her playfully. "Now we know where he buried it. So, the more pressing question is who stole the map, and why is he so eager to find the treasure that he's willing to kill for it?"

Mary took the notebook from Charles and placed it back in her purse. "Come with me."

They left the room and headed back to the front desk, where they had first met the young lady that had helped them earlier. She was on the phone in obvious distress. Whoever was on the other line was giving her the business. She kept saying "sorry" and "yes, sir."

When she finished the call, she turned to face them. Still in distress, she said, "Sorry about that. As you can imagine, my boss is not thrilled that a three-hundred-year-old document has suddenly gone missing on my watch."

They both tried to console her by telling her it was not her fault, and everything would be all right. Even if they were simply trying to appease her, she was grateful for the gesture, nonetheless.

To lighten the mood a bit, Charles told her, "I promise the will is still in the plastic bag. You can search us if you would like."

"That won't be necessary," she replied. "But if you don't mind, I'm going to run to the room just to make sure."

As she left, Mary had an idea. "I know how we can find out who stole the will and attacked us," she said to Charles in her best detective voice. He raised his eyebrows with interest.

Mary walked to the front desk, grabbed an open book, and spun it around so she could read it.

"We had to sign in today to view the documents, so the person who stole the map must've done so as well. We just need to see who checked in yesterday."

She flipped the page back one day and saw only one person who had signed in:

Samuel Goldsmith.

25

Now that they knew what was in the safe deposit box, that a treasure could be at the end of the rainbow, and someone else knew about it, they realized that time was of the essence. Goldsmith was one day ahead of them. He was the attacker, and he was likely already in South Carolina.

The librarian who'd helped them find the will was still in the back, securing it. They left the library without saying goodbye. If they waited for her, they feared her supervisor would show up and start asking questions. They were willing to help, but it was not worth the risk of being delayed with questions about the will and map.

Union Station was bustling as always when they arrived. "Two tickets to Boston, please," said Charles. Even though a train could take them directly to Hinesville from New Haven, they had to go back to Boston to get their luggage.

"The last train to Boston leaves in four and a half minutes. Better hurry!" explained the man behind the glass.

Minutes later, they were on the train again. The ride to Boston did not feel like five hours. They spent the time talking about the treasure and Samuel Goldsmith.

After hours of contemplation and thinking aloud, it was likely that the Goldsmith family knew about the will but somehow did not have access to the safe deposit box. Goldsmith must have hidden the receipt in the Cotton Mather book but told no one where it was before his death. They presumed the tale of the treasure had been passed down for generations in the Goldsmith family and became a reality when the Plymouth Savings Bank failed in the 1800s, and they had revealed the contents of the safe deposit box.

The problem they now faced— one they'd never expected —was that someone else was involved with this adventure, someone with hundreds of years of history behind the passion for finding the buried treasure and seemingly willing to kill for it.

"Charles, I have a question for you," Mary said sternly. It was time to approach the elephant in the room. "Samuel Goldsmith seems to know more about this treasure than we do. He is obviously one step ahead of us. He was behind the attacks on us, right?"

After hearing that Mary was attacked, Charles knew one person had to be behind both assaults. He just didn't know who or why. Now he did.

"Of course. He must feel that his family has a right to the treasure, and if he is the one behind our attacks, then he is willing to do anything for it."

Mary continued the train of thought. "But doesn't it seem odd that a generation of Goldsmiths would believe they have a right to someone else's treasure? It's obviously William Hilton's, not theirs."

"Agreed. Regardless, he's dangerous, so we need to keep that in mind. At this point, we need to decide if it's worth continuing," his voice got lower and lower. "Personally, it's more important to me that Goldsmith pays for what he did to us than finding the treasure. I want him behind bars."

"True. He can't get away with it. What do you suggest we do? We can't call the police. They'd laugh at the idea that someone tried to kill both of us because of some long-lost treasure."

Charles paused. "Even so, by the time we could get the police to Hilton Head, he would have likely found the treasure and be long gone. We get justice by ensuring Goldsmith does not find the treasure and never hurts anyone again."

"And how do you suppose we do that?"

"The element of surprise," added Charles. "For all he knows, I am still in a coma or even dead. He probably thinks you're still in the hospital as well. He doesn't know we're on his tail."

Mary was impressed with his intuitiveness. "That's true! All we have to do is be discrete, and we shouldn't be in any danger. Plus, imagine if we find the treasure. What would life be like?"

"My only motivation is to make sure he doesn't get it. If we find it… let's promise to do good with it. It's our chance to make the world a better place."

Mary nodded in agreement and made one last declaration. "Promise me this. If it gets too dangerous, we call this whole thing off."

Unfortunately, Charles didn't hear her request. He was too busy dreaming about a life with the woman sitting next to him.

****

When they arrived at Boston's South Station, they were told the next train to Hinesville wasn't until the next morning. They expected that answer but were still disappointed at the thought of losing precious hours to Goldsmith. Charles purchased one-way tickets for both of them and suggested they get rooms at the Parker House for the evening.

Since it was only about a mile to the hotel and they didn't bring luggage to New Haven, they walked to the hotel. Mary knew her way, so it was an easy walk. It was perfect timing, too. Once they arrived and checked Mary in, afternoon tea was just beginning.

They decided to dine at the Union Oyster House that evening. It was one of the oldest restaurants in the city and was renowned for its seafood. Mary had been there several times and was always fascinated that the likes of John Adams and other Founding Fathers had dined at the same establishment. They were seated at the semi-circular oyster bar that looked out to the bustling street through the large, front-facing windows.

During dinner, they mapped out the next few days. Mary expressed concern about taking too much time off from work for the reunion and being by Charles' side in the hospital. She needed to return to work for fear of being fired. His eyes widened a bit at her admission. He knew that Hilton Head Island was sparsely inhabited, so the terrain would likely be difficult to maneuver. Although Mary had proved herself to be strong-willed and intelligent, this part of the adventure might be too dangerous. Of course, he would never admit that to Mary.

"So, you go to work when we get back, so you don't get fired," said Charles. "And I'll meet with my father. He has visited Hilton Head many times over the past couple of years looking for land to buy. He must have made some contacts there who might help us get to the southernmost part of the island where Hilton hid the treasure."

Mary chimed in, "Then what? Would you simply start digging holes at random? I hate to break it to you, but you're not a treasure hunter."

After a dozen oysters and a couple of glasses of wine, they finally figured out the answer.

"I'll use a metal detector!" said Charles. "I had one as a child and spent hours during family vacations in Florida looking for lost coins and valuables at the beach. I never found anything of significant value, but I have a feeling that my luck is about to change."

"But what about Goldsmith?" Mary interrupted his stroll down Memory Lane. "Isn't he already there?"

Charles was too consumed with getting to the south side of Hilton Head that he had forgotten about Goldsmith. That was a rookie mistake.

Their plan was flawed, naïve, and dangerous. They would need more than a metal detector and a little luck to find Hilton's treasure and avenge Goldsmith.

They didn't know, yet feared, that their adventure was about to turn into a nightmare.

26

The train pulled into Hinesville at 11 a.m. Mary was going straight to the paper mill, expecting some nasty looks from her coworkers about her extended absence. Charles chose to walk to his apartment, shower, change clothes, then head to the lumber yard to speak with his father.

They hugged each other goodbye, and Mary kissed Charles on the cheek. This was the most affection they had shown each other since they'd met. They exchanged telephone numbers, and Charles promised to call later that evening to update her on his meeting with his father.

About an hour later, Charles pulled up to the lumber yard. The parking lot was almost full, so he suspected it would be a busy day. He entered the office and was immediately approached by the receptionist, who had been worried sick when she found out about his injuries.

Her name was Madeline. She was in her early sixties, overweight but with the energy of a teenager. She had been with the lumber company since they opened and was one of the family's dearest employees.

"Well, aren't you a sight for sore eyes!" she said while giving Charles one of her famous hugs. "I have been praying for you, child. I've been praying for you night and day. Blessed be God that he returned you home unharmed."

Madeline was a big part of the Gramer family. He had known her since he was a little child, so he considered her a second mother. "It is great to be home, Madeline. I thank you for your wishes and prayers. It appears I needed them more than I knew. Is my father in his office?"

Madeline put both hands on his head while touching up his hair. "He is upstairs. I am sure he is dying to see you."

Charles walked up the stairs like he had done hundreds of times before, but he appreciated it a little more this time. He had been feeling the same way lately with other things in life that he'd taken for granted before his injuries.

He knocked on his father's office door and let himself in. Before he could say hello, his father jumped from his desk chair, ran over to him, and gave him a big hug. "It's so good to see you, son. Welcome home. Have you seen your mother yet?"

"Thanks," he replied. "It is good to be home. No. I haven't seen her yet. I came straight here from the train station. I need to share some developments regarding the safe deposit box with you."

Charles explained to him about William Hilton's will, the hidden treasure, Samuel Goldsmith, and the stolen map. With every word, Joseph grew increasingly intrigued but angry at the same time. He could not believe a book purchased at auction for his wife could have provided such a mystery... and danger.

"Well, we have to get to Hilton Head Island," Joseph declared.

"We?" asked Charles.

"Yes. We. I will bring you to Hilton Head and introduce you to some folks who can help us get to the south side of the island. Plus, if Goldsmith is on the island, I'd prefer to have a lieutenant general by your side for protection."

Joseph continued, "If he was the one who put you in a coma, you need to be very careful… and so does he now that I'm involved."

27

After visiting Pearl and packing a bag, Joseph and Charles set off on their trip to Hilton Head Island. They didn't tell her the real reason why they were going to the island, fearing she may put a stop to it. The island was dangerous enough, but the idea that Samuel Goldsmith could already be there kicked it up a notch or two. Vengeance was never easy and would not be any different this time.

They took Joseph's car. Savannah was about halfway there, so they stopped to buy metal detectors they would need to find the treasure. The Army/Navy store had everything they needed. Besides the metal detectors, they bought binoculars, shovels, tents, canteens, and guns just in case they came across Goldsmith. They purchased five metal detectors, hoping they could rally a few men on the island to help with the search. The ride took a little over three hours. Assuming everything went as expected, they would stay in Savannah while they searched for the treasure.

Joseph drove to the May River in Bluffton, South Carolina, to charter a boat down the May River to the Mitchellville section of Hilton Head, where most residents lived. The island was home to a little over one thousand Gullah people. Gullah is a west-African-inspired culture comprised mainly of men who were former slaves freed after the Civil

War. On his last trip to Hilton Head, Joseph had befriended a few Gullah men he had hired to help him explore the land.

Joseph pulled into a small marina where he'd met his friends on his most recent visit. The marina had a small wooden building and a few long docks that could secure ten mid-sized boats. Only two boats were tied up since the rest were out on their daily fishing excursions.

When Joseph and Charles exited the car, the smell of dead fish hit them like a straight jab in a prize fight. The muggy, humid air did not help the pungent smell either.

They walked towards the building, where three men sat on benches playing dominos. Joseph recognized one gentleman and waved to him.

"Tamba. Remember me? Joseph Gramer. You took me to the south side of the island earlier this year."

The middle-aged African man rose from his seat and extended his hand to Joseph. "Of course, Mr. Gramer. It is good to see you again. What brings you back to the island? Still looking to buy acreage for your lumber yard?" he asked in a thick African accent.

Joseph was hesitant to answer the question honestly. He didn't know Tamba very well.

Can I trust him to help find the treasure? What would stop him from taking the treasure for himself and leaving us to die on the remote island?

Unfortunately, the Gullahs were the only ones that could help them at this time. No one knew the island better than them. Plus, they didn't have time to round up a crew of their own. There were no other options. He had to tell him.

"I am always looking for lumber, but today I am here for another reason. This is my son Charles. He believes there is a treasure buried on the south side of the island."

Charles shook Tamba's hand. Instantly, he tilted his head. *Was the first time I've ever shaken a Negro's hand?* By no means was he racist. In fact, he recently joined a protest in Savannah to press for racial change in the south. All people, regardless of their color, should be able to vote. That was especially true since so many Negros had fought valiantly in the Second World War.

Tamba explained to Charles that there had been many stories of treasure hidden on the island. It started with the Civil War and still existed today. Unfortunately, he didn't know anyone who had actually found any treasure, so he told him that they likely would come up empty.

He continued, "In fact, in recent years, the waters on the other side of the island near Spanish Wells have seen drug boats hiding their stash and money in fear of it being taken by the authorities. We have had several of our boats attacked by them. They drive PT Boats with machine guns attached to them. That's likely the only riches you will find on this island."

"Why hide money and drugs on Hilton Head?" asked Charles.

"As Joseph knows, our island is very remote, and the terrain can be treacherous. The island is full of large pine trees that block the sunlight from reaching the ground," Tamba gladly continued. "The ground is thick with brush and soaked pine straw. It makes for great hiding places. It's also a perfect breeding ground for alligators, so travel by boat is the only way to get on the island."

Tamba impressed Charles with his intimate knowledge of the island. "We need to go to the southernmost point. That is where I believe he buried the treasure," he said. "We have five metal detectors in the car's trunk. Do you think you could find a few men to help us search? We will pay them handsomely for their services and share the treasure when we find it."

Tamba pointed to the two men he was playing dominoes with earlier. "These two over there know the island as well as anyone. They are hard workers, and Bala is the best boat driver we have."

Charles and Joseph introduced themselves to the other two men as they got up from the bench. Like Tamba, both men looked to be in their mid-thirties. They both were huge. They each looked to be almost two hundred fifty pounds of pure muscle.

"When can we start?" asked Joseph.

Bala replied in an equally thick African accent to Tamba's, "It takes about a half hour to get to the south side of the island from here. If we leave now, we could have an hour or two of daylight to set up camp and begin the search."

Tamba directed the two men to collect supplies and prepare the boat for launch. As the men turned to enter the building, Bala stopped and asked Charles and Joseph a question, "Do you have weapons in the car as well? If so, I would bring them. We might need them."

28

Joseph and Charles were a bit surprised when Bala asked them about weapons. They expected an encounter with an alligator or rough seas but never considered gunfire to be part of the trip. Then again, Samuel Goldsmith could be on the island, and they were ready to defend themselves while trying to avenge what he did to Charles and Mary.

After Tamba warned them about the ever-present danger involved with the drug trade on the island and realized that they might encounter Goldsmith at some point, the trip became more dangerous.

Joseph was no stranger to weapons because of his military background. He'd been a sharpshooter during his stints in both World Wars. Charles also knew how to shoot a rifle, having partaken in several hunting trips with his father and brother. Over the years, it had become clear that Charles was the better shot than his older brother Joseph, Jr.

The boat the crew was going to take to the south side of the island was a twenty-eight-footer. It was white with black trim powered by a Chrysler marine engine. It had a cover housing that could fit about five men, which was perfect for their voyage.

The Gullah used the boat mainly to export cotton to Savannah. Cotton picking was the most profitable trade on the island. They learned how to do it during their slavery, but now they owned the land and sold cotton weekly to merchants on the docks of the Savannah River. Each trip was long and profitable but dangerous, as well, due to the drug traffic.

After the men stocked the boat with the metal detectors, guns, ammunition, a tent, shovels, and some food and water, Bala started the engine on his third turn of the key. The loud engine roared and spewed dark smoke from behind while warming up. It was an older boat, but by the sound of the engine, it had some horsepower.

"All aboard!" yelled Bala as everyone complied. He directed Joseph and Charles to sit at the back of the boat while the other three men stood in the galley.

As they untied the boat from the dock and pushed away, Joseph asked Charles, "We are off. Are you nervous, son?"

"No. I can handle myself despite what you might think after being attacked in Boston," he replied. "I think I have had enough bad luck in the past few weeks. It's now time to turn the tide, so to speak."

As they pulled away from the inlet, Joseph and Charles admired the island's beauty. The green of the landscape and size of the pine trees were unbelievable. Joseph kept seeing dollar signs with every single one.

In no time, Bala had the boat humming at twenty-five knots. The seas were calm, so they were due to arrive a little earlier than expected. That was, of course, if they did not encounter any problems along the way. One such problem could be the boat that Tamba noticed beached in the distance on the southside close to where they planned to stop. Bala took the binoculars from him and confirmed that the boat was probably hiding drugs and money on the beach. The men asked Charles and Joseph to join them in the galley to discuss the situation.

"That boat presents the danger that I have spoken about," said Bala. "I suggest we turn around and try again tomorrow."

Charles was hesitant to continue as well. "I agree. As much as I want to search for the treasure, I think it's too dangerous right now. Although, I think I know whom that boat belongs to, which makes me want to proceed."

Bala looked at Tamba and raised his shoulders, suggesting that he give his opinion.

Tamba glanced at Joseph and said, "If anyone is on that boat, we could be in grave danger if we proceed."

"I don't think it's drug dealers. I trust my son's instincts. I think it is the other treasure hunter," warned Joseph. "And for all we know, he could be more dangerous than a drug dealer."

By the time they had agreed to turn around, the boat on shore was moving. When Bala saw the boat leaving shore, he immediately turned around to return to the marina. He pushed the throttle to the max as the boat begrudgingly rose to its maximum speed.

The other boat was a PT Boat that the US Navy used in both World Wars. Bala turned the boat around and fled, but that was not satisfactory for the boat following them, apparently. Instead of heading to the open ocean to return to Savannah, the boat headed north in pursuit. When Tamba saw this, he directed the men to arm themselves. Joseph and Charles grabbed a rifle and positioned themselves at the back of the boat, lying on the floor with the rifles resting on the back lip. If there was going to be trouble, the Gramers were ready for it.

The PT Boat continued to follow the fishing boat while slowly gaining ground. When they got close enough, the gunfire started. Before the Gramer men could pull the trigger, rounds of automatic gunfire surrounded them. The marina was within sight, but the fishing boat was being riddled with bullets. In a matter of a minute, the boat had dozens of bullet holes in its stern. The windows of the galley had already been shattered too.

Charles and Joseph returned fire, but their rifles were no match for their enemy's weaponry. It didn't help that the PT Boat was metal, so their shots did not affect its structure. When they'd each expelled the bullets in their guns' chamber, they lay down to reload. Joseph directed Charles to crawl to the bow of the boat for safety. "I'm not going anywhere without you!" yelled Charles. "We either stay here and fight together, or we go to the bow for more cover."

"All right, let's head to the bow then," replied Joseph. "We're no match for the artillery they have."

As they crawled to the bow of the boat, they came across the Gullah in the galley lying down on the floor except for Bala, who had his head just high enough to steer the boat to the marina.

Tamba saw the Gramers and explained that drug dealers would not enter the marina. They had tried before but found that the Gullah could defend themselves on shore. It was a death sentence for them if they attempted to approach it. This was music to the Gramer's ears since they were not overly optimistic about their chances against the approaching boat. Now all they had to do was get to the marina without dying.

Bala pushed the fishing boat to its limits. The assault continued. Bullets flew over the heads of the men lying on the floor with the walls of the boat protecting them. They were almost at the marina.

When Joseph and Charles finally reached the bow of the boat, Joseph raised his head above the threshold to see how far they were from the coast. Just as he did so, another round of gunfire started. This time one of the many bullets hit its target. Joseph fell to the floor and looked at his son with fear in his eyes, "I've been hit."

29

Bala decided not to dock the boat. Instead, he steered full throttle for the sandy beach next to the marina. Tamba blew a horn several times as they approached the land to notify the Gullah that they were in trouble. The chase continued with a seemingly never-ending spray of gunfire. The fishing boat was covered with bullet holes, so too should have been the men on the boat, but they were lucky... everyone except for Joseph.

Charles rolled over to see his father reeling in pain while grasping his left side. Blood trickled from a wound that Joseph's hand was applying pressure over to stop the bleeding. His first thought was how calm he appeared. For the last fifteen minutes, Charles had been hysterical inside, and his heart rate was pumping at an unhealthy speed. Everything happened so fast. He had no control over what was happening and was truly little help to those on board.

"Father! Are you ok?" he screamed. "Where have you been shot?"

Joseph rolled over to see his son. His eyes were glazed, and he squinted in a sign of pain. This was not the first time someone had shot him. As a young infantry soldier in the First World War, he'd been shot in the leg. Twenty years later, the injury still nagged him, but he never complained.

He still had a powerful voice when he answered his son, "They got me in the shoulder. I'm fine. Just keep your head down. There's too much gunfire to fight back."

Just as he finished his warning to Charles, the boat came to a crashing halt against the shore. Neither of the Gramers could see where they were going, so the impact came as a surprise. They both crashed hard against the front edge of the boat and then were driven back by force through what had recently been the front windshield. Now it was just an empty window. Charles flew into the galley where the Gullah men were strewn on the floor in various positions.

Joseph bounced back to almost his original position on the floor. When the shock of the crash had worn off, he noticed that he still heard gunfire, but it was different. For one, the bullets were not hitting the boat anymore. He cautiously looked up, still holding his bloody shoulder. What he saw was a phrase they'd used in the World Wars: the cavalry was coming.

The attacking boat had made a U-turn and was heading away from shore. They continued firing but not at their fishing boat anymore. They were defending themselves from the dozens of Gullahs hidden in bunkers on the beach, opening fire on them. Some had automatic weapons while others had rifles and pistols. There were enough of them to make the boat retreat. One thing the drug dealers and treasure hunters were learning about Hilton Head Island was that the Gullahs had proved that were willing and able to defend their land.

When the gunfire stopped, the men in the boat looked around to ensure everyone was okay. They immediately all went to Joseph, who appeared to be the only one seriously injured. The others were bloody and bruised from broken glass and being thrown about the boat, but none of their injuries were severe. They approached the injured Joseph and saw that he was sitting up, leaning on the side of the boat. His white shirt had turned crimson.

He continued to clutch his shoulder and said with a weak chuckle, "I haven't had that much fun since the war. Someone help me up. I need to take care of this wound."

Charles and Tamba both grabbed him by the waist to help him stand. They nodded to each other amazed at how calm he was after being shot. He was a true soldier.

"Let's get you to the car. We need to drive you to the hospital in Savannah," directed Charles.

"Nonsense. It's a flesh wound. I'll be fine. I'm sure there is a doctor on the island who can take a look at it," replied Joseph in the sternest voice he could muster.

The men helped him get off the boat because, despite his bravado, Joseph was still severely injured and had lost quite a bit of blood. They brought him into the marina and called for a doctor to examine him. While waiting for the doctor to arrive, the Gramers thanked the Gullah men who had helped fend off Goldsmith's presumed attack. They were not fearful of the danger. It had become part of their lives since they had to take the boats to Savannah each week. Joseph promised he would reward them for their bravery. All the while, in the back of Charles' mind, he was questioning whether this was all even worth it.

My father has already been shot. Bala's boat is ruined. Is the treasure worth his life or the lives of others? Should he just let Goldsmith have it and go free?

The doctor arrived in about thirty minutes. He was Gullah but looked nothing like the other men the Gramers had met. He was only five feet, six inches tall and appeared to be wider than that. The man had a bald head and was in his fifties. He removed Joseph's shirt to reveal his wound but determined that the bullet had not entered the body. It had simply scraped across his shoulder. The good news was that there was no puncture wound, but there was nevertheless a three-inch gash in his shoulder that needed to be stitched up.

"I'm going to dress the wound for the time being," explained the doctor. "Then you can take him to Savannah to get stitched up."

Joseph disagreed. "No need, Doc," he said. "You can just stitch me up here. It's not the first time this has happened, but I certainly hope it will be the last."

The doctor explained that he had nothing in his bag to ease the pain. That did not faze Joseph at all. For the others in the room, it was another story. They looked away while Joseph received ten stitches with no pain relief and without saying a word.

When he was all bandaged up, Joseph promised to return tomorrow with money to pay him for his services. He also promised Bala that he would buy him another boat. Both men appreciated the offer.

After the doctor left the building, Charles saw his father who was shirtless and covered in blood from the procedure. "Let's go. We need to get back to Savannah, so you can get some rest."

Joseph got up and walked over to his son and placed his good hand on his shoulder. "Good idea. I will need as much strength as possible if we are going to the south side of the island again tomorrow."

Tamba, Bala, and the other crew member, who had a name that both Gramers had a difficult time pronouncing, all turned to Joseph impressed. They were standing in front of a man in his mid-fifties, covered with blood, a gunshot wound on his left shoulder, who still wanted to do this all over again tomorrow.

Acting as the lieutenant general he was, Joseph directed, "Bala. Find us another boat for tomorrow. We will be here before dawn. I suspect that will be a safer time to travel."

Charles was surprised that the team was still willing to continue his treasure hunt despite what had happened to them. They would reach the south part of the island the next morning but wondered how, or even if, they would get back. He continued to doubt whether it was worth it, but his father gave him strength, and Mary gave him the motivation he needed to proceed.

Also, what about Samuel Goldsmith, who was probably responsible for shooting his father?

Was Goldsmith already on the south side of the island searching for Hilton's lost treasure or had they just encountered drug dealers?

Would he finally meet the man who nearly killed him weeks ago? Part of him hoped so.

30

Samuel Goldsmith had a head start on Charles. He had known about William Hilton's lost will since he was a small child. His father told him a false tale about how their ancestor, after whom he was named, had discovered the Carolinas while William Hilton took all the credit for it. He was also told that Hilton had stolen money from all the mariners that risked their lives to discover the new colony. The name "Hilton Head" had always angered Samuel. He thought it should be "Goldsmith Head." If he had anything to do about it, he would avenge Hilton, find the treasure, and tell the world what he earnestly believed to be the actual truth about the island.

Today, Goldsmith sat on a wooden chair on a long sandy beach at the southernmost part of the island. It was low tide, so the tight, compact sand stretched almost one hundred yards to the soft waves crashing on the coast. There was little wind, so the ocean was calm and a bright blue.

Goldsmith was not interested in doing any of the labor to find the treasure. His job was already complete: He'd stolen the map, bought the supplies, arranged for travel to the island, organized the team, and told them where to dig.

His team consisted of five men, each with a particular skill. One was a sailor who knew the island and had gotten them safely to their destination while avoiding drug dealers. Two others were the muscle, heavily armed former marines hired to protect the team against natives or anyone else who got in their way. The other two were simple farmhands interested in the payday if they could find what Goldsmith had assured them was there.

Life is good, he thought. *In the next few days, I may be one of the wealthiest men in the United States.*

****

Dawn approached quickly for Charles. The alarm clock in the Savannah hotel room sounded like it was a million miles away. It didn't faze him at all, however. He slept through the annoying bells until his father, who had been awake for over an hour, turned it off and shook Charles awake.

"Let's go, son. Get dressed. We need to leave for the island."

Charles wiped his eyes and shook his head to clear the cobwebs. "What time is it?"

Joseph, already dressed and ready to go, replied with a familiar tone, "05:00. Let's go, soldier."

Following the orders of Lieutenant General Joseph Gramer, Charles got out of bed and went to the bathroom to get ready. Joseph was feeling good despite his injury. That may have had to do with the painkillers a local pharmacist had prescribed him, or it could have been the great steak dinner and red wine they'd had the night before that put him to sleep quickly.

When they were ready and about to leave the hotel room, there was a knock on the door. Charles rushed to open it. "Mother... Mary," he asked with a voice cracked by surprise. "What are you doing here?"

Pearl walked right past Charles and ran to her husband to make sure he was okay.

Mary hugged Charles and said, "Your mother called me last night and explained that your father had been shot. We were both horrified, so we decided to get up early and make the trip to Savannah to talk some sense into you."

Pearl continued threateningly, "As I told you last night on the phone, this treasure hunt has gone too far. At first, I thought it would be fun, but now I want you to stop this foolishness and return to the lumber yard."

The women's concern for each of them was obvious and justified. Neither one of them wanted to stop now though. They had come too far. Sitting on the bed next to Pearl, who was inspecting his gunshot wound, Joseph attempted to defuse the situation.

"Granted, our encounter with some pretty bad people was a surprise to both of us, but I guarantee that will not happen again. It was an error of judgment on my part. We must be more discrete as we approach the dig site. As you know Pearl, I have never made the same mistake twice."

Mary challenged the older and presumably wiser man. "If you say it is not so dangerous, then I guess you wouldn't mind if I came along as well."

Charles saw that coming from a mile away. Mary had been eager to join them on the adventure she'd been such an integral part of.

"Since we never actually made it to the dig site yesterday, I propose that Father and I go back to Hilton Head today alone. After we confirm it is not dangerous, we will meet back here tomorrow, and Mary will come to the island with us."

"I don't like it," Pearl warned. "Is the treasure really worth it?"

Charles hesitated for a second before responding. "It's not about the treasure, Mother. It's about retribution. Samuel Goldsmith can't get away with what he did to us. He needs to be stopped."

"Plus, he has a lieutenant general on his side for protection," assured Joseph. "We will be fine."

Pearl and Mary begrudgingly agreed with the proposal. They would stay at the hotel, waiting for a call later that evening with an update. If the coast is clear, Mary would join them the next day. If things got worse, they would put a stop to it.

Charles made one last proposal. "The one thing we need to make perfectly clear is that the treasure is not worth any of our lives and the lives of others. Finding it would not be worth a cent if I had blood on my hands. Let's agree that if a weapon needs to be fired, we do so only in self-defense."

"No truer words have ever been spoken," replied Joseph. "I see no reason for violence except for Goldsmith. If he was the one who tried to kill us, I don't think I have the strength not to seek revenge."

The room fell silent at Joseph's statement. Mary tried to lighten the mood. "The best revenge for what he did to us is to never let him get a hand on that treasure."

****

When they arrived at the marina, the Gullah team was waiting for them. The Gramers had revisited the Army/Navy store the day before, so they were stocked up with necessities. While opening the trunk of the car, Tamba asked Joseph how he was feeling from the gunshot wound. He explained that he was fine and thanked him for his concern. When he opened the trunk, the men were impressed by the stockpile of weapons and ammunition they'd bought.

"These are for you," said Joseph. "These are to be used for this mission and any future danger you encounter. This is your land, and you must be able to defend it properly. Take this as a token of my gratitude."

The men looked at their new arsenal. "Those are American M1 Garand semi-automatic rifles. They are what soldiers use in the World War," explained Joseph. "Once the drug dealers see you shooting at them with these, they will think twice about coming to your island."

The men were gleeful and thanked the Gramers graciously for their new weapons. They most certainly would come in helpful in protecting them from the drug dealers on their trips to Savannah.

They immediately stocked the new boat with all the supplies. The boat left the dock before the break of dawn. Unbeknownst to one another, each crew member said a short prayer as they left the dock. After all, they knew the danger they were about to face… or at least they thought they did.

Bala drove as fast as he could along the coast. The other three men were on each side of the boat, pointing their machine guns at the open water in search of danger.

About fifteen minutes into the ride, Tamba announced, "We are likely out of the danger zone. The drug dealers visit the west side of the island rather than the south side. The current and tides on the south side are too rough for them to drop off their cargo easily."

Bala waved to them, "Join me in the galley for the rest of the trip so you can regain your strength. The other two should keep watch just in case."

As they neared their destination, the Gramers rejoined Tamba at the bow of the boat and gazed at the island's beauty. Joseph had been here before, but only on the east side. He wondered at the beautiful crashing waves on the coast and the seemingly endless dunes that Bala skillfully avoided. Tamba pointed ahead and said they were about five minutes from the southern tip of the island where Charles told them the buried treasure lay. While doing so, Charles looked ahead with a pair of binoculars they'd purchased the night before.

"I think we have a problem," said Charles.

He handed the binoculars to Tamba. "It's the boat again," he responded.

"Goldsmith," Charles muttered under his breath.

31

"Samuel Goldsmith is a descendant of the man who stole the will and treasure map from William Hilton, the founder of this island," explained Charles. "And he also took a priceless map from Yale University a few days ago. Oh… and we also think he tried to kill me a few weeks ago."

The 'killing' part of the story did not surprise Tamba. He had encountered many treasure hunters over the years. The one thing they all had in common was that they were very territorial and dangerous.

"One cannot just approach a treasure hunter and inquire about their excavation. If you did," Tamba explained, "you should expect to be attacked like yesterday. Several Gullahs have gone to their grave without knowing such danger."

Bala spun the boat around in hopes of not being noticed again. They were far enough away this time that they all agreed no one could have seen them. After a lengthy discussion about what to do next, they decided to dock the boat on the beach and walk through the woods to the excavation site. Hilton Head Island had over twelve miles of pristine beach, so the walk to the site could have been relatively easy. However, they would have to travel through the dense woods if they didn't want to be noticed.

They exited the boat, each carrying a firearm for protection. Bala also carried a machete in case they encountered alligators. He found he could defend himself with a knife better than a gun when encountering wildlife. Unfortunately, he had had several encounters with gators and had the scars to prove it.

Tamba led the way into the woods. They each walked behind him in a single file. It was morning, but the sun was already intense. The humidity would be unbearable to most, but the team was used to it. That didn't prevent each one from sweating profusely, however. Luckily, they were in the forest, so the large pine trees blocked the sun.

They stopped and took cover when they got to about one hundred yards from Goldsmith's camp. Each of them hid behind a tree or bush and lifted a pair of binoculars that dangled from around their necks.

Two tents stood on the sand. One appeared to be used for preparing and eating food. There was also a table with large canisters of water and a grill to cook. The other tent was closed, so it was safe to say they used it for sleeping. There were five men in the woods. Three of them were digging, and two were watching guard with rifles on their shoulders.

Charles pressed a finger to his lips. He'd assumed Goldsmith would beat him to the site but was surprised at how organized he was. He'd expected to see one guy with a shovel, not a well-oiled treasure-hunting machine. They had their hands full.

"What do you suggest we do?" he asked. "We can't just walk up to them and tell them to leave. I imagine the two guys with guns wouldn't welcome us to the camp."

Joseph agreed. He gathered the team behind a large bush covered with Spanish moss to hide while they formulated a strategy. "If we are going to prevent Goldsmith from finding the treasure, we need to get them away from the site. It appears there is a tent for sleeping, so I suspect at least two of them stay here overnight to guard their position. By the looks of it, they have been here a few days. If the treasure map they have is accurate at all, they could find the treasure at any moment."

Charles asked how they could stop them from digging.

Tamba replied, "It's simple. We need them to feel like they are in danger. They will continue to dig if there are no obstacles. If they encounter a danger like we did yesterday, it will force them to stop searching and defend themselves."

Charles sucked his teeth. His father was a decorated soldier. If anyone would know how to formulate a plan, it'd be him.

"Father, what do we do?"

"I like Tamba's suggestion," he answered. "We need to create a distraction. The advantage we have right now is the element of surprise. If we engage them, I think they will take cover and maybe even leave the site. It all depends on the extent of their arsenal."

Charles agreed with his father's assessment, but it was only a short-term solution. If they scared them away today, Goldsmith would be sure to return tomorrow and with more firepower. They need to force him to abandon his search altogether. Considering Goldsmith's passion for finding the treasure, that might be impossible.

Joseph suggested they all spread out and take cover behind a large tree, then create a semi-circle around the site. They would space each other about twenty-five yards apart.

"Take fire upon my command," Joseph instructed. "Remember, we're not here to kill anyone. Our goal is to simply scare them."

The men agreed with his assessment, but Tamba's curiosity got the best of him. He asked, "So what do we shoot for then?"

Joseph gave a half smile. "My first shot will be to scare one of the armed men. I will not hit him, but the bullet will come so close to his ear that it will ring for a day."

The men chuckled at his wit as he continued, "Charles, I know you are an excellent shot too, so I want you to take out the water canteens. For the others, I want you to aim at objects near people. I want them to hear the distant gunshots and hear them hit something close to them. We will each take two shots, then return here. I will stay in this position and cover each of you in case they return fire. Be careful. On my count."

The men scattered and got into position. When they were ready, Joseph raised his good arm as if to say, *Take your aim.* He raised his rifle with his left hand, which was no effortless task since he had ten fresh stitches on his left shoulder. He didn't think the injury would affect his aim. If it were his right shoulder, that would be a different story.

His first shot went right where he wanted it. The man holding a rifle went straight to the ground after the bullet whizzed past his head. The first thing everyone noticed after Joseph's shot was the shock and awe on each man's face. They all turned their heads from side to side and then dropped to the ground to take cover.

Four more shots went off immediately from various directions. Charles' aim was almost as good as his father's. Two large water jugs went flying off the table. One of the other shots hit the grill, causing a loud metallic clang. One more round of gunfire from each man caused Goldsmith's men, including the armed security, to crawl from their positions in the forest onto the beach. There, they found a fuming Goldsmith standing tall with a look of evil in his eyes.

Team Gramer gathered back behind the Spanish moss where Joseph was positioned. None of the men returned fire. It would not have mattered anyway. They were so hidden that it would have been a futile attempt if they did. Goldsmith only had two men to protect him. If they had fought back, it would have been a grave mistake.

To the dismay of Goldsmith and against his demands, his men scurried to get into their moored boats, fearing another round of gunfire. The boats took off hurriedly into the open ocean.

They would be back with more firepower like yesterday, so they didn't have much time.

"Let's get back to the boat to fetch the metal detectors," Charles urged. "It is time to find a treasure."

32

Charles was so excited to begin searching. It had been over a month since Joseph found the safe deposit slip in Pearl's book, but it felt like a year with everything he had been through. He roamed Goldsmith's camp while the Gullah men retrieved the metal detectors. Charles directed his father to sit on the beach where Goldsmith had been lounging so he could regain his strength while keeping watch to make sure they did not return.

In a matter of an hour or so, the realization dawned that searching for buried treasure was quite monotonous. The constant beeping sound of the metal detectors became annoying after a few minutes, but he muscled through it.

A metal detector would go off five or six times during the search. A loud, high-pitched beep would ring throughout the forest, telling them it had found something. Each time it did, the men each grabbed a shovel and started digging in anticipation of riches and gold. They were so excited that they would whimsically tell each other tales about what they would buy with their share of the fortune. Bala was going to buy a new boat. Tamba would use the money to send his children to college. They both dreamed of moving to faraway places. Unfortunately, they found nothing each time.

Their spirits remained high despite each false alarm, but that changed the instant Joseph came running from the beach, yelling, "Incoming!"

The men looked to the water to see two boats hurtling towards the beach. It was Goldsmith's men. They grabbed their gear and ran to the boat Bala had hidden from sight. Knowing there was a likelihood that Goldsmith would return seeking revenge and the treasure, Bala made sure they would not be exposed to a defenseless attack. After a brisk walk back to the boat, he started it up for their escape back to the marina.

The ride back was tense since they had to keep watch for drug dealers. This was the time of day when Gullah fishermen were often victims of unprovoked attacks. Charles kept watch of the open sea using binoculars, and Joseph did the same with the coast. While they did, the two men brainstormed about how they could stop Goldsmith from searching for the treasure. If they kept trying to scare them off, they would continue to defend themselves, and their lives would be in danger. They also agreed that the treasure was not worth any more bloodshed.

Charles then had an idea. "What if we buy the land?" he asked his father tersely. "If we own the land, we can forcefully and legally remove them from it."

"Great idea, son. As you know, I have been wanting to buy more land for logging. The sea pines on the south side of the island would be very profitable for the company."

The idea, in theory, was a good one, but time was not on their side. Goldsmith could find the treasure at any moment, so before they bought the land, they needed to continue delaying Goldsmith's search.

Charles suggested, "Let's return to Savannah immediately and call your attorney to start making arrangements to purchase the land. In the meantime, we can hire Tamba and his men to continue scaring off Goldsmith."

Joseph knew where his son was going with this. "I will develop a tactical strategy that will keep the Gullah safe but simultaneously keep Goldsmith guessing," replied Joseph. "It is important that they keep the attacks random and continuous. At the same time, they can't injure any of Goldsmith's men."

"Boat... 45 degrees west!" yelled Tamba looking through a pair of binoculars.

The men all turn to confirm his discovery. Unfortunately, he was correct. Another highly armed boat was heading to them at a rate of speed that Bala could not compete with.

"Take guard, everyone!" ordered Joseph. "We're not going to let these guys get us again."

The men each grabbed a semi-automatic machine gun from the galley. This time, they would have the rifle power to defend themselves. Each man took position at the stern, ready to fire when they got close enough.

Bala was driving at full throttle approaching the marina, preparing to hit the beach like he did the day before. The men braced themselves for another crash while ready to defend themselves at the same time. Bala blared the siren as they were close enough to the marina for the other Gullah to hear the alarm. The other boat was ready to open fire when the alarm sounded.

Instead of attacking, the boat chasing them slowed down and turned around. This time, rather than Goldsmith, it was drug dealers chasing them. History had taught them that they should retreat when the siren went off. They knew not to mess with the Gullah in the marina.

A collective sigh of relief came over the men while releasing the clinch of their guns.

"Weapons down," said Tamba. "We are in the clear."

Bala slowed down since they were safe from the drug dealers. When the tension subsided, the Gramers entered the boat's galley to speak with Tamba and his men. They explained how they intended to stop Goldsmith.

After hearing the idea, the Gullahs were amenable to it and impressed with Joseph's military acumen. They would gather five more men with whom to make trips to the excavation site once per day. They would attack from the water, place booby traps in and around the site, attack from the land like they did earlier, and vandalize their equipment. If they did that for the next week, Joseph would have enough time to purchase the land and then be able to remove Goldsmith permanently.

On the ride back to Savannah, Charles was filled with excitement about the purchase of the land. When they crossed the South Carolina/Georgia border, Charles asked his father a question that had been bugging him ever since introducing the idea of purchasing the land.

His heartbeat raced when he asked, "I know I do not have the money to buy the land, but I want to. I feel like it could be profitable for the lumber yard, but it could also be profitable to me. The area is so beautiful and untouched. When we find the treasure, I believe I could build houses and hotels to make Hilton Head one of the most beautiful places in this country."

Joseph digested his son's monologue and asked, "How do you suppose you could buy the land without the funds to do so?"

Charles expected the question and had an answer ready. "You could lend me the money, and I will pay you back with interest when I find the treasure. If I don't find it, I will deed the property back to you to do whatever you wish with it. Obviously, you will remove the trees from the land for logging so that it would be a profitable investment for you either way."

"We have a deal. You will buy the land, and I will lend you the money for it," agreed Joseph. "Now, I just need my attorney to find out who owns the land and convince him to sell it to us."

It was the perfect plan, thought Charles… *unless Goldsmith had already bought the land.*

Regardless, the most challenging part would be managing to execute it flawlessly. If not, they could lose the treasure, Goldsmith, or even worse, their lives.

33

The Gramers returned home to Hinesville that evening rather than stay in Savannah again. Pearl fixed them a delightful meal attended by Joseph, Jr., and Mary as well. It had been a while since the family had all been together, so it was a joyous evening. Mary left right after dinner to give the Gramers some family time, but it was not a late night for the Gramer men. They were so tired they were practically asleep before their heads hit the pillow.

Before going to sleep, Charles called Mary, and they talked for a while. Since they didn't expect to return to the island for another day or two, they thought having dinner at the local diner the following evening would be fun. Charles dozed off to pleasant thoughts of him and Mary together forever.

The following morning, the Gramer men got to the lumber yard early. Work had been piling up because of their absence, so they knew they needed extra time to catch up, especially knowing they could return to Hilton Head any day. This workday was like any other at the lumber yard except for the anticipation of the call from Joseph's attorney about the land deal. Unfortunately, the call did not come, so at the end of the day, they said goodbye and agreed to meet again early the next morning.

Charles drove his two-seater almost recklessly to his apartment after work to take a quick shower and clean up for Mary. They were meeting at the diner at 6 p.m. He offered to pick her up, but she declined. She knew he was within walking distance of the diner, so she didn't want him to drive across town just for her.

Severe thunderstorms had come through the area earlier that afternoon, so the humidity had dropped significantly by dinner time. This pleased Charles because when he left his apartment, jumping two stairs at a time, it was still hot even though the sun was weakening. He didn't want to be all sweaty when he saw Mary. Nothing was worse than a big sweaty Georgia summer bear hug to impress a pretty girl.

The ten-minute walk from his apartment consisted mainly of dodging puddles while admiring the blue and red sky with its spongy white clouds.

When he entered the diner, Mary was in a window booth facing away from the door. He approached her from behind, gently put both hands over her eyes, and jokingly asked, "Guess who?" It was cheesy, but it was the first thing that came to his mind.

"Ronaldo! My big and strong Spanish lover," Mary replied instantly as if she was expecting the question.

They both laughed. Mary had a quick wit about her for sure.

Each ordered a cup of coffee to start while they looked over the menu... and each other. Charles placed his menu on the table and reached out both hands while Mary did the same. Hand in hand, he said, "Mary, I have to admit, I am beginning to think I have a little crush on you."

"Well, if it doesn't work out with Ronaldo, I'll be sure to look you up," she continued to tease. Then she looked him in the eyes and admitted, "I have a big old crush on you too, Mr. Gramer."

Now that the lovey part of the dinner was complete, they got to order their meals. While Charles enjoyed his open-face turkey sandwich and Mary dined on a large dinner salad, he filled her in on all the excitement that had happened earlier that day.

"You guys shot at Goldsmith and his men?" she exclaimed. "So, you're telling me that you could have died again and could have killed someone?"

Charles raised his eyebrows and shook his head in disagreement. "It wasn't like that. We never considered shooting anyone. We simply scared them off. No one was injured. They jumped in their boats and ran for their lives. Then we started searching for the treasure, but unfortunately, they came back, so we got out of there quickly."

Needless to say, this did not thrill Mary at all. She was sitting next to the first guy she'd really liked in a long time, and she felt he was purposefully putting himself in danger.

"I don't like this one bit. Whether you choose not to harm anyone, the people you just shot at will now look for revenge."

Charles was confused. "You're probably right. We shouldn't have shot at them, but it seemed like a good idea. In hindsight, it was likely a mistake."

Knowing there was little chance she could stop him from trying to get the treasure from Goldsmith, Mary asked exhaustedly, "So, what's the next step?"

With a stoic expression, Charles immediately replied, "I am going to buy the land where Hilton buried his treasure so I can legally remove Samuel Goldsmith from the site and prevent him from continuing to search for it."

"Of course, you're going to buy the land," Mary quipped. "Why am I not surprised?"

Charles did not answer the rhetorical question. Instead, he folded his arms and simply smiled at the woman he was falling in love with.

34

When Charles arrived the next morning just after eight, Joseph was already at the lumber yard. This part of the morning was the time of day that made Charles' heart beat slowly. Often it was just him and his father in the office, so it was quite peaceful. The rattling of machines and endless telephone calls wouldn't start for another hour.

Charles walked to his father's office to say good morning and, while doing so, learned that his attorney had called the night before with details on the Hilton Head land. Joseph made an appointment to visit the law office at 9:30 a.m. His office was only ten minutes from the lumber yard, so they left at nine-fifteen. That gave them plenty of time to catch up on the day's most pressing issues that involved logging, not finding buried treasure, or seeking revenge.

The Gramers' attorney was Michael Gray. He was a prominent figure in the Hinesville community and, over the years, had become close with Joseph. They considered each other friends besides their attorney/client relationship. Attorney Gray's office was in a small white Victorian home just a half-mile from downtown. The yard was filled with Georgia pines that helped to cool the office down during summer days like these.

185

The men entered the office with the familiar bell ringing as they opened the door. Directly to their right was the receptionist, who was talking on the telephone. She knew the Gramers, so she waved to them and signaled for them to sit, all while talking to a client on the phone. She had not finished the call when Attorney Gray came from his office to welcome them.

They all shook hands as he guided them into his conference room. The room appeared to have been a dining room in a former life. Today, it was home to a large wooden conference table surrounded by ten leather-bound chairs. Attorney Gray sat at the head of the table in front of a folder marked 'Gramer Land' scribbled with a black marker. The Gramers took a seat on each side of him.

The portly, bald attorney dressed in an expensive gray suit opened the conversation by saying, "So, I have some information about the land on Hilton Head that you inquired about. It is a twenty-thousand-acre parcel of land. It is not for sale, but the owner would consider an offer."

Their eyes popped open by the possibility of the purchase, but their jaws dropped by the sheer size of it. Charles asked with a trace of concern in his voice, "How much do you think we would need to offer to purchase the land?"

"The owner's attorney told me that he thinks $60 per acre would get the deal done."

The Gramers started doing math in their head. It didn't take long for Joseph to add it up. He looked at his son. His eyes were stern and focused. "That is over a million dollars!"

"I know it is a lot of money but consider the value of the lumber. Those sea pines are worth their weight in gold. Plus, white sand beaches surround the land on three sides. Once people get access to the island, the land will be invaluable. Not to mention if we find what we are looking for."

He said the last four words with hand quotes since they had decided not to tell their attorney about the treasure, which made more sense to stay on a need-to-know basis.

Joseph paused for a minute to consider his son's reasoning. Charles' line of thought made sense. He had been wanting to buy land on Hilton Head for quite a while, so he knew the profit potential. It was just so damn expensive.

The difficult aspect of the transaction, he thought, *would be getting the funds so quickly.*

"Try to get the owner down on the price per acre," said Joseph. "We needed the land yesterday, but that does not mean I will overpay for it."

Attorney Gray slowly got up from his chair and poured a glass of water into a tumbler sitting on a matching credenza on the other side of the room.

"Here is where we might have a problem," he replied, trying to appear nonchalant. "I am not sure the owner will be flexible on the price."

"Why not? There is always room for negotiation," asked Charles, his eyes narrowed.

"I don't think there will be room to negotiate with this owner. Does the name Ron Martin ring a bell to either of you? Ron 'The Hangman' Martin?" asked the attorney, hoping that he looked composed but was afraid they could see the terror in his eyes and the trembling of his hands.

The Gramers were silent in shock until Charles replied, "Ron Martin… as in the mafia kingpin?"

Rubbing his eyes as if he had just gotten out of bed, Attorney Gray replied, "That's right. The owner of the land is none other than Savannah's most ruthless and notorious mob boss. He is linked to hundreds of murders, most of which were done by hanging. Hence his nickname. This is not the kind of guy you want to be in business with."

Everyone in Hinesville knew about Ron Martin. His reputation preceded him. He was cruel, mean, wealthy, powerful, and could seemingly do anything he wanted without any interference from the police. After all, most of Savannah's finest were on his payroll.

"Okay. Just put the deal together. If he wants $60 per acre, we pay him that amount. Just get it done by the end of the week, Michael," Joseph ordered his friend, hesitant but eager to get down to business.

Attorney Gray sat back and took a sip of the water he'd just poured. "We can get the deal done this week… maybe even earlier. Martin has requested that the potential buyer of his Hilton Head land meet him in his Savannah office today at 3 p.m."

Charles and Joseph's eyes revealed shock and surprise. "The Hangman wants to see us in his office this afternoon?" Charles stammered.

"If the Hangman calls you to his office, I suggest you do what he wishes," replied Gray, above the sound of the ice rattling in his glass from his hands that were now visibly shaking.

Joseph hesitated momentarily, gazing at an open window overlooking the bustling street. He then relented with a deep sigh, "Let's go meet The Hangman."

35

Both Charles and Joseph had a tough time concentrating on work for the rest of the day. After all, it was not every day that one gets invited to a mob boss's office to discuss buying land from him. Of course, there was the inherent danger of dealing with a guy like Ron Martin, but it was a good business move for the lumber company and for Charles, the aspiring treasure hunter.

Joseph drove them to Savannah after a lengthy discussion about how much he disliked Charles' car and the fact that he would never drive two-plus hours in it. During the drive, they deliberated on their strategy on how to approach The Hangman. They both agreed to call him Mr. Martin and refer to him as "Sir." It was also agreed that Ron Martin could not know about the potentially buried treasure on his land. Knowledge like that would undoubtedly unravel the deal.

Also, if The Hangman learned about the treasure after the deal came together, then they knew a particular mob boss who would be interested in a sizable portion of the loot they found. That would not be good for anyone involved… other than Martin.

Ron Martin's office was in a penthouse suite on East Bay Street in downtown Savannah. It overlooked the Savannah River, one of the busiest cargo ports on the east coast. While pulling into to a parking space right in front of the building, Charles looked at the large ships slowly maneuvering down the river. He wondered what The Hangman's tariff was to have these ships bring items into "his" city.

Attorney Gray followed them to Savannah and parked a few spots behind them. After locking his Edsel, he approached the Gramer men and asked, "Are we ready to do this?"

The men entered the building through a pair of large, glass double doors leading them into a marble lobby with three gold elevators at the rear of the room. Behind a large round desk sat a large, round security guard. They explained they were there to see Ron Martin, so they were told to take the elevator to the top floor, where they would be welcomed by another set of security.

They rode silently up the gold-adorned elevator surrounded by mirrors on all sides. When the bell rang, indicating they were on the penthouse floor, the tension in the elevator could be thick enough to spread over toast. Each man tried to play the part of a confident businessman, but blank stares gave them away. In unison, they all took a deep breath, released it, and thought… *it's time to meet The Hangman.*

When the elevator door opened, two large men in black suits wearing sunglasses approached them. They directed them to turn around, spread their legs, and put their hands against the wall as if they were being arrested. None of them were dumb enough to carry a weapon, but when dealing with mob bosses, one can never be too cautious.

After they finished frisking them, one guard led them to a conference room comprised mainly of glass walls and doors. The view of the

Savannah River was breathtaking, but none noticed being overcome with fear. One man ordered them to sit at the right of the large glass table and wait quietly until Mr. Martin arrived. Needless to say, they did as they were told. They sat silently for over a half hour with no sign of Martin. The longer they waited, the more nervous they got.

It was apparent that Martin was delaying them on purpose to create a sense of tension and fear before he appeared. It worked. The men were nervous wrecks by the time someone finally entered the room. He was an older man who wore a black suit and had a full head of bushy white hair with a matching beard. He was intense but cordial.

"Which of you is Attorney Gray?" asked Martin's attorney. Michael stood up, shook his hand, and introduced himself. They had spoken on the phone the day before, so they were familiar with each other.

After some minor pleasantries, he sat down and explained that Mr. Martin would be with them in a few minutes. He opened his briefcase and handed Gray some documents. They were the same ones they discussed earlier on the telephone, so he offered Gray an opportunity to review them. The Gramers' hearts pounded while they watched their attorney flip through them, nodding in approval while doing so.

"Everything seems to be in line," said Attorney Gray. "Has Mr. Martin agreed to these terms?"

"I cannot speak on behalf of Mr. Martin. You can ask him when he joins us," he replied impatiently.

Just then, a man entered the conference room. Like all the others, he wore a black suit, a black shirt, and a black tie. He appeared to be in his forties and in relatively decent shape. He slicked his jet-black hair back, so he looked the part of a mob boss and was proud of it.

He walked into the room and took a seat at the head of the table. He put his elbows on the table and folded his hands. Looking at his attorney, he asked in a southern drawl, "Are these the gentlemen who want to buy my land?" His attorney nodded in approval.

Charles stood up and introduced himself. "Mr. Martin. My name is Charles—"

Martin waved his hand in disgust, telling him to sit down and stop talking. "I know who you are, Mr. Gramer. You would not be allowed in this building if I did not know who you were. A man in my position does not deal with strangers. I have found in the past that doing so could be detrimental to my health and my business… if you know what I mean."

Charles settled back in his seat and apologized. The Hangman got up from his chair and continued his dissertation. His drawl surprised the men. He looked like he should have an Italian accent rather than his southern charm. He was low country through and through.

"Joseph Gramer and Charles Gramer. Owner of Gramer Lumber. A successful company in Hinesville. I have done some research on both of you. You run a good business. You are well respected in your community. In fact, you are the former mayor of Hinesville. Is that not correct, Mr. Gramer?" The Hangman asked Joseph.

Joseph chose to remain in his seat when he answered the question after seeing how he'd responded to Charles getting up. "You are correct, Mr. Martin. I am indeed the former mayor of Hinesville. I am a retired Lieutenant General in the US Army and am now proud to run a successful business with my son, Charles."

"I appreciate your military service, Mr. Gramer. I wished to fight beside you in our last world war but could not because of matters here that demanded my attention," Martin continued.

"It would have been an honor to serve beside you," Joseph said, obviously trying to butter him up. "I am sure you would have made a fine soldier."

Shrugging off Joseph's attempt at flattery, Martin replied, "Don't jump to conclusions, Mr. Gramer. As I am sure my reputation precedes me, you can imagine that I am a good fighter. I doubt, however, that I would have been a good soldier. You see, I am used to being the one giving orders, not taking them."

The Hangman was now standing behind Charles and put his hands on his shoulders. "So... Charles, why do you want to buy my Hilton Head land?" he asked without emotion.

Charles was shaking. Twenty-six-year-old lumber executives were not used to conversing and negotiating with reputed mob bosses. "Well, Mr. Martin. My father has been considering buying acreage on the island for some time now. He has visited several times over the past year. The sea pines that grace your land are valuable in our line of work."

"Your aspirations are solely based on lumber? Are you simply going to cut down all my trees and sell them for profit?" asked The Hangman. His hands were still on Charles' shoulders, so he could tell that Charles was trembling.

"The land is still valuable without the trees, Mr. Martin. I believe if there was a bridge built from Bluffton to the island, it could become a tourist destination. It is a short drive from Savannah. I believe the city's elite, like yourself, would find the island a beachfront paradise."

Martin unlocked his grip on Charles and returned to his seat, keeping his eyes glued on Joseph. A minute passed before The Hangman spoke again. "Mr. Gramer, you raised an intelligent young man in Charles here."

"Thank you, Sir," Joseph replied. "In fact, he just—"

"He just graduated from Yale Law School," said Martin irritably. "I know, Mr. Gramer. Again, I always do my homework. I too, believe that there is development potential on the island, and I agree with your son that if a bridge is built to the island, it could become one of the east coast's finest resort communities."

Martin began to leave the room. While walking out, he said, "What I am selling you is only a portion of the land I own on Hilton Head Island. I will sell you the southernmost portion of my holding and intend to follow the progress of your logging and any potential real estate development. When development begins, I suggest you contact me. I am someone who can help build that all-important bridge."

He turned and walked out the door, then spun around, surveying the room without emotion, and ordered his attorney, "Sign the paperwork and have the money in my account by this time tomorrow. Otherwise, the deal is off."

36

After Charles signed the paperwork to buy the land from Savannah's most notorious mob boss, Joseph got a ride back to Hinesville with his friend and attorney. He spent the rest of the afternoon and most of the next day arranging with the local banks to have the funds deposited in The Hangman's account. In the meantime, Attorney Gray drafted the promissory note and mortgage for Charles to sign to secure the loan he'd be taking out from his father to purchase the land.

Charles borrowed his father's car and drove to the Beaufort County sheriff's office. The trip was about halfway to Hilton Head, so it did not take him more than an hour to reach the police station. He parked in front. It was no bigger than a typical low country house. Beaufort County was still mainly rural land at the time with few residents, so a large police force was unnecessary.

Inside the station sat three wooden desks facing the front door and a cell in the back of the one-room building. There was only one person there. Charles asked if he could speak to the sheriff. The man behind one desk stood up and introduced himself as Hubert W. Randall, sheriff of Beaufort County, South Carolina.

Sheriff Randall was a tall man. He towered over Charles, standing about six foot four inches tall. The sheriff wore glasses and a uniform. He appeared to be in his forties, although he could have been younger. His receding hairline was the determining factor in how he looked.

Charles explained that he had just purchased land on Hilton Head, and there were trespassers on the land whom he wanted to be removed.

"How do you know there are trespassers?" asked the sheriff. His tone was careful at best.

Charles tried his best to sound convincing. "My father and I visited the land yesterday and found a group of men setting up camp on the south side of our land. We told them to leave, but they refused. We know they are armed and dangerous and also believe they are stealing our natural resources from the land."

"What makes you claim they are dangerous?" asked the sheriff as he wrote notes in a small notebook.

Charles continued, "When we approached them yesterday, they opened fire on us. One of them shot my father. Only by God's grace did he survive. The bullet just grazed his shoulder."

Sheriff Randall did not stop writing. By the look on his face, he was taking the accusations seriously.

It was time for the final dagger. "One other thing, sheriff. We paid over one million dollars for that land. Twenty thousand acres worth. We did not pay that amount to be shot at and have someone steal from us."

The size of the sale and cost made the sheriff raise his eyebrows. "Wow. That's a lot of land. You boys are serious," he said in an impressed tone.

"We are, sir. We own a lumber company in Hinesville, Georgia. We plan to use the lumber for our business and then develop the land when we are finished with the logging," explained Charles with a hint of confidence. "There is one thing I should make you aware of, however." He hesitated. "We bought the land from Ronald Martin."

The sheriff's face instantly turned a shade whiter. "Ron 'The Hangman' Martin?"

Charles nodded, testing the sheriff's resolve. "Is that going to be an issue?"

"There is always an issue when you deal with The Hangman," replied the sheriff dismissively. "We just need to be a lot more careful. One wrong move and either of us could find a noose around our necks."

The sheriff explained that he was willing to help them with the trespassers but could not do so for forty-eight hours. Only three officers were on duty that day because of a funeral for an officer from another county who'd passed away the week prior. All the officers he could spare were at the ceremony to pay their respects.

They agreed to meet at the station on Saturday morning. Sheriff Randall asked that he bring the deed to the land and told them he would arrange for a boat to take them from Bluffton to the southernmost point of Hilton Head Island. Charles thanked the sheriff on his way out of the station and sat in his car. He put his hands on the back of his head and took a deep breath.

I just bought over a million dollars of land on a remote island from a mob boss. I'm about to confront the man who tried to kill me. Everything is going as planned... yeah, right! What have I gotten myself into?

37

Since Charles was already in Beaufort County to visit the sheriff, he hoped to visit Tamba and the guys to see how it was going holding off Goldsmith on the south side. Unfortunately, it was getting too late in the day to charter a boat from Bluffton to the island. Instead, he returned to the same hotel in Savannah where he'd stayed with his father a few days before.

Checking into the hotel was a little more complicated than before. Since it was a Thursday at 6 p.m., the lobby was much more crowded than earlier in the week. Four other groups were in front of him, so he waited in line and surveyed the scenery. The first thing he noticed was a lobby bar where a gentleman was playing the piano.

Room service, then I'll stop there for a nightcap.

People were coming and going from the elevators. Some were rushing for a late reservation or the theater. Others were returning to their room for an early night's sleep. Everyone seemed to move in unison with each other except for two men. One was standing next to the revolving door, and the other was reading a newspaper on a red leather loveseat in the lobby. Charles had noticed that neither of them looked down at their watch, so he assumed they weren't waiting for anyone. The only place either of them looked was subtly at each other or at the line of people checking into the hotel, where Charles was coincidentally standing.

Are they looking at me?

He would not let the paranoia get to him. Sure, he was purchasing over a million dollars worth of land from Savannah's most notorious mob boss. Sure, there were two men in all black in the lobby of his hotel.

Just check in. It is your mind playing tricks on you.

After a ten-minute wait, Charles got his keys and proceeded to the elevator. He entered it as soon as the door opened, hit number three, then subtly looked up as the elevator door closed. Both men in black suits were looking right at him.

Clearly, The Hangman already had his guys tailing Charles, and he hadn't even bought the land yet. However, he was not overly afraid. One thing was for sure: they would not hurt him until Ron Martin got his money.

Why put the shakedown on the guy before he can even finish the deal? It makes little sense.

Before jumping in the shower, Charles made two phone calls. The first one he made was to room service. He ordered a tomato soup and grilled cheese sandwich to be delivered directly to the room. He ordinarily would have ordered a glass of wine with dinner but chose not to this evening because of the two goons in the lobby. That wouldn't stop him from having one after dinner at the lobby bar, though. He wanted to see if they were still there.

His second call was to his father in Hinesville. Charles was anxious to see how the financial aspect of the land transaction was going. His father explained that he would have all the funds by tomorrow at lunch and that he and Attorney Gray were going to drive to Savannah to deliver the funds to Mr. Martin in person the following afternoon.

It was hard to believe that this was all coming to fruition. Even without the buried treasure, he knew that acquiring this land could make him and his father rich men. Correction: It would make Charles a rich man. It would simply make his father even richer.

After a quick shower and finishing the cold soup and burnt grilled cheese sandwich, he could use a nightcap. At 8:30, he headed down to the bar. When the elevator doors opened to the lobby, he found the two men in black in the same position as they'd been in over an hour ago. Charles walked with his back to the gentlemen and took a seat facing the piano player and the two goons.

He sat next to a man who looked to be just about his age. He had a buzz cut, chiseled jaw, and appeared to be in particularly good shape. He was dressed casually and looked to be alone. He was drinking something on ice in a tall glass. The next couple of seats to his left were empty.

The pianist was playing "As Time Goes By" when the bartender asked Charles what he wanted to drink.

"Glass of red wine, please?" asked Charles. The bartender nodded without saying anything, turned his back to him, and returned with a healthy pour of Bordeaux and a bowl of peanuts to snack on.

Charles was now getting used to subtly assessing his surroundings. This might have to become an acquired skill if he did not want to get on the wrong side of The Hangman. There was only one couple at the bar who appeared to be on a date. Other couples sat at cocktail tables, enjoying the entertainment. There was healthy applause after each song, which was visibly appreciated by the African American gentleman providing the skilled piano playing and an even better voice.

The only two people that did not seem to be openly enjoying the music were the two men who, by now, were obviously Martin's men. One continued to stoically stand at attention near the door while the other read his newspaper for the fifth time.

They may be dangerous, but they are not the brightest guys.

"Excuse me, Sir," asked the man sitting next to Charles. "Would you mind if I had a few of the peanuts? I have not had dinner yet."

Charles slid the bowl to a distance where each man could help themselves to the dry-roasted nuts. He was still hungry after his less-than-satisfying room service dinner, so giving the nuts away hurt a little.

"Sure," Charles replied. "Here you go, my friend. My peanuts are your peanuts," Charles replied.

"Thanks. I wonder why they gave y'all peanuts and did not offer any to me? Do I look like the kind of guy who couldn't go for a good peanut now and then?" the stranger joked.

Charles openly laughed and continued the banter, "You are totally a peanut guy. I knew it the minute I walked in. Hi. I'm Charles."

The gentleman reached out his hand to clinch Charles' outreached one and introduced himself as Jim Lisenby. He explained that he was visiting Savannah for his cousin's wedding the following day and was trying to escape the endless stream of relatives who were all staying at the hotel across the street.

"You have only been here less than twenty-four hours and are already avoiding your family?" asked Charles.

"What can I say? I have an annoying family. What are you in town for, Charles? By your casual attire, I would guess it is not business."

"I am here on business. I just purchased a sizable piece of land on Hilton Head Island. We are completing the deal tomorrow."

"Hilton Head Island?" asked Jim with a quizzical look on his face. "You just purchased a large piece of land in Hilton Head?"

"Yes. Twenty thousand acres on the south side," bragged Charles. After all, it was over a million dollars worth of land. *How many times does a guy get to brag about that to a stranger?*

Jim rubbed the back of his neck with his right hand, put his elbow on the bar, then turned to Charles and whispered, "So you are the guy buying the land from The Hangman?"

38

Jim pulled out a few dollars from his wallet to pay his bill. Without looking at Charles, he asked what floor he was staying on.

"What is this about? Who are you? Why did you ask about Ron Martin?" Charles asked, his mind now racing.

"I have to leave now. Immediately. What floor are you on? Have one more drink. Pay the bartender, then meet me upstairs. Trust me," ordered the stranger.

Charles told him he was staying on the third floor. Jim left without a handshake but looked at his watch as he headed to the elevator doors. He did so openly and purposefully as if to say he was late for something. No one in the lobby gave him a second look.

Following Jim's request, Charles gladly ordered another glass of wine, which he was going to do anyway. The only difference now was that, instead of losing himself in the live music, he was consumed with who this man was and how he knew about his business. Something made him think Jim was not attending a wedding. The second glass of wine went down a little quicker and easier than the first. It was not because of the expected relaxation the alcohol should provide; it was more the anxiety of the moment and the anticipation of finding out who Jim was.

Charles paid his bill and thanked the bartender for the peanuts. He rose from the barstool towards the elevator doors. He waved to the piano player in gratitude, who returned the gesture by giving him an appreciative nod without missing a note.

Again, he entered the elevator to find the two men in the same positions. He could not figure out if they were there for show or just terrible at their jobs. Anyone in his position would know they were there to monitor his whereabouts. He stepped into the hallway when the doors opened to the third floor. From around a corner, Jim walked casually towards Charles with his hands in his pockets. He stopped near him and asked if anyone else was with him in the elevator.

"Are you asking if one of the two thugs in the lobby followed me?" Charles asked all knowingly.

"Do not say another word. Just take me to your room," replied Jim stoically.

Charles walked down the hallway to his room and let the mystery man in. Jim did not provoke a sense of danger. After all, The Hangman already knew who Charles was and knew he was buying the land.

"So, what exactly is going on here, Jim?" asked Charles while taking a seat at the small table covered with the remnants of his dinner.

"It appears you didn't like the tomato soup, huh?" Jim said, while looking at the half-eaten meal on the table. "My name is Jim Lisenby. I am a deputy for the Beaufort County Sheriff's Department. Sheriff Randall asked me a few hours ago to stake out Mr. Martin's office. I saw two of his guys leave the office a little over an hour ago and enter this hotel. After a half hour, I exited my car and went to the bar to monitor their actions, but I didn't notice that you entered the hotel about ten minutes prior."

"I assumed they were following me," replied Charles. "It just seemed a bit too obvious in the lobby. They could have been a little more conspicuous, don't you think? They must have been trailing me since this afternoon's meeting."

Jim agreed. "The Hangman wants you to know that he is watching you. Believe me, if he wanted those guys to go unnoticed. They would be invisible."

"Why are you staking out The Hangman's office?"

"The sheriff thought it would be best if we kept track of him and his men during the transaction to make sure they are not doing anything suspicious," explained Jim. "You are delivering over one million dollars to a mob boss tomorrow for a precious, yet very remote, piece of land. It would not surprise me if you found some company on your land when you visit. Believe me; they will not welcome you with open arms."

Charles rubbed his head in confusion and took a deep breath. "You are telling me that besides the men already on my land who tried to kill us yesterday, there may be mobsters there as well looking to do the same thing?"

"It might not be today. It may be tomorrow, but I promise you this will not be the last time you hear from The Hangman," warned Jim. He then turned around, abruptly left the room without saying goodbye, and walked down the emergency stairwell, where he exited the hotel from the back service entrance.

39

The following day, Charles awoke in his hotel room after a restless night of dreaming about mafia thugs. His subconscious kept him tossing and turning all night. He rubbed his eyes wondering if he was kidding himself.

While waiting for room service to deliver him his breakfast, he thought about whether he could ever release the grip of The Hangman. What if the mafia interfered with any development and profit he would make from the land? And what if he had unknowingly "partnered" with a known killer instead of signing for a bit of land?

When the breakfast arrived, he called Mary to say hello and update her on recent developments. He was going to call the night before, but by the time Jim had left his room, and his heart had stopped racing, it was too late to call. She left for work at 8:30 a.m., so they would have plenty of time to talk. He told her he was going to visit Hilton Head to see Tamba and his other Gullah friends and to find out how it was going with Samuel Goldsmith. She continued to share her fears but asked if she could come with him. Charles skipped a beat. No everyone has someone who cares for them as much as Mary did, but her safety was his main concern.

"I don't know. As we've discussed, Hilton Head can be a dangerous place," he said in a concerned yet loving tone.

Mary replied sternly, "I'm not some delicate flower who goes to tea parties and cotillions. I can take care of myself. I'm coming with you. I want to avenge Goldsmith as much as you do."

Charles tried to think of the proper rebuttal, but Mary was convincing. Deep down, he didn't want her to go to the island for fear of something happening to her, but she had been by his side right from the start and was a victim of Goldsmith's wrath as well.

Reluctantly, he told her to meet him in the hotel lobby as soon as possible. She agreed, knowing that she had a lot of vacation days at her job. Her boss would not be happy, but this was more important than work. They planned to meet in a couple of hours.

After talking with Mary, Charles showered and made one last call. "Father. It's Charles. I wanted to let you know I will be heading to the island today to see Tamba." He filled him in on Martin's men, who were most likely still in the hotel lobby waiting for him, and on his meeting with Sheriff Randall and Deputy Jim.

"I was afraid of this," sighed Joseph. "Martin is skeptical of our intentions with his land. Skeptical may not be the right word. I think Paranoid is a better word for it."

His father's voice trembled. He tried to console him by expressing confidence and a lack of fear. "Don't worry. I can handle myself. Now that I know I am being followed, I am in control of the situation. I will be sure not to do anything foolish or tip our hand."

His words comforted Joseph. "Good. Be careful and be sure not to go to the south side of the island today. I suggest we wait and visit tomorrow with the sheriff and deputy."

The two of them now had their strategy for the day. They agreed Joseph would stay in Savannah that evening. They would meet for dinner after Charles had visited Hilton Head and Joseph had delivered the funds to The Hangman.

A little later, Charles left his room for Hilton Head. When the elevator door opened to the lobby, Charles spotted Mary sitting on a loveseat near the entrance. He waved, walked over to her, hugged her, and whispered in her ear, "Play it cool. There are two of Ron Martin's men following me. They are in the lobby. Just pretend we're going out to lunch together."

Mary pretended to laugh, held his hand, and turned to leave. They kept their eyes focused on the revolving door to exit the hotel.

While walking out of the hotel towards his car, Charles wondered how long it would take the man in the black suit who was on the lobby pay phone to follow him. It didn't take long.

****

Martin's men were already tailing Charles soon after leaving Savannah. It did not take a genius to see the black car following him along the deserted country road that led to Bluffton. The overtness of their tail continued to convince him that he was not in imminent danger. At least, he hoped as much.

The problem now was that, besides Goldsmith, Charles had to worry about Ron Martin finding out about the treasure. If he did, this adventure they embarked upon might be over sooner than expected.

The ride to Savannah was much less exciting than what the Gullah men were up to. The day before, they'd done a drive-by shooting at

Goldsmith's excavation site. While Bala sped down the coast, Tamba and his men opened fire on the camp. The barrage took less than a minute but was effective enough to delay the digging and continue to place fear and doubt in the mind of Goldsmith and his men. As the boat sped off, they noticed the men lying face down on the ground with their hands over their heads, fearing being shot. Today, they were going to ignite the booby traps they'd placed in the camp after Goldsmith had retreated the day before. Joseph's plan was working like a well-oiled machine.

When Charles and Mary finally arrived at the marina, they chartered a boat down the May River, where they met with Tamba, who was again sitting on the benches in front of the building.

"Tamba, it is good to see you. I would like you to meet my friend Mary," Charles said, reaching out to shake his hand.

Tamba reached for Mary's hand and coupled it with both of his when he said, "Mary, it is my honor to meet you. You are a most beautiful woman with the eyes of an angel."

Mary was flattered by the compliment and impressed with Tamba's politeness. She had never met a Gullah before, so she was intrigued by his accent. "Is that a hint of creole I hear in your accent, Mr. Tamba?"

"Please call me Tamba, Miss Mary." He beamed. "We call it 'Sea Island Creole' here on Hilton Head Island. The accent designates 'Gullahs' from 'Geechee.' I'm very impressed. How did you recognize it?"

Mary revealed that she took a dialect course in college and was most interested in southern dialects since so many people of African descent lived nearby. The room fell silent for a moment while everyone tried to grasp the intellect displayed by the beautiful woman. Each of them was impressed in their own way and a bit jealous of Charles for bringing such a pretty and intelligent woman to the team.

Charles cut through the silence. "How are things going with our friends on the south side?"

Tamba was eager to see his new friend and proudly explained how well the mission was going. They also had seen no drug drop-offs in the past couple of days. He hoped they were beginning to scare them away with their defense of the marina the previous week.

Charles explained they were buying the land today and that the south side of Hilton Head would soon be a source of employment and wealth for the Gullah, whom they intended to hire to help excavate and develop the land. Tamba bowed his head at the Gramers' generosity to him and his people.

"Tomorrow, we will return with some help," explained Charles. "We will be here early in the morning and arrive on a boat driven by the Beaufort County Sheriff and his deputies. They are going to kick Goldsmith off our land."

The news thrilled Tamba. Even though the Gramers' mission would be very lucrative for him and his men, there was still an inherent danger. He did not wish for anyone else to get hurt. He just wanted to do his job. With the sheriff involved, the violence would stop.

Tamba was kind enough to take Charles and Mary by boat back up the May River to Bluffton. The ride took only about fifteen minutes, but this trip consisted of more contemplation than previous conversations. After several minutes of silence, Tamba finally broke the ice with a question, "Mr. Gramer, what do you think will come of all of this? Do you think there is a treasure?"

Charles took a moment to ponder the question. Everything was happening so fast that he hadn't had time to wonder what would happen when this was all over. "Yeah. I believe there is a treasure, and we will find it in the next couple of days. You will be rewarded greatly for your help. I just fear Goldsmith won't go away so easily."

Tamba continued to look at the waters ahead rather than at Charles. There should have been a joy on his face, but instead, his brows furrowed in concerned.

He cleared his throat and muttered, "I just pray we survive."

40

When Charles and Mary returned to the hotel in Savannah, the front desk told them that his father had checked in and that he was in the room next to him on the third floor. He thanked them and asked if he could get another room for Mary close by. They obliged. After getting her room key, they walked hand in hand to the elevator purposefully, not looking at the man pretending to be on the phone or at the other sitting on a couch pretending to read the paper.

He knocked on his father's door and entered when he opened it. "It appears your friends are still in the lobby. Did they ask you how your day went?" asked Joseph jokingly.

"No, but they sent flowers to my room with a nice card," quipped Charles.

When Mary entered the room, Joseph covered his mouth with his hands. "Mary, what a surprise. What are you doing here?"

"Hello, Mr. Gramer," she replied. "I couldn't let you and Charles have all the fun. I convinced him to let me come along today."

Joseph took a deep breath. "With all due respect, Goldsmith has already shot me. The island is dangerous. It's no place for a lady."

Mary giggled at the surprised look on his face. She would have been more surprised if he were indifferent.

"I tried to convince her to stay home," explained Charles. "She's not gonna budge."

Mary folded her hands and squared her shoulders. "Don't worry Mr. Gramer. I can take care of myself. The island does not scare me. My father took me camping every summer growing up. He taught me how to hike, fish, and hunt. You name it. I can shoot a gun. I won't be a liability. I promise you."

Joseph's shoulders softened, he agreed to add her to the treasure hunting team.

The three went to dinner at a restaurant across the street that served classic low country cuisine. It was nestled in a typical Savannah brick brownstone. It had lofty ceilings with exposed ductwork. They dimmed the lights purposely to enhance the ambiance.

They feasted on fried chicken and gravy, macaroni and cheese, and collard greens. The Gramer men agreed that the chicken was not as good as Pearl's, but the collard greens were to die for. During dinner, Joseph told Charles how uneventful it was delivering the funds for the land to The Hangman. Apparently, he had other things on his plate, so he was too busy to attend the meeting. It was like any other business transaction that he'd made in the past, except that, this time, he was dealing with a cold-blooded killer.

Towards the end of dinner, Joseph handed Charles an envelope. He took it from him and asked, "What is this?"

"This is the deed to your land. Congratulations, son. You are now the owner of twenty thousand acres of land on Hilton Head Island... and you owe me over one million dollars," Joseph joked, raising his eyebrows as if to say he wanted it now.

"Let's cheers to that," said Mary as they all raised their glass of red wine and clinked them together.

"Here's to justice being served," blurted Joseph as they clanged glasses again.

"And here's to our health and safety." Charles paused. "I'm afraid that may be more important with what is yet to come."

41

The Gramers and Mary chose not to check out of the hotel the next morning fearing that it might tip off Martin's guys as to their plan. Instead, they let them presume that it was just another day. They left Savannah in Joseph's car with The Hangman's guys not far behind. It took over an hour to reach the Beaufort County Sheriff's office, where four squad cars waited in front. They parked as close as they could and made their way in.

The station was bustling more than it had been when Charles was there two days before. There were five officers present. Some were at their desks. Others gathered around the coffeemaker. Each turned and looked at the Gramers when they entered.

Sheriff Randall welcomed them and introduced himself to Joseph and Mary. Jim walked over to Charles to greet him as well.

"So, what's the plan of action, sheriff?" asked Joseph after a little small talk about their mutual service in the war.

"Do you have the deed, Charles?" asked Sheriff Randall.

Charles pulled an envelope from his shirt pocket and waved it at him instead of answering.

The sheriff grabbed his hat and rallied his men. "Then let's go. We have a boat waiting at the May River to take us to the south side of the island."

Everyone hurried to their cars and drove to the marina in Bluffton. One officer stayed back to cover the desk at the station. The others seemed thrilled to take a road trip via boat rather than a squad car.

Sheriff Randall confirmed that all the officers properly armed themselves and made sure that the Gramers were not. They entered a large blue boat with "Beaufort County Sheriff" painted on the side. It was similar to the boat being repaired by the Gullah men that had been riddled with bullets just days prior. The one exception was that it had a blue light on the roof of the galley to let boaters know they were the authorities.

The boat captain, who was not a police officer, explained they would go south down the east side of the island rather than the west side to avoid any drug dealers that might drop off in the Spanish Wells area, where they often did. The boat was faster than Bala's, so the trip took about half the time. At least it seemed that way to the Gramers.

As they approached the south side of the island, Sheriff Randall instructed the Gramers and Mary to enter the galley and sit on the floor.

Randal and his team were no strangers to being on the water and encountering criminals. They had been trying to stop the drug dealers for years but eventually felt it was not worth their time to patrol the waters. They only had so much manpower in his precinct. He just could not afford to have two men stationed on the water each day. He had appealed to the coast guard several times to monitor the waters but was continually told they were low-staffed because of the recently ended war.

The sheriff turned on the blinking blue light on the roof of the boat and started pushing a crank that made a very loud wailing siren. It could be heard from hundreds of yards away.

When they made the final turn west to the southernmost part of the island, they spotted two boats moored, and a group of men lying on the beach, facing the open sea, with rifles pointed at them.

"Take your positions, gentlemen, and have your weapons locked and loaded. It appears we may have a situation here," said Sheriff Randall.

The police siren wailed as the boat idled fifty yards from shore. The tension cut through the humid air. Five men lay on the beach with rifles pointed at them. Sheriff Randall made the first move. He walked to the bow of the boat, held up his right hand, and waved his badge.

"Put your guns down! This is the sheriff's department. Put your guns down now!" he screamed.

Goldsmith came out from a tent when he heard the sheriff's warning. He confidently walked up in front of the armed men on the beach and directed them to unarm themselves. They did so accordingly.

When Randall saw no more imminent threat, he directed the captain to steer the boat toward the beach. The small waves allowed them to glide onto shore, where it sat comfortably in the sand with no need for a mooring.

"You three stay in the galley until I tell you otherwise," he said to the Gramers and Mary.

In unison, the officers jumped out of the boat while continuing to aim their guns at the now unarmed men standing together on the beach. "Everyone, drop your guns and step away from them," ordered Randall.

"Listen to the sheriff," Goldsmith announced. "Do as you're told. Drop your weapons. They are no danger to us."

Randall led his team in a triangular position as they approached Goldsmith and his men. "I want everyone to put your hands behind your heads so we can frisk you. We need to make sure you don't have any other weapons on you. Tell us now if you are carrying any other weapons. It will make things a lot easier on you," ordered Randall.

The men complied, so the officers spread out to frisk them. Randall went directly to Goldsmith. He had to be sure he was unarmed.

The sheriff explained firmly, "My name is Hubert Randall. I am the Beaufort County Sheriff. Please identify yourself."

"My name is Samuel Goldsmith," he replied in a kind and polite tone. "Is there something I can help you with? Have we done anything wrong?"

Randall reiterated Charles' claim that Goldsmith and his men had opened fire on nearby boaters in the past week.

"That is ridiculous!" Goldsmith lied, with his voice full of frustration. "We are the ones being shot at. Every day we have been attacked by ground and sea. Yesterday, one of my men almost lost a leg by a booby trap set by someone."

The sheriff was listening intently but didn't believe his story. After all, just minutes ago, Goldsmith's men were ready to fire at them but did not because they were the sheriff's department.

"Regardless, you need to collect your things, leave this property immediately, and never return," replied Randall.

Goldsmith's lips fell towards the ground. He figured that he would have the treasure by now, but the ever-important treasure map he stole proved not to be as helpful as he had hoped. He should have taken the will from Yale as well. It may have given him a more specific place to dig. Now they were held at gunpoint by the sheriff and were ordered to leave.

"Why do we have to leave? We are not disturbing anyone," he rebuked.

"Whether you are disturbing someone is irrelevant, Mr. Goldsmith. You are trespassing on another person's property. They want you off their land because they fear you will continue retaliating against them when they order you to leave. I am here to enforce their rights."

Goldsmith's mind was now racing. In the past few days on the island, they had spent more time dodging bullets than digging for treasure. Now he was being forced to leave with no results.

"There must be some way we can work this out, Sheriff," he suggested, his voice now icy with anger. "I am sure the owners would allow us to stay if I could just speak with them. We're only going to be here for a few more days. Maybe I can talk to them. Do you know how I can reach them?"

The sheriff didn't need to ask Goldsmith why they were there or what they were doing. It wasn't any of his business. His job was to remove the trespassers from the land, and that was all.

"I know how you can reach them. They are in my boat with the deed to the property."

Goldsmith looked at the boat and saw two men and a pretty woman standing at its bow overlooking the situation. The sheriff waved them over. Charles asked Mary to stay put while the Gramers jumped out of the boat and approached Goldsmith and his crew.

"Mr. Gramer, may I introduce Mr. Goldsmith," said Sheriff Randall.

Samuel Goldsmith's mouth was wide open. The man he left for dead in a Boston alley no less than a few weeks earlier was walking towards him. *He survived the attack.* If he had known he was still alive, he would have whacked him one more time with the baseball bat to finish him off.

Charles glared at the man who tried to kill him, seething angrily and overwhelmed by revenge. He spoke first, shaking his head. "I want you to leave my property immediately. Take all your things and leave."

Goldsmith was furious now. He spat at Charles' feet. *How could this guy own the land?* He bickered with the sheriff for a few minutes until Charles pulled out the deed from his jacket and waved it in front of Goldsmith.

Randall finally gave him an ultimatum. "Mr. Goldsmith, I suggest you pack now, or I will have to arrest all of you for trespassing. It is up to you, sir. Do you want to leave peacefully, or do you want to spend some time in my jail cell?"

Now broken and distraught, Goldsmith dropped his head in despair. He knew it was over for the moment because he needed to comply with the sheriff for fear of being arrested. The only thing he knew was that he had to find the treasure. It was his family's destiny, and it was his job to fulfill it.

He cursed at himself, then picked his head up to gain some composure. "Pack it up, boys. We are leaving," he barked to his men while giving Charles a death glare. When the men had disbursed to pack, Charles asked Sheriff Randall if he could speak privately with Goldsmith. The sheriff complied and walked into the forest with the others to supervise the cleanup.

After they were alone and no one could hear them, Charles looked Goldsmith in the eye and said in a low and powerful tone, "I have to warn you, Mr. Goldsmith. I have the legal right to defend my property. The second amendment of the Constitution tells me so."

Without blinking or taking his eyes off Charles, Goldsmith smirked and replied in a condescending tone, "And?"

"And... if you return to my property, I will be forced to defend it and am not afraid to do so. In addition, if I ever see you again, I'll be tempted to contact the New Haven police department and let them know where they can find the person responsible for stealing a priceless map from the Yale University Archives last week."

Goldsmith's face turned pale white when he heard the threat. *How could this guy know I stole the map?* "This isn't over, Gramer," threatened Goldsmith. "That treasure belongs to my family, and I will do whatever it takes to get it."

"Would you give up your life for it, Mr. Goldsmith? I know what you did to me in Boston."

Without hesitation, he smirked. "I would gladly give up my life for that treasure, and I would expect no less from you. It just may come down to that if I have anything to do with it."

42

It took a couple of hours for Goldsmith and his men to pack up their camp and leave the site. When they were done, Charles asked Sheriff Randall if he could drop them off at the Gullah's marina in Mitchellville. The sheriff had no qualms with the request and dropped them off a half hour later. Before they said goodbye, Randall warned them about Goldsmith and his men. He feared they would return and continue to terrorize them. After some contemplation, Joseph suggested that the sheriff or one of his men work security detail for the next week or so to help protect them. Charles added that they would pay handsomely for the job. The officers agreed. They never passed up paid detail work. Charles then asked if one of them was available today since they planned to return to the site immediately. His friend, Deputy Jim Lisenby, explained that he had the rest of the day off, so he was willing to return with them and work on the detail.

They thanked the Sheriff and his men, then left the marina and waited on a bench hoping that Tamba and his men would be there soon. It didn't take long for the Gullah men to arrive.

The men packed the boat with supplies, tents, shovels, metal detectors, and weapons. Jim was initially concerned about the amount of

ROBERT J. PERREAULT

weaponry, but Charles reminded him of the danger inherent in the drug trade and Goldsmith's threat. The deputy was satisfied with the explanation, so allowed it.

The trip to the excavation site was timely and uneventful for everyone except Mary. She had not been on a boat very many times, so like earlier, she spent the trip in awe of the island's surroundings and the vastness of the open sea.

Jim stood guard on the beach after they arrived while the other men entered the forest to set up camp. Charles was eager to start the search for the treasure, so he and a few other men began using the metal detectors. Joseph, Mary, and the others focused on setting up camp.

They searched until just before dusk with no luck. There was a constant parade of beeping while they looked. Every half hour or so, someone's detector would start beeping louder, hinting that it had found something, so the Gullah would run over and start digging. Unfortunately, each time they dug, there was no treasure to be found.

As the sun started going down, most of the team packed up to head home for the evening. The Gramers and Tamba stayed back to continue searching. Unfortunately, Mary would have to stay on the island as well because, since it was her first time on the island, she was afraid she couldn't find her way back to Savannah on her own. It was dangerous for her to stay on the island overnight, but he felt like there was no other choice. Plus, she told him that she made a mean pot of coffee to help them get an early start the next morning.

As they were putting the last few items in the boat, Deputy Lisenby, who was using binoculars to search the open waters for intruders, announced that he saw a boat approaching at high speed from the west, about three hundred yards from the coast.

228

"Everyone get in the galley and lay on the floor!" he ordered.

By the boat's speed, Jim could tell they only had a minute before it was within shooting distance of the camp. They all jumped into the boat quickly. Jim put down his binoculars and grabbed his rifle, slung around his shoulder. He stood at the front of the boat, shielding him from any potential danger. His gun rested on the top of the stern, cocked, and loaded.

The boat continued to speed towards the camp, then halted. It was now close enough that he could throw a rock at it.

"I am sheriff Deputy Jim Lisenby of the Beaufort County Sheriff's Office," he screamed. "This is private—!"

A loud single gunshot echoed in the evening's silence. It was then replaced with the sound of gentle waves splashing on the shore. The next thing was the sound of a boat accelerating full throttle away from the shore.

"Stay down Mary," whispered Charles as he jumped up from his position on the galley floor to assess the situation. He looked to the open water to see a boat in the distance driving away from them at high speed. He couldn't determine who was on the boat but knew for sure that it was Goldsmith. Then he turned and looked toward the back. There was no sign of his friend Jim.

"Jim. Jim. Are you all right?" he asked, his voice trembling.

The deputy did not respond. Charles jumped off the port side and ran to the back of the boat, where he found Jim lying face first in the shallow water. "Jim!" he screamed as he ran towards him to help.

When he rolled him over, he saw a shadow of the man he had met just two nights before. His face was covered with blood dripping into a gaping mouth full of ocean water. There was no sign of life, but the cause of death was clear. One eyeball was now just a hollow eye socket oozing blood. The sniper aimed for his right eye and hit the target perfectly.

Joseph and Mary approached the stern, looking down at Charles and the deceased deputy. Charles glanced up at his father with Jim's head resting in his lap. "He did it again. He killed a police officer," he sighed, his voice trembling. "Has this gone too far? Mary was right. Goldsmith will kill for the treasure… He must be stopped."

Mary's knees were like rubber as she looked back to make sure there was no imminent danger. The reality of the situation had just hit her. She had never seen a dead body nor seen Charles so vulnerable. "Goldsmith will not get away with this. Don't give up. We can find the treasure. I promise."

As a father, Joseph tried to find the words to console his son and make him feel like everything was going to be okay. He considered that, in the past few days, he had been shot, and a sniper had just killed a deputy. Unfortunately, optimism was not the first thing that came to mind while consoling his son. Joseph had to go back to his military roots to make sure that they lost no more souls on this mission.

"Charles, gather the men. Bala and I will return to Bluffton immediately to deliver the deceased to Sheriff Randall and advise him on what just transpired. You, Mary, and the others search for the treasure. Search all night if you have to. We need to find it before Goldsmith comes back. And son… he will come back. Be careful."

43

Joseph and Bala wrapped the deputy in a blanket and laid him on the floor of the galley before heading to Bluffton. They said goodbye to the others and promised to return the following morning. They expected to reach Bluffton just after sundown and had to wait until the next morning to return because it was too dangerous to make the trip back in the dark.

Being that it was dusk, Bala believed the trip would be uneventful since the drug dealers do not make drops in the darkness. At the same time, he would not take any chances, so he had Joseph armed at the bow with binoculars to keep a watch for any more danger.

They stopped at the Mitchellville marina on the way to Bluffton to refill the boat's gas tank and to call the Beaufort County Sheriff's Office. While Bala tended to the boat's needs, Joseph walked to the phone booth next to the docks to make the dreaded call. After a few rings, someone picked up the phone.

"Sheriff's office, can I help you?" asked the person on the other line.

"Hello, this is Joseph Gramer. I was with Sheriff Randall and some other deputies in Hilton Head today. I was hoping to speak with the sheriff."

Sheriff Randall picked up the phone and asked Joseph how he could be of assistance. Joseph had been thinking about how to break the news to the sheriff on the boat ride. *Should I break it to him gently? Should I just rip the bandage off?* He never actually came up with a definitive answer, so he just went from the cuff.

"Sheriff, I have some sad news. It is about Deputy Lisenby."

"What about him?" he asked timidly.

"Goldsmith and his men came back after you left. They approached the shore via boat and apparently had a sniper on board. They fired only one shot. That shot hit the deputy in the right eye. He died instantly. Sir, he protected all of us. We owe our lives to him."

The line went silent. Randall had been sheriff for about three years. During that time, he had never lost an officer nor even come close. His eyes welled up. He replied carefully, "Where is the body?"

"Bala and I have him in the boat. We are in Mitchellville now and wanted to deliver him to you in Bluffton. It will only take fifteen minutes to get up the May River," Joseph answered reluctantly.

The sheriff hung up the phone after agreeing to meet Joseph and Bala at the marina in Bluffton, where he would have an ambulance waiting for the fallen officer. He then gathered the officers at the station and gave them the sad news. The room was filled with tears and anger. Objects were thrown, and they promised justice. Only minutes after hearing the news, each man instinctively got into their squad car and followed Randall to pay their respects to their friend.

The officers arrived at the marina before both the ambulance and the body. The marina was empty except for a black car with two men sitting in the front seat. Unbeknownst to the officers, the car had been sitting there all day, and the men in the car were waiting for the Gramers.

The officers exited their cars and lined themselves along the water in salute to their fallen comrade. Joseph and Bala pulled up to the dock. After tying up the boat, Joseph stepped off and shook the sheriff's trembling hand.

Under the sound of the distant whining of an ambulance siren, Joseph said to the sheriff, "The deputy and his family will always be in my family's thoughts and prayers, sir. We will have him in our memories for the rest of our lives. He was never fearful and was confident in his actions. He is a genuine hero."

The sheriff did not respond. Instead, he turned to the two officers next to him and directed them to board the craft and prepare the body for the ambulance. The two officers did not hesitate as Bala led them into the galley.

The ambulance arrived five minutes later. There had been no other discussion between anyone since Joseph's well wishes. The sheriff pointed the EMTs to the galley where they could retrieve the body. They carefully and respectfully placed the deceased on a cot and carried it into the back of the ambulance amidst the line of officers in salute to their fallen comrade.

Sheriff Randall turned to Joseph as the ambulance door closed. "Tell me what happened. Tell me everything you know… including why this piece of land on Hilton Head Island is worth shooting a police officer for."

44

Even though Charles and Mary were distraught over Jim's murder, they knew they had to find the treasure before Goldsmith and his men returned. To protect themselves from another attack, Charles directed the Gullah to take turns keeping watch on the beach as the others kept searching.

While the Gullah searched with the metal detectors providing a constant beeping symphony, Mary took out her notebook and reread the passage of the will describing where the treasure had been buried.

"Starting at a group of 10 large sea pine trees, walk to the north and then to the east, and there I buried the treasure."

"Are you confident Goldsmith has been searching in the right spot?" asked Mary.

The question surprised Charles. He just presumed that Goldsmith knew where the treasure was since he had the map. *Maybe he didn't?* He took the notebook from Mary and read the passage out loud. He then grabbed a pair of binoculars and walked to the beach. In the darkness, he used the light of the nearly full moon to look up and down the beach for a noticeable cluster of ten trees. He and Mary walked the beach, hoping to find an obvious spot while knowing that over the past three hundred years, there was a good chance that other trees had grown around the ten that Hilton had written about.

After walking seventy yards north of the excavation site, Mary noticed a small opening in the forest. The rest of the coast had been a continuous line of large pine trees. *Maybe this is a clue*, she thought.

She pointed to Charles and said, "Look over there. I might have found something."

Charles looked at each side of the opening and counted the trees to see if there was any sort of grouping of ten. He found no obvious cluster, which was frustrating. Then he had a thought. He left the edge of the forest and rushed to where the water met the shore. The waves gently covered his shoes, soaking his feet while he pointed his binoculars to the sky.

Are any trees different heights from others?

Lucky for Charles, there was a blood moon out that night, so even though the sun had already set, the moon and the stars lit up the sky like it was dusk. He looked until he found a grove of trees that were significantly higher than the ones next to them. He didn't count to see if there were ten of them, but that didn't matter.

"I think we found the treasure!"

He turned to Mary, grabbed her by the shoulder, and gently shook her. "With your help, I think we found where Hilton buried his treasure."

Charles called out to Tamba and the others to stop searching at the camp, collect the detectors and shovels, and follow him.

"I walked at least 500 paces to get to that spot, but I was not more than 500 paces, as the crow flies, from the large sea pine trees. I am sure that I walked farther in the northerly direction than in the easterly direction."

"Follow me," Charles said to the Gullah men as he counted his steps while walking north from the opening in the forest they had just found. When he reached five hundred steps, he stopped and looked towards the woods for a clue where Hilton may have entered. The group formed a line parallel to the coast, with each person ten feet apart. They walked west into the forest, mimicking the walk that William Hilton had presumably done centuries before. The metal detectors beeped as they slowly searched the area for any open spot where Hilton may have found the perfect place to hide his fortune.

It didn't take long for one of the Gullah's metal detectors to go off. The sound differed from other times when they thought they might have found something while searching earlier. This time the detector sounded louder, stronger. Charles hurtled to the spot and ran his detector over the area as well. The quiet, low country night was now shattered by the loud stereo beeping of metal detectors going off in unison.

"Tamba! Grab a shovel and start digging. I think we found it!"

Tamba and two others started digging in the area where Charles was standing with his arm around Mary. After a dozen or so shovels of dirt were removed, one man dug into the ground, but it did not give way this time. He hit something hard. It might have been a tree root. Maybe a rock. It might have been the treasure…

It was time to find out.

The men carefully removed the dirt from the top of the solid object until they made an outline. It was fairly dark because the sea pines above blocked the moonlight, so they used flashlights to see what it was. It appeared to be about three feet long and two feet wide. They began digging around the object until it seemed they'd reached the bottom. Then they used the shovels as leverage to loosen the thing from its earthen grave. After a few minutes, it was loose enough that they could remove it from the hole. Each man grabbed a side of the object and lifted it.

"One, two, three, lift!" encouraged Charles, who was covered in dirt and sweat in the hole with the others.

"Lift!" he repeated several more times.

On the fourth attempt, the men gathered enough strength to raise the object out of the hole and rested it on the dirt above them. In complete exhaustion, the men fell to the ground panting to catch their breath. Charles was as tired as any of them but could not take his eye off the large object. Mary passed around canteens of water to refresh the parched men.

After taking a deep gulp, Charles looked at Mary and said, "This is it. It is time to see what William Hilton left on this island."

He and Tamba brushed off the object quickly while two others pointed their flashlights at it. Soon it became clear that it was a large wooden chest. When all the dirt and debris had been removed, Charles took a deep breath and reached to open the chest. As he was about to open it, a light from a boat quickly approaching the shore lit up the beach.

"Shit!" Charles grimaced. "Goldsmith is back."

45

"**G**rab the chest and come with me!" barked Charles. "They must have seen the flashlights."

Four of the Gullah men each grabbed a side of the chest and followed Charles and Mary through the forest heading back towards their camp. They could not use flashlights anymore for fear of being seen by Goldsmith. Luckily, the moon gave off enough light through the tall sea pines to allow them safe passage. They had only brought one weapon with them to the dig, so the priority should be to return to camp and arm themselves in defense of their newfound treasure. Charles' thoughts then focused on the danger he put Mary in. If there were any harm to her, the treasure wouldn't be worth it.

The pace back to camp was methodical. The Gullah struggled to carry the chest and simultaneously walk at a brisk pace. It was heavy but not heavy enough to strain the muscles of the men. Nevertheless, it was awkward to maneuver it through the trees and brush.

When they finally arrived at their camp, Charles directed the men to put the chest in a tent. When he exited, he found Mary standing guard outside with a semi-automatic rifle in her hands, ready to defend the fortune.

"Get yourself a weapon, Gramer," ordered Mary, her head turning from side to side in search of danger. "It's time to light this guy up!"

Charles shook his head in amazement and laughed seeing Mary holding a rifle. "I'm going to have to start calling you Mary the Mobster."

Mary shrugged her shoulders as if to agree, then ordered the others to scatter behind trees circling the camp with weapons locked and loaded, expecting an attack from any side.

From this point, they made all communications via whisper since the night air was still and the sea was calm. The sound of the boat pulling onto shore was not too far away. The camp was too deep into the woods to see how many men were on the boat. But they could clearly hear the engine when the boat hit the beach. When the captain turned the boat off, the beach became eerily silent again.

Moments passed, which seemed like hours, as Charles and Mary waited for Goldsmith's imminent attack. There was nothing they could do but hide for cover and prepare for a counterattack. Being aggressive and hitting them as they approached would leave them too exposed. Plus, Goldsmith had a sniper on board who could have easily picked them off one by one. Their position now allowed them a better opportunity to defend themselves.

Charles flinched at the sound of guns being cocked and footsteps in the forest. Goldsmith's men were now only feet away from their camp. He prayed that the moonlight was strong enough to light up the battlefield so they could attack before Goldsmith could determine their positions.

The moonlight provided just enough light to reveal two men walking through the forest. Right before Charles was about to yell "Fire," a familiar voice asked, "Charles, where are you? It's Bala and me."

Everyone felt a collective sigh of relief as they put down their weapons.

"Holy smokes! You almost got yourself killed," screamed Charles. "You cannot just sneak up on us like that. What's going on? I thought you were returning tomorrow morning."

Unfazed, Joseph and Bala continued to walk toward the camp while the others turned on the lanterns. Joseph looked around at the men recovering from the tension and said, "Okay. The drama is over. Let's get back to work. We have a treasure to find."

The men laughed and went back to what they were doing. Joseph was annoyed at the lack of discipline that the men were showing, so he turned to his son and asked with a firm yet sarcastic tone, "Am I the only one here who believes that time is of the essence?"

Charles looked at Mary, grinned, and replied, "Follow me." He led Joseph into the tent and pointed his flashlight on the large, dirty chest sitting smack dab in the middle of it. "We did it…" he beamed, placing a hand on his shoulder. "Mary and I found the treasure."

Joseph stood motionless. He had been gone for less than two hours, and they had already found the treasure. *Amazing.*

Charles explained how Mary reread the passage of the will and realized that Goldsmith had been looking in the wrong place. Not knowing what was written on the map he had stolen; one thing was almost certain—whatever was on that map must have been incorrect. Either that or else, Goldsmith must have misread it in his haste to find the treasure.

"Have you opened it up yet?" asked Joseph.

"No. We were about to when two strangers came rambling onto the beach ready to attack us, so we were forced into a defensive mode," Mary replied sarcastically.

Joseph gave her a playful look. "Hilarious. Let's waste no more time. Open the damn chest and see if everything we've been through this past month was worth it."

Charles lit a lantern to illuminate the tent. Joseph grabbed two flashlights and handed one to Mary.

"The moment of truth," said Charles.

He walked over to the chest with a crowbar and jammed it below the cover. It had been closed for over three hundred years, so he did not expect it to pop open like some jack-in-the-box. After a dozen attempts at jimmying it open, it gradually loosened up. It would not be long before he discovered what was inside.

Suddenly, with one last jam of the screwdriver, the cover unlatched slightly with dust pouring out on all sides. The three looked down and nodded in unison. Charles then opened the chest fully.

Their flashlights revealed piles of gold, silver, and jewelry. There were hundreds of gold coins, countless large gemstones attached to ornate necklaces, pendants, rings, silver spoons, and place settings. They looked in amazement at what they had unearthed.

In unison, they whispered, "Holy…" They then stared in awe, had a group hug, and started jumping up and down in celebration.

Joseph was the first to release their embrace. He grabbed his son's shoulder and shook him violently. "You did it! By God, you did it! You found William Hilton's treasure. You are now an extraordinarily rich man!"

The weight of the moment overwhelmed Charles. He fell to the ground in exhaustion. His mind raced with thoughts of what transpired to get him to this moment. He remembered waking up in the Boston hospital bed. Hearing the news Mary had been attacked ran through his mind. He pictured his father being shot. He saw Deputy Jim's blood on his hands.

Then he quickly realized that revenge had finally been served. Goldsmith would never get the treasure. He wished he could see his nemesis' face when he approached the shore and found a large empty hole where Hilton's treasure once lay.

Next, he imagined all the good he and Mary could do together with the fortune. Their efforts and prosperity could make the world a better place. That made everything they had been through worth it, so he hoped.

It took a few minutes for them to collect their thoughts and embrace the enormity of the situation. Joseph left the tent to give Charles and Mary privacy. They sat on the ground, resting their backs against the treasure chest in silence.

Mary eventually broke the silence. "What's next?"

"I suggest we get the hell out of here immediately and return to Hinesville," replied Charles. "We need to leave before Goldsmith returns or our mafia friends decide to pay us a visit. I'm tired of people trying to kill us."

46

The boat ride back to Bluffton may as well have taken hours. The reason was that Bala had to be careful driving in the dark of night. Hilton Head's coast was full of sandbars, so if he was going too fast and hit one, the boat could capsize. Being they had a veritable fortune in the galley, no one on the boat complained about taking it slow on the way back.

During the trip, Charles and Tamba sat at the stern of the boat gazing at the vast universe and discussed how his men would be compensated for their arduous work and bravery. After the debacle with Goldsmith, the Gramers agreed to pay for a new boat for Bala. They also agreed to pay the men handsomely once they'd determined the value of the treasure. Each man would never have to work again with the riches afforded to them via the treasure.

Charles suggested, and Tamba agreed, that each of the men would receive one of the many gold coins when they reached Bluffton as a gesture of good faith. To make sure that he fully compensated the men, Tamba agreed to return to Hinesville with the Gramers to collect the final payment for his men, which was fair.

When they arrived in Bluffton, the Gullah men placed the chest in Joseph's car. Before they left, Charles gave each of the men one gold coin. He explained to each of them that the value of each coin was likely more than their total annual income and that more was to come when they returned.

The men couldn't believe their good fortune. Each man lived a humble lifestyle, like every other Gullah on the island. They did not have time or money for frivolous things or luxuries that others on the mainland had. All they had was their land and the profits they could make from it by selling their goods on the docks in Savannah. With a coin grasped in each of the men's hands, they rushed off to spend the night at the Mitchellville marina, drinking every spirit they could get their hands on while celebrating their newfound fortune.

Charles covered the treasure chest with a blanket in the trunk of Joseph's car. They also filled the trunk with necessary guns and weapons, considering the fortune they were carrying. When finished, they said goodbye to the Gullahs and hurried off to Hinesville. Unfortunately, their excitement clouded their judgment. As they were driving away from the marina, none of them noticed the black car parked in the back of the lot with two men in black suits watching their every move.

The Gramers took turns driving during the night on the way back to Hinesville with Mary and Tamba in the back seat. All the while, a black car followed them from far enough away that none of them had seen the tail.

Dawn was just breaking when the three men finally made it to Hinesville. A couple of hours prior, they had dropped Mary off at her car in Savannah so she could drive home on her own. While saying goodbye to Mary, Charles proposed they meet later that evening for dinner so he could keep her apprised of the treasure's worth.

Joseph drove directly to the lumber yard because he had a safe in his office that was large enough to fit the treasure. It was early enough, so no one was at work when they arrived. It was perfect timing. The three men carried the treasure up the metal stairs and across the balcony to his office. Joseph unlocked a door behind his desk, which was hiding a safe bigger than a refrigerator. Joseph twirled the dial on the safe until it opened and directed Tamba and Charles to place the chest inside it. It fit. He closed the safe and locked it.

"Now that the treasure is safe, pun intended," said Joseph, "we need to determine its value. I will call my contacts at the local banks and the owner of Hinesville Jewelry to visit us today to get an idea of what this might be worth."

Charles and Tamba had already sat in the two leather seats across from Joseph's desk. They nodded in agreement with his suggestion. In the meantime, they needed to visit Charles' apartment to take a shower and get breakfast before the banks and jewelry store opened.

They quickly left the lumber yard and jumped in the two-door coupe. It was the nicest car that Tamba had ever been in. He told Charles the same. In return for the compliment, Charles fishtailed out of the dirt parking lot like a race car driver, to Tamba's delight.

As they sped out of the lumber yard's parking lot, again, they did not notice the black car hidden down a side road monitoring who entered and exited the facility. They cruised right past the car that exited the side road and drove towards the lumber yard.

The Hangman's men had seen what went down on the docks in Bluffton. Something valuable was in the back of the old man's car, and they intended to find out what it was. They slowly drove up to the lumber yard parking lot and noticed one car in the lot. It was the old man's car from the docks. The men exited their vehicle and drew their pistols. They opened the main door to the lumber yard and were disturbed to hear a bell ring as they entered.

They closed the door quickly, then heard someone in the distance ask, "Charles, is that you? Did you forget something?"

The two men looked up and saw Joseph Gramer exit his office and peer down at them from the balcony. The men pointed their weapons at Joseph, and one of them fumed, "We did not forget anything, Gramer, but it appears that you forgot to invite us to the party on Hilton Head Island last night. From what we saw this morning on the docks, it looks like you had some fun."

Joseph instinctively raised his hands over his head without being asked to show them he was not a threat. The men pointed their guns at him as they walked up the stairs. When they reached the second floor, they directed Joseph to return to his office. All three men entered his office but did not close the door behind them. "Show us what you put in the car, old man."

"I don't know what you're talking about," replied Joseph right before one man pistol-whipped him for his unacceptable answer. To the surprise of the two goons, Joseph simply wobbled from the blow. They assumed the old man would have hit the floor like a sack of potatoes. His cheek swelled, and a gash opened that would certainly need medical attention.

"Listen, old man. It looks like you have a lot to live for. I am sure you have a nice family. You obviously have a successful business. Do you want this to be the reason you lose it all? Just give us what you found, and we'll be on our way."

Joseph continued his denial. "We found nothing. I don't know what you're talking about. We just went fishing."

One man walked up to Joseph and shoved the tip of his gun into his mouth. "That must have been one enormous fish you caught because it took four men to put it in the back of your car. Before coming to visit you here in your office, we noticed that the trunk of your car is empty... so where is the fish?"

Joseph's luck was running out. The two men knew that whatever had been in the car's trunk was now on the premises. The office would not open for another couple of hours, so there was only so much he could do to delay the inevitable.

He doubled down while gagging on the gun, blood filling his mouth. "As I told you, we simply went fishing. What we put in the car was our catch. That's it." His head was now pounding from the blow.

One of Martin's men slammed his fist on the desk. The man then removed his gun from Joseph's mouth and turned around while the other man walked up to Joseph and kicked him straight in the groin. Joseph crumbled to the floor in agony. He would have screamed, but the pain was so excruciating that he could not catch his breath. He simply squirmed on the floor, holding the injured area, hoping it would ease the pain. Unfortunately, it did not.

"One last time," said the man standing over him with his gun pointed at his head. "Just tell us where it is, and you live. If you choose otherwise, you will die on this floor with your balls in your hands."

Joseph gasped for breath and tried to answer, but it was hard to talk because of the pain. He gathered energy and shuddered his last words to Martin's men, "Fuck you."

The two men looked at each other, shook their heads, and aimed their guns at his head. Joseph closed his eyes and said one last prayer.

When he heard the two gunshots, he raised his hands to his face hoping that he could somehow deflect a speeding bullet. Then came a thud. He looked up to see Mary in the doorway with a gun pointed at the ground where The Hangman's two thugs lay face down in pools of their own blood.

47

The boats had almost crossed paths. Samuel Goldsmith and his men were on their way from Savannah back to Hilton Head to confront the Gramers and reclaim the treasure Goldsmith believed was rightfully his. Bala and his men had a boat full of cotton and other commodities they brought to Savannah to sell, just like they did each week.

Today was different for the Gullah men, however. Most of them on the boat were now wealthy, thanks to the Gramers' discovery. The exuberance showed on their faces. They couldn't hide their joy. Slavery to riches was the dream of every Gullah man, but only a rare few ever experienced it.

The men tied the boat up at the River Street docks as they always did and made their way to the open-air market to sell their goods. Bala and a couple of the men were still feeling the effects of their booze-laden evening of celebration and continued with the festivities. In his thick African accent, Bala instructed the crew to continue the job while he and a few others went into the local watering hole for a few more drinks.

Fishermen and dock hands often went to the River Street Saloon for drinks. The Gullah men frequented the place often since it welcomed people of color, unlike many other establishments in the city.

Over the past few years, they had been threatened, spat on, and even attacked while trying to enter bars and restaurants. It wasn't surprising that the state of Georgia was about to elect a white supremacist as governor. The Gullah men often talked about the fact that racial inequality would never end until the minority got the right to vote. However, that was unlikely since the Georgia Democratic Party just ruled that only white men could vote.

The welcoming bar was on the first floor of a brownstone building. It was long and narrow. They cleaned it maybe… once a year. The smell of stale beer, dirty floors, and stained bar stools was evidence of the same.

The Gullah entered the bar where music played on the jukebox. Since it was only two in the afternoon, the place was mostly empty. It stayed open until the wee hours of the night, so the real action didn't start until after midnight. The only other people in the place were a few tough guys drinking beer at the bar and a group of four at a table playing cards.

"A round of beers, barkeep," ordered Bala. "And another round for the house!"

The Gullah cheered, and the other six patrons of the bar all raised their glasses in thanks to their good graces. While placing the frosted beer mugs in front of the men, the old gray-haired bartender asked, "What's the occasion for your celebration, y'all?"

Bala took a long chug of his beer and exclaimed, "We are rich! We no longer have to spend countless hours in our fields picking cotton for a few shingles. We can now sit on our front porch and watch the days go by."

"Here here!" hailed the other Gullah men as they raised their glasses for a hearty toast. They clinked their nearly full mugs, causing beer to drip on the floor. The bartender didn't mind since it would be the first of many beer spills that happened every day.

"How did you get rich?" asked one man sitting next to them at the bar.

Bala replied, "We helped a couple of white folks find a treasure. They gave us each a gold coin worth more than our annual profits. They promised to bring more once they sell the loot."

The strangers sitting next to them raised their eyebrows, surprised by the story they had just overheard. One interjected, "Y'all found a treasure? That don't happen every day. Congratulations and thanks for the beer."

Bala grabbed his mug and raised it to his new friends for a toast. "Here's to the treasure hunters."

The bartender was now curious. "How did y'all find the treasure? Did you search for a long time?"

"We found it after two days of searching. It seems the fellas knew exactly where it was. They were so confident that it was there that they went out and bought the land the day before... 20,000 acres of land on the south side of Hilton Head Island. It must have cost them a fortune."

The three men at the bar sitting next to Bala spun their heads and looked at each other with no emotion. "Check, please," they said to the bartender in unison.

After the three settled their bar tab, they exited the bar, congratulating the Gullah men on their way out. When the door behind them closed and they set foot on River Street's cobblestone walkway, they peered straight ahead and said while walking briskly, "Before we go back to work, I reckon Mr. Martin would like to know there was buried treasure on that land he just sold to those two fellas from Hinesville."

****

When Goldsmith and his men returned to the excavation site, they expected to see the Gramers and their entourage. They'd prepared for an all-out war, but it was for naught. The campground was empty, which was strange. They had been here just twenty-four hours earlier when they forcefully removed him from the grounds. They wouldn't just abandon the site or take their leisurely time looking for a priceless treasure. Then again, maybe his attack on them yesterday successfully scared them away.

"Scatter about, men. Look for any clues if the Gramers have been here and if they found anything," he said while spinning around and looking for any sign of activity. "I highly doubt they kicked us off their property only to abandon it."

Goldsmith now had a team of ten men. Each started looking around the site where they had been previously digging and where they had set up camp. After a lengthy search, they determined that the ground was the same as when they'd left. No one had dug anything in that area.

Then one man called out to Goldsmith, "Look here, sir. I see several footprints going north."

"Good work. Let's follow them," replied Goldsmith.

The crew followed footprints and broken branches. There was a path carved out through the woods. It appeared they were onto something. Goldsmith feared the worst. After a few minutes, his fear became a reality. Standing right in front of him was a large hole... a hole big enough to fit a treasure chest.

"Shit!" he roared. "They found my goddamned treasure. Those bastards. I'm gonna get them and get my treasure!"

"I don't think so," said a voice from behind Goldsmith and his men, all circled around the large hole in the ground.

Goldsmith turned around to find Sheriff Randall and his men lined up with rifles aimed at each of his crew.

Randall then beamed and exhorted with more of an attitude. "Drop your guns. Lie face-down on the ground with your hands behind your back. You are all under arrest for trespassing and the murder of Deputy Jim Lisenby."

48

Before the employees of the lumber yard came to work that morning, Mary called Charles to tell him what had happened. After hearing the news, he drove faster than ever before to be by her side. The police arrived a few minutes after him and taped off the office since it was now considered a crime scene. When employees arrived for work, the police told them to return home and come back the following day.

Inside the building, the Gramers and a visibly shaken Mary sat in the reception area, answering questions from the police. Hinesville was a small enough town that everyone knew his or her neighbor. As a result, the Gramers recognized the officers who arrived on the scene. That certainly lightened the severity of the situation. This was the first shooting in Hinesville that anyone could remember. The town would be abuzz the next day when the local paper hit the newsstands.

The head detective was a short, stocky man in his thirties. Unlike the other officers, who were in uniform, he wore a suit and sunglasses. He had a small notebook containing everything said and every observation of the crime scene.

"Again, Mr. Gramer. You say these men broke into your office and held you against your will at gunpoint," the officer asked while trying to get another version of the story Joseph had told him four times already in the past two hours.

Joseph sighed while losing patience. "Yes, detective. That's what happened. They were about to shoot me when Mary stormed in and shot them both from behind. If she were even ten seconds later, I would be dead."

The officer asked Mary why she was at the office and where she got the gun. Mary explained that when they dropped her off in Savannah, she noticed a black car following the men as they left for Hinesville.

"I knew they were Ron Martin's men and that the Gramers could be in potential danger," she said. "So, I followed them."

The officer was jotting down notes as she was interrogated. "And the gun, Ms. Wheaten... where did you get it?"

"Charles told me that Martin's men had been following him since the land purchase, so when I left for Hilton Head yesterday, I took my father's gun from his safe and put it in my glove compartment," she continued. "When they arrived, I parked far enough away that no one could see me. After Charles and Tamba left, I saw the two men exit the car and enter the building. I knew Mr. Gramer was in trouble, so I grabbed my gun and entered the building."

The officer applauded Mary for her bravery, then directed his questioning back to Joseph. "And you say these men are Ron 'The Hangman' Martin's hitmen?"

Holding an ice pack to his cheek to lessen the swelling, he replied, "You are correct, detective. My son purchased a large parcel of land from Mr. Martin two days ago, and he has been following us ever since."

Before calling the police, Joseph had decided not to tell them about the newfound fortune. If he did, they might take it as evidence. The treasure was theirs, fairly. That being so, it was unnecessary to share that part of the story with the authorities.

"The Hangman must have buyer's remorse," fibbed Charles. "I am not sure what they want with us."

The detective continued taking more scrupulous notes while not bothering to look up when he said, "I've heard stories of this fella, Martin. He's a bad man. Ms. Wheaten just killed two of his men. This is not the last you will hear from The Hangman. That's for sure. I hope the land y'all bought from him is worth it because you might live to regret it."

It took about five hours for the police to inspect the crime scene, identify the bodies, and interview all the witnesses. At first glance, it looked like a straightforward case of self-defense, so no one needed to visit the station. The detective gave his business card to each of the Gramers, as well as Mary, just in case they had any encounters with Ron Martin. It also prepared them for the possibility that he may ask them to come to the station in the future if any other issues arise from the case.

During the investigation, Joseph pretended he needed to make phone calls for business since the lumber yard was closed for the day, so he periodically stepped away for privacy. In reality, he arranged for his contacts to come to his office later in the day to evaluate the fortune and estimate its worth.

Throughout the day, Charles continually consoled Mary. He cursed himself that he put her in a situation where she was forced to shoot two men. "I am so sorry for this. This is all my fault. I regret ever finding that damn bank receipt."

Mary trembled in his arms, still in shock at what transpired. "If you hadn't found that bank receipt, you would never have found me. Whatever happens, please know that none of this is your fault. I chose to be a part of it and don't expect to back down now."

Charles held her in his arms, never wanting to let go. "Let me drive you home. Maybe you can try to get some sleep; then we can get some dinner and try to put this behind us."

"I don't know if I'll ever be able to do that… but dinner would be a welcome distraction."

Charles couldn't shake the guilt. She didn't deserve this. At the same time, it warmed his hear knowing he met a woman brave enough to do what she did. As they walked out of the lumber yard, he thought, *With God as my witness, I'm going to make this right.*

****

His jeweler was the first to arrive. He owned Hinesville Jewelry, which had been a staple on Main Street for over forty years. He entered the office wearing a brown suit with a top hat.

As the Gramers led him to Joseph's office, they made pleasantries with one another. Tamba was not there. The Gramers did not think it prudent or necessary for him to be there for the evaluation process, so Charles returned to the lumber yard by himself after dropping him off at his apartment. Mary was still really shaken up from the encounter, so she drove home to rest. The thought of the two men lying dead in pools of blood would leave a lasting toll on her.

"It is imperative that anything you see, hear, or say this afternoon does not leave this room. Do you understand?" asked Charles.

He agreed. Joseph opened the safe and, with the help of Charles, dragged the heavy chest into the middle of the room. The jeweler got up from his seat when they opened the chest. The sight of the treasure caused the man in his sixties to remove his black horn-rimmed glasses and fall back into his seat. He had never seen anything like it.

"My God on Earth. I have never seen... Look at the rubies, the emeralds, the diamonds!" he exclaimed while picking up an enormous diamond and viewing it with a jeweler's loupe in his right eye.

"It is flawless. I have seen nothing like it."

For the next five minutes, he continually picked up jewel after jewel and analyzed them through his magnifier. Each time he seemed more amazed. Finally, he put the magnifier in his pocket and fell back into the leather chair, apparently exhausted.

Charles was the first one to speak. "I can presume from your reaction that the jewels are valuable."

The jeweler widened his eyes in disbelief at the question. "Valuable?" he asked sarcastically. "I would consider them 'invaluable'... to the level of being priceless."

"If you had to estimate the value of the jewels, what would you guess right now?" asked Joseph.

He rubbed his chin vigorously. He then took his glasses off again and guessed. "If I had to predict, I would say you are sitting on over five million dollars worth of jewels here. If I were you, I would take them immediately to my store on Main Street and place them in my safe."

After their hearts had stopped racing from the jaw-dropping assessment, the Gramers thanked him for his time and expertise and told him they would be in contact with him shortly to discuss storing the items, then figure out how to resell them.

An hour later, the manager of the local savings and loan visited the lumber yard. He was an enthusiastic young man in his thirties who looked like he could have been the quarterback for the Georgia Bulldogs. He was tall and handsome but acted like he did not know it. He had moved to Hinesville from Atlanta about five years earlier, so he was a newcomer to the town. Since becoming bank manager, he had fostered a close business relationship with Joseph and his family. He managed most of the lumber yard's accounts, so he saw Joseph two to three times a week in his office.

Like the jeweler, they all walked into Joseph's office and requested that he keep privileged what he was about to see. He agreed as Joseph opened the door. In the middle of the room was an open chest half-full of gold and silver coins. The Gramers had removed the jewelry since they agreed that the vastness of the treasure was on a need-to-know basis.

The banker walked to the chest and kneeled beside it. He grabbed a handful of coins in both hands and turned to the Gramers in amazement. "What on earth do you have here?" he asked, bewildered. "Did you find a buried treasure?"

"Something like that," Charles smiled. "Can you give us an estimate of what the gold and silver are worth?"

He asked for a pencil and paper, which Joseph retrieved from his desk. He appeared to be counting by how he kept pointing his finger. For a few minutes, he kept pointing and writing notes on the tablet given to him. After he finished counting and weighing several coins in his hands, he asked for an adding machine. Joseph pointed to his desk, where the banker sat, and started punching in numbers. The white paper kept spitting out of the machine with every keystroke. When he was finished, he ripped the paper off and handed it to Charles, who read it in bewilderment.

"What does it say?" asked Joseph.

Charles took a deep breath, exhaled, and said, "Two million dollars. The gold and silver are worth two million dollars."

Again, after catching their collective breath from the immensity of the estimated value, the Gramers asked him to arrange for a large safe deposit box in his bank to place the fortune. He agreed and said it would be ready by the end of the day. They asked if he could keep the bank open later to afford them the time to organize and deliver it that evening. With the potential business that such wealth would provide to his bank, he would keep the bank open 24-7 if they wanted, so he had no complaints about their request.

After he left, the Gramer men sunk into the two leather seats in Joseph's office and sat quietly for a few minutes.

Joseph was the first to speak. "You are now a multi-millionaire, son. You are likely one of the richest people in the state of Georgia. I have one piece of advice for you, considering this change of circumstances."

Charles turned in his chair to face his father and said, "You have always guided me on the right path and provided the knowledge and advice to succeed in this life. I would appreciate any advice you have to give."

Joseph got up from his seat and kneeled in front of his son. He looked him straight in the eyes and shared, "I wish I had told you this before all of this started. With great fortune comes great danger. I am so happy about your windfall but fear the ramifications that may follow. I hope it was worth it."

49

Ron Martin was sitting at his desk in his Savannah office when he received a phone call. It was from one of his men who told him he and two other colleagues would like to meet with him regarding the sale of his Hilton Head land. He said he'd heard a rumor that Martin would be interested to hear about. The Hangman ordered the three men to appear in his office later that afternoon to discuss their findings. They arrived promptly as required and, like everyone else, were frisked by Martin's security guards prior to entering his office. Afterward, they were asked to wait in the conference room for their boss.

When Martin arrived, he sat at the head of the table without acknowledging his subordinates. He simply sat in his seat and demanded, "Speak."

The men divulged what they'd heard in the River Street bar. They explained that a bunch of Gullah men had been bragging they'd just gotten rich after finding buried treasure on Hilton Head Island, and the guys they were working for had just bought a large amount of acreage on the island just days before.

"The Gramers? They told me they wanted my land for lumber, but what they actually wanted was a fortune that was buried there… on MY land," Martin fumed, "Do you know what that means?"

"I don't know, boss. What does it mean?" one man asked nervously.

Martin shook his head, frustrated at being so much more intelligent than the three goons he relied on for certain aspects of his business.

"It means that treasure is mine, you buffoons! I intend to find the Gramers and reclaim my fortune. That I can promise you."

He then ordered the men to leave the conference room and to tell his consigliere to come in immediately. Even though The Hangman was not Italian, he preferred calling his most trusted attorney "consigliere." He felt like it gave the man more clout and prestige that he could use over his other employees when necessary.

David Summer entered the conference room with a briefcase in hand. He was a fifty-year-old family man who'd spent most of his legal career as a prosecutor. Ten years ago, after putting one of Martin's henchmen in the slammer for twenty years, The Hangman made him a job offer he could not refuse. With four kids at home and college tuition coming up, Summer had taken the job as Martin's right-hand man and never looked back. He simply tried to ignore the crime and death associated with the job and focused more on providing for his family.

Summer sat across from Martin and asked how he could be of service.

"We need to find the Gramer men who bought my Hilton Head land," Martin said before explaining what he had just learned about the treasure.

"Arrange for the two guys who've been tailing them to come in at once. I need to speak with them and see what they have learned over the past few days."

Summer never enjoyed sharing unwelcome news with his boss. Martin did not take bad news very well. "I am afraid our men cannot meet with you, sir. I was just notified that they were both killed this morning," said Summer.

"Killed? What the hell happened?" asked a now fuming Ron Martin.

"They were both shot... at the Gramer Lumber Company," Summer said hesitantly.

The Hangman pounded his fist on the marble table and stormed out of the office. Summer heard him mumbling in the hallway as he walked away, "Charles Gramer is a dead man."

****

The Beaufort County Sheriff's Office was busier than it had been since Hubert Randall had been appointed. In his jail cell were ten men, including Samuel Goldsmith. He and his deputies had arrested the men without incident in Hilton Head and brought them to the station via boat earlier that day.

"You can't lock me up like this, Sheriff," threatened Goldsmith. "We did nothing wrong."

"Shut your mouth! You killed one of my deputies. You will never see the light of day again if I have anything to do with it," replied the sheriff.

Goldsmith continued to argue, "I know my rights. I have a right to a phone call. I want to call my attorney."

"Very well," said Randall. "Someone let this prick make a call."

Goldsmith called his attorney and spoke with him for about ten minutes. He explained what had happened and ordered him to get him out of jail immediately. When he got off the phone, he smirked and said to Sheriff Randall, "My attorney is calling the prosecutor right now. We will be out of here by the end of the day. He says you have no evidence that I or any of my men killed your deputy. As for the trespassing charge, he tells me he can get me off with a simple fine."

Randall had feared exactly what Goldsmith had just bragged about. He had no supporting arguments regarding the murder of his deputy, but he wanted to arrest the guy anyway. Ever since he met Goldsmith, the guy had rubbed him the wrong way. In cases like this, his philosophy was simple: Arrest the asshole and let the prosecutor deal with the specifics. That often meant letting the perpetrator go, but that was all right with Randall. It still allowed him to kick some criminal ass and show them who was boss in his county.

By the end of the day, Goldsmith was proven correct. His attorney had come to the station with communication from the prosecutor that Sheriff Randall could no longer hold the men in jail. They would not be filing murder charges without further evidence, and the trespassing charge did not warrant incarceration.

He cordially said goodbye to his attorney and warned Goldsmith on the way out, "Do not go far. This is not over. You will pay for killing Deputy Lisenby. I promise you. You will pay."

"Blah, blah, blah. Have a nice life, Sheriff. See you in hell," he said while slamming the precinct door on his way out.

50

The first place that Charles went was to meet Mr. Eaton, the owner of Hinesville Jewelry whom he'd met earlier in the day. He didn't want to put all the jewels in the store's safe because he did not know their security level. He planned to place some jewels with him and allow him to sell them on the market to cash in. There was no need to give him everything at once. It was prudent to provide him with a certain amount of the jewels at a time so he could prove his worth.

Eaton was the only one present. Per Charles' request, the jeweler locked the door behind him and turned over the sign in the window so that it now read "Closed." Then Charles followed him to the back room, where he opened his briefcase to show him a dozen jewels that were more grandiose than anything that had ever been in his store. Eaton showed him his safe, which was rather impressive. It was significantly larger than his father's and would indeed prove to be a safe spot to store his riches.

Eaton explained he would visit Savannah the next day to meet with several of his buyers to notify them of his new holdings. He was confident that he could sell the jewels quickly for top dollar. It was thrilling news that Charles would be able to liquidate his fortune.

There was one other point of business he wanted to discuss with Eaton before he left. "I need to ask you a favor. If it is not too much trouble, I would like to take an advance on my sales profits."

"Anything, Charles. Just name it," Eaton responded eagerly.

Charles walked back to the front of the store, tapped on one of the glass displays, and said, "I would like you to find me the most expensive diamond ring you have."

Eaton face became flush. "I assume this is for someone special?" he asked.

"I've arranged to meet my girl for dinner tonight and ask her to marry me. I want it to be extraordinary," said Charles seriously.

Eaton knew just the ring. He ran to a display and pulled out a three-carat, European cut, solitaire ring that screamed opulence. Charles looked at it and fell instantly in love with it.

"I'll take it," he said with a glimmer in his eye.

"Would you like to know how much it cost?" asked Eaton.

"Just box it up. I don't care to know how much it costs. It is for the girl of my dreams. Price is no issue."

Eaton placed the ring inside a felt-covered box. Charles put the box in his coat pocket and walked out of the store with a kick in his step.

Mrs. Mary Gramer... that has a great tone to it!

Charles hurried home to see Tamba and get ready for his big night while his father was at the bank, securing the gold and silver in the safe deposit boxes. When he arrived at his apartment, he found Tamba sleeping on his sofa. He laughed at the sight, knowing that he well deserved the rest. After all, they had been through a lot together over the past week. Charles was also exhausted but had been running on pure adrenaline, so there was no need to sleep.

"Wake up, Tamba," he said while shaking his friend's shoulder.

Tamba awoke suddenly from a deep sleep. It took him a few moments to remember where he was. When he'd cleared his head, he asked Charles about how the rest of the day had gone, and Charles explained how they'd met with the jeweler and banker.

"Let's put it this way, my friend," Charles said gleefully. "You and your friends are now the richest men in Hilton Head. By the end of the week, I will set up bank accounts in each of your names at a Savannah bank and deposit one hundred thousand dollars into each account."

Tamba almost fell to the floor after hearing the news. He could not believe the good fortune and generosity of Charles. How lucky was he to have been sitting at the Mitchellville marina when the Gramers had appeared and asked for a ride to the south side of the island? His decision to help them would change his and his family's lives forever.

Charles explained that he had plans to go out that night with Mary, so he suggested that Tamba visit the diner down the street to eat dinner. He gave him a few dollars to treat himself and told him to get the meatloaf. Charles then jumped in the shower to clean off. Then he left for his big night.

Tonight, he was going to pick up Mary at her apartment. As he got in his car and pulled out of the parking lot, his excitement again blurred his instincts. Unfortunately, he did not see the large black limousine pull out behind him. Unbeknownst to him, in the car's backseat sat Ron "The Hangman" Martin, on a mission to seek his revenge and reclaim his treasure.

51

The ride to Mary's apartment did not take exceptionally long. Hinesville was not a sizable town, so getting from one place to another was not all that time-consuming. Charles parked on the street in front of her building, then sat in the car for a few minutes to catch his breath. He was even more nervous than he'd expected. He had only known Mary for a brief time, but he already knew beyond doubt that he wanted to spend the rest of his life with her. The nerves were probably because of their short, intense time together. Hopefully, she felt the same way and would take this huge leap with him.

Mary answered almost immediately after his first knock. She'd been standing at the door, waiting for him. Like always, when she opened it, her beauty took his breath away. She seemed to get prettier each time he saw her. Her eyes lit up with joy when she saw him, and her arms were outreached, seeking a big hug.

"It is so good to see you, Charles. I've been trying to rest today, but every time I close my eyes, I see the image of those two men," she muttered, still wrapped in his arms. "Do you think it will ever go away?"

A muscle in his jaw twitched. After all, it was not every day that someone kills two men to save another man's life. "Everything will be fine," he sighed. "Goldsmith shot my father and killed a deputy. You saved my father's life… It's been a rough week, but one thing I know for sure, those men deserved what they got. You shouldn't feel an ounce of guilt for what you did. I'm proud of you."

"Do you promise?" she asked, undecidedly. "This feeling will go away someday?"

"I hope it will go away sooner than you think," he replied as he got down on one knee and pulled out the ring he had just bought.

He raised his eyebrows and asked, "I know we have only known each other briefly, but I fell in love with you the day we met. I want to spend every day together for the rest of our lives. Mary Wheaten… will you marry me?"

Mary stood there with her mouth wide open, looking down at Charles. Her mind was racing. She'd realized she loved Charles a couple of weeks ago when she'd seen him unconscious in the Boston hospital bed. She hoped to marry him, but she was surprised with the proposal. He hadn't even met her family yet. In fact, he probably didn't even ask her father for permission which was expected. It was all happening so fast. Her head was spinning. The man of her dreams was on one knee, holding out the biggest diamond she had ever seen.

She got down on one knee so she could be face to face with him. She answered in her pathetic English accent, "What took you so long, chap? Of course, I will marry you!"

Charles placed the ring on her finger. They then shared the longest, most passionate kiss of their relationship. And all the while, they still hadn't remembered to close her front door. If a neighbor had walked by at that moment, they would have wondered why two people were making out on the floor of her apartment.

"Where did you get this gorgeous ring? Did you get an estimate of the treasure's worth?" she asked while getting up from the floor, her knees shaking from the excitement.

"Let's go to dinner. We have so much to talk about," he said while grabbing her hand. "And yes. The treasure is estimated to be worth about seven million dollars."

Mary's mouth dropped. Her eyes widened. In truth, her eyes nearly popped out of her head. "Seven million?"

Charles squeezed her hand and interrupted, "Come on, Mrs. Gramer. I'm getting hungry."

She plastered a smile on her face.

Mrs. Mary Gramer. That has a nice ring to it.

They went to a fancy Italian restaurant on the outskirts of town to celebrate their engagement. The Gramer family always went there for special occasions, but Mary had never been. Charles spent most of the dinner filling her in on their meetings with the banker and jeweler. She could not believe that the man across the table owned twenty thousand acres of land on Hilton Head Island and was now a multi-millionaire. What she found most fascinating was that his personality had not changed a bit. He was still the same old Charles sitting next to her on a train to Boston. He talked about everything like he was talking about buying groceries. It was almost like he'd expected it to happen, so he acted like being a millionaire was no big deal.

"The best part of the wealth that we now have," Charles promised, "is that it provides us the ability to protect ourselves from Martin and Goldsmith. I will build us a big house surrounded by gates, and we will always have security. I promise you a happy life with no chance of further danger."

Mary smiled and took a deep breath. "Seven million dollars is more money than we're ever going to need. Promise me that we will use it to help people. If William Hilton was unable to give the treasure to his family as he wanted, I think he would want us to use it to make the world a better place."

Charles took her hand and gazed into her eyes, "If I have my way, Mrs. Mary Gramer will become one of the most philanthropic people the low country will ever know."

After talking about the treasure's worth and the good they could do with it, they started discussing their engagement. They both agreed that it was too soon to make any decisions, but they enjoyed discussing the possibilities for their wedding, honeymoon, and future living arrangements. It was all happening so fast, but that didn't stop them from enjoying every minute of it.

As dinner continued, Mary constantly played with her ring finger and gazed at the diamond in awe. Charles kept asking her if she liked it. He always answered the question with, "I can get you another one if you don't like it."

His insecurity was charming. She loved the ring and would never take it off.

After eating more lasagna than any two people should and sharing a gigantic piece of tiramisu, they planned to have Charles meet Mary's parents on Saturday. At the same time, Charles invited her to the Gramer Sunday dinner to share the big news. His mother would be thrilled because she had constantly asked about Mary since they met.

After Charles paid the bill for the long romantic dinner, the couple walked out of the restaurant hand in hand, glowing in their love for one another. When they got to the car, Charles opened the passenger door for her. "Classy move, Mr. Gramer," she said jokingly.

"Nothing is too good for my fiancée," he replied while closing the door for her.

Then Charles heard a familiar voice behind him say, "Congratulations, Mr. Gramer."

Charles turned around to see who was speaking to him. When he did, he saw a man in the darkness walking toward him. As the man got closer, a shiver went down Charles' spine, and a droplet of sweat ran down his temple. He was now standing face to face with Ron 'The Hangman' Martin and two of his goons. Each of them had a gun pointed at his chest.

"Here is what I'm going to do, Mr. Gramer. I am going to take your fiancée on a brief trip. I will keep her safe and sound until we meet tomorrow at my warehouse in Pooler. Unlike my Savannah office, I prefer doing my dirty work there. Mostly because I have what I like to call a 'noose room' there for people who do not cooperate with me," explained Martin.

His mind racing, Charles said the first thing that came to mind. "If you hurt her, by God I promise—"

"Tomorrow, you will deliver the treasure you found on my land. Then, if I am in a charitable mood, I will hand over your beloved Mary. If not, she will endure the same fate two of my best men faced today at your lumber yard. Did you think the fact that you killed two of my men would go unnoticed, Charles?"

If only he knew Mary is the one who pulled the trigger.

Charles was defeated. There was no way out of this situation.

How does he know about the treasure? News indeed traveled fast about the death of his two goons.

Charles shuddered. He knew what The Hangman was capable of, so he feared for the worst. "I don't know what you are talking about, Mr. Martin. Do you think I found a treasure? I have not even been to the island since I purchased it," he tried lying since it had worked so well for him earlier in the week.

"Now, now, Mr. Gramer. The one thing I dislike more than someone who steals from me is someone who will lie about it to my face," threatened Martin while pushing him aside so the two thugs could grab him.

Martin then reached into the car, grabbed Mary by her red hair, yanked her out, and dragged her onto the pavement. She screamed and tried to resist, but Martin was too strong.

"Listen here, pretty lady. Don't fight me," he said while pulling her by her hair. "Any resistance will be met with pain and violence. Trust me. Do you really want me to mess up that pretty little face of yours?"

The sight of Mary crying while trying to escape the grasp of The Hangman horrified Charles. He struggled to break free from Martin's men, but it was no use. They were bigger and stronger than he was, and there were two of them.

"Don't lay a finger on her! If you do, you will live to regret it. I promise you," threatened Charles with anger in his voice.

Martin now had Mary's right arm behind her back, pushing it upward, causing significant pain. Any attempt that Mary made to free herself would just result in more pain. There was no way that she could escape his grasp.

Martin smirked while he walked Mary past Charles and laughed. "That is ridiculously cute, Mr. Gramer. You're threatening me. I will see you at noon tomorrow. Otherwise, you will never see this beauty again. Oh, and I want you to know that if I kill her, it will be a slow and excruciating death... And it will be all your fault."

Martin threw Mary in the back seat and ordered his men to get in. They threw Charles down on the cement parking lot and ran to the car. By the time Charles had gotten up from the ground, they were already driving away.

Charles got up and started chasing after them while yelling obscenities until they disappeared into the darkness.

52

The sporty two-door sedan zoomed through the streets, getting Charles to his destination in what felt like five minutes. He rushed into his apartment. Tamba sat on the sofa, reading a book. He looked up as Charles bolted into the room.

"Get up quickly! The most horrible thing happened." He beckoned Tamba off the couch and turned back to the door. "Ron Martin kidnapped Mary!"

Tamba did not know who the man was, but Charles' expression sent a bolt of fear through his mind. He followed his friend closely and lunged into the passenger seat as Charles had already revved the engine.

The whole interaction took less than a minute. In the car, Charles explained to him what had happened. Tamba had never heard of Ron Martin before, so he didn't know what danger they were in, but one look at Charles' aggrieved face told him it was serious.

Charles sped off to his father's house. Besides going to the police, he would be his best ally in this situation, considering his military background.

They arrived at the Gramers' home at about 9 p.m. Charles knocked frantically on the door, which Joseph finally opened after being awakened from an early night's sleep. Pearl was up as well and went to the kitchen to put on a pot of coffee. Whatever was going on warranted strong black coffee, she presumed.

They all sat at the dining table, and Charles explained what had happened outside the restaurant. Each time he told the story, he got increasingly angrier. At this moment, he didn't care about The Hangman's reputation. He would do whatever it took to get Mary back safely.

"Martin has gone too far," said Joseph in his military voice. "We need to find a way to get that poor girl back unharmed. The one thing I know for certain is that we cannot go to the police. If The Hangman finds out we got the police involved, we will find Mary hanging by a noose."

The thought of Mary's dead body hanging lifelessly beside a smirking Martin brought chills down Charles' spine. There was no time to waste. They had to do something and do it fast.

"Let's just give him the treasure. Mary is more important." Charles grunted.

Joseph knew what he had to say to his son but didn't know how to say it. It was one of the hardest things he would ever tell him. "Giving him the treasure is your safest bet. However, I hate to say this," he paused, "but that doesn't guarantee that you will see Mary alive again."

Joseph took a deep breath and continued, "In situations like this, dealing with a psycho like Martin, most times, the hostage does not survive. He will probably want to make an example of her in retaliation for killing his two men."

Tamba jumped into the conversation, "So, you think he will just kill her?"

Joseph blew on the hot mug of coffee Pearl had just brought to the table and took a small sip. "She may already be dead."

Charles put his head on the table and sobbed. His worst fear had just come true. Pearl approached him from behind and wrapped her arms around her son.

Joseph got up from his chair with coffee in hand and continued thinking. He was in full military mode now. "So here is how I think it should go down. Charles will pull up to the warehouse in my car. The treasure will be in duffle bags in the trunk. Martin and his men will probably be inside with a couple of goons holding Mary."

"So, I carry duffel bags into the warehouse? That's suicide. He'll kill us both," Charles barked.

Joseph lowered his voice to calm his son, "Do you think The Hangman will make this easy on you?"

The severity of the situation was becoming ever so clear.

Joseph continued with his idea, "You'll have a bulletproof vest on and in one of the bags will be a gun. I hope you won't need them, but I suspect you will. The Gullah and I will hide in the woods not far behind."

"You need to negotiate or stall for five minutes. At which time, we will storm the warehouse and take the men out." Joseph's voice was still low since he did not want Pearl to hear of the imminent danger her son would soon face.

"Here is the most important part: Once we barge in, you must drop to the ground immediately. There will likely be a lot of gunfire, so if you are standing there, you will probably be in the middle of it."

Tamba interjected, "I will call the Gullah men first thing in the morning to provide us with the backup we need."

Joseph asked Tamba to call them immediately. They needed help now. "Tell them to meet us at the Savannah Airport at 9:00 a.m. and bring all their weapons."

****

Ron Martin did not bother to blindfold Mary while driving to the warehouse. It wasn't necessary to hide the location from her. After all, she would not live to see her next birthday, so what did it matter whether she knew where she was going to die?

During the ride, Mary was combative and uncooperative, which was annoying to Martin. As a result, he was forced to tie her hands behind her back. It was no simple task with her resistance, so he happily smacked her around a few times to show her who was boss. Dark bruises spread across her face like water soaking into a paper towel.

He tried to feign friendliness and assure her everything would be all right, but Mary read right through his façade. She knew The Hangman did not have a gentle bone in his body. If she was going to make it out of this alive, it would not result from Martin's generosity. There was only one way she would escape this mess: Charles would rescue her. Her belief in him gave her the confidence to keep fighting.

They drove up a secluded, wooded road about two hundred yards to get to the warehouse. At the end was a paved parking lot surrounding a large brick building. It had four loading docks in the front, with two trucks backed up to the stalls. When they arrived at the warehouse, half a dozen men greeted them, all in the same attire, standing in front of the building. It was apparent that Martin liked his men wearing black suits, black shirts, and black hats. Some would call it cliché; Martin called it professional.

The Hangman exited the car without speaking to anyone and walked into a door on the left side of the warehouse. Above it hung a sign that read 'Office.' The other men lifted a garage door next to the office and dragged Mary into the warehouse. They turned on the lights to the large space while closing the door behind them.

Mary looked around to find a mainly empty room. The ceilings were over twenty feet high. The floor was concrete, and the walls were brick. There was an echo anytime someone spoke, and there was a distinct odor in the room. It smelled like a hospital: clean and purified, but the stench of death was hard to hide.

"Take a seat here, beautiful," said one man as he pushed her onto a wooden chair in the middle of the room. "You know, if things go the way I want, you might get some loving from me and my friends before The Hangman has his way with you. Think of it as a little going away present from us to you."

It was clear to Mary that she was not leaving this place alive unless Charles came to save her. She trembled at the thought. Anybody would be in the same situation, but a sense of calm came over her when she thought of Charles. He would not allow her to die at the hands of these criminals. Unfortunately, the calm she felt momentarily while thinking of Charles turned to hate when Ron Martin entered the large room.

"I hope you find my accommodations comfortable," he said as he walked toward her. "Unfortunately, you were less cooperative than I had hoped on the way over here, so I need to make sure that you do not cause any further problems for me. Lower it."

One of Martin's men walked over to the wall and pushed a large red button inside a plastic cover. Mary looked up when she heard a humming noise. Directly above her head was a thick rope being lowered. Martin grabbed the rope and put the noose around her neck. He tightened it and nodded to the man again. This time, he raised a lever next to the red button. The rope slowly rose upwards, tightening around Mary's neck with every inch higher. Once it got sufficiently tight, she was forced to stand up to avoid being choked. When the rope was firm around her neck and she was standing on her tippy toes, The Hangman gestured for him to stop.

Now Mary stood in the middle of the hangar with her hands tied behind her back and gasping for air. The men all laughed at the fear in her eyes. They had seen this countless times before and knew how it would end. No one crossed The Hangman.

Tears covered her face as the reality of the situation hit her. She tried to scream for help but couldn't get out any words. The noose was simply too tight. She could barely breathe. In a last act of desperation, she whispered, "Save me, Charles. Please save me."

53

Morning arrived at the Gramers' home with no one getting a moment of sleep the night before. They spent the evening going over the details of how they would rescue Mary while spending an equal amount of time worrying about her.

Charles had told no one about their engagement the evening before. Such news would simply cloud the judgment of everyone involved. The time would come to tell them, and he decided that time would be when he and Mary could share the news with them together.

Thankfully for the Gramers, Joseph still had the stockpile of weapons they'd bought before confronting Goldsmith on Hilton Head Island. He had guns, plenty of ammunition, and even bullet-proof vests packed in his trunk. They planned to meet the Gullah men at the Savannah Municipal Airport at 9 a.m. Joseph chose the meeting site because it was close to Martin's warehouse in Pooler, and there was plenty of space in the parking lot to organize.

They left the house with Pearl saying goodbye to her husband and son, praying they would come home safe. Joseph reminded her he had always returned home safely from war, so this instance would be no different. The Gramers jumped into the front seat of the car while Tamba sat in the back seat.

Before heading to the airport, the three men visited the jewelry store and bank to collect their riches and placed them in duffel bags. They had arranged the night before that each would open early for them since time was of the essence. Both agreed to do so wholeheartedly.

When they arrived at the airport, the Gullah men were nowhere to be found. They waited, and they waited. Tamba grew concerned. When he spoke to Bala the night before, he was told that the men were eager to help. Something went wrong.

It finally got to the point where a decision had to be made. "I'm leaving," declared Charles. "I can't afford to be late. If so, who knows what Martin will do to her."

Joseph agreed. He went into the trunk of his car and took out one of the bullet-proof vests. He handed it to Charles and said, "You're going to need this."

Charles put on the vest and a harness around his shoulder to hold a pistol. Joseph gave him a powerful hug. "Be careful, son."

He now adopted the military tone his father had perfected over the years. "I don't care about the treasure anymore, but I'm willing to die for Mary. It's just not going to happen today."

As Charles drove away, Tamba said to Joseph, "So much for your master plan. I can't help but think something has happened to Bala. He would not be late."

"So far, we have been lucky enough to have things go our way. That resulted in finding the treasure," replied Joseph. "Inevitably, however, a hitch always presents itself. I hope this one does not cost me my son's life."

The two men agreed to wait another ten minutes for the Gullah. After that, they had no choice but to follow Charles and be his backup. They would much rather prefer having more men, but if it were only going to be them, so be it.

A few minutes later, a rickety old pickup came stumbling into the parking lot. Bala was driving. When he got out of the car, he explained that the truck overheated on the way which caused the delay.

"No need for explanations," ordered Joseph. "We need to leave immediately!"

They drove about a quarter mile from the entrance to Martin's warehouse, where they parked the truck hidden in the woods. During the ride, Joseph explained the plan to the men. Each man had a semi-automatic machine gun resting on their shoulder. Around their waists were belts holding extra ammunition and hand grenades.

Joseph led the men through the woods in a single file line towards the warehouse. No one spoke while they approached an opening and saw the parking lot and large brick building. Joseph ordered the men to scatter about by crawling on the ground. Each man took position behind a tree for protection with a clear view of the warehouse where they pointed their guns. Then they simply sat and waited.

The tension was unbearable. Charles had already arrived. His car was in the parking lot but stopped far short of the building. At 10:00 a.m. on the nose, one of the warehouse's garage doors opened. Inside the hangar were six men standing in a 'V' formation with guns pointed at Charles. Behind them, The Hangman stood next to Mary with a noose around her neck.

54

Martin's men walked cautiously out of the warehouse, pointing their guns at Charles' car all the while. When they were twenty yards away, one of them demanded that he exit it.

So much for my father's plan, thought Charles. *Now it's time to improvise and hope for the best.*

He couldn't take his eyes off Mary. He had to do something.

Did he have support or was he on his own?

Either way, there was only one choice. He slowly got out of the car, closed the door, and stood passively in front of it. From there, he could get a good look at The Hangman and Mary in the warehouse. His heart sank when he saw her hanging helplessly and crying uncontrollably.

"Untie her, Martin!" he warned. "Untie her now, or you will never see the treasure."

Now that Charles had exited the car and Martin's men had taken their positions, Joseph was hiding nearby trying to think how he could salvage this mess. He waived to Tamba, who was hiding not too far away. He whispered for Tamba to take two of his men and sneak to the back of the warehouse so they would then have the men surrounded. Tamba made a hand signal to his men, and within seconds, they were quietly changing positions.

"Give me the treasure, Gramer, and then I will release the girl," demanded Martin in an echo-distorted voice.

Charles held his ground knowing he needed to delay. He hoped the five minutes his father planned the night before were still an option. "There's no way you will see the treasure without releasing her. It is that simple."

"Looks like we have ourselves a classic 'Mexican standoff,' young Charles," quipped The Hangman while he pushed the lever he was holding, slowly raising the noose. Mary tried to scream as she was now barely able to stand. "Give me the treasure now, or the girl dies right in front of you!"

Five minutes were about to elapse. Charles prayed that the next part of their "plan" would come into effect soon, or he and Mary would soon be dead.

"I am going to give you one last chance, Martin. Release the girl now, or you are going to face the wrath of Hinesville, G-A," he warned, trying to sound tough while shaking in his boots.

Martin's expression hardened. Charles was not cooperating as he assumed he would. "You're one crazy motherfucker, Gramer; I'll give you that. I was going to make this nice and easy for you, but you have forced my hand. Now it is time—"

BANG!

The Hangman never saw the gunshot coming and forgot that, while studying up on the Gramers during the land deal, that a US Army sniper could be hiding in the woods. The bullet hit him in the stomach. His temperament instantly turned from anger and frustration to shock as he looked down and saw blood-smeared hands. He fell to his knees, then staggered forward with his head hitting the concrete. Joseph had taken a perfect shot.

When the gunshot echoed through the parking lot, Martin's men saw their boss lying face down on the ground. When they turned back to confront Charles, they faced several Gullah men with semi-automatic rifles, running from the forest, ready to attack. Martin's goons then turned again to see Tamba and the other two men rushing up behind them. They were surrounded.

Charles was the first to break the tension. "Put your guns down now, fellas, and you get to leave here alive. Understood?"

"Fuck you!" yelled a man, then aimed his pistol at Charles and fired. The shot hit Charles square in the chest. The force of the bullet caused him to jerk backward, slamming him into the front of the car, and then tumble to the ground.

Before Charles hit the ground, Joseph put another bullet into the shooter's forehead. Again, the guy never saw it coming, and again, it was a perfect hit. All-out gunfire erupted after the two gunshots. The Gullah had much more firepower with their semi-automatic rifles than Martin's men, who relied solely on the pistols they were holding. The Gullah quickly unloaded their magazine clips on the men until each of them lay on the pavement, riddled with bullet wounds and drowning in pools of blood.

The firefight didn't last more than a minute. It was too overwhelming. At most, each of Martin's men got off one shot before catching a barrage of bullets. The combination of Joseph's aim and the number of hidden Gullah men with semi-automatic weapons caused it to be over quickly.

When the dust had settled, Joseph came out from his perch to see how his son was doing. Tamba raced to the side of Bala, who was lying on the ground and suffering from a clear gunshot wound.

"Son, are you ok?" Joseph frantically asked while rolling Charles on his back so that he could inspect the wound.

Charles appeared groggy. It felt like he passed out for a minute. He looked at Joseph, who was kneeling over him. He then ripped his shirt open to reveal his bulletproof vest. "I think it is going to leave a mark, but I'm okay. Get Mary!" he whimpered out of breath.

Joseph ran into the warehouse, where he found Mary on her tippy toes, struggling to stand thanks to the noose tight around her neck. She cried as he reached into his coat pocket and pulled out a Swiss army knife compliments of the US Army. With a swift motion, he cut the rope above her head. The release of tension forced Mary to fall to her knees, where she wept uncontrollably. It was loud enough that Charles heard it from where he was lying.

"It's okay, Mary. It's over. These men won't hurt you again, dear."

Joseph then picked her up and carried her back to the car. Charles was still lying on the ground recovering from the brunt of the gunshot. Joseph sat Mary next to Charles. She was still shaking and crying uncontrollably. She reached for Charles and fell on him, wrapping him tight in her quivering arms.

"Are you okay, Charles? Were you shot?" she tried to ask; her voice still weak from the hanging.

Charles' face grew pale at the sight of his fiancée with a bruised face, a black eye, and the markings of a noose around her neck. Then again, she'd never looked more beautiful to him. "I am fine, my love. The Hangman will never hurt you again. I promise."

Tamba's cry interrupted their heartfelt moment. "Bala has been shot! Someone, please do something." Joseph and the Gullah men ran to his side. Unlike Charles, Bala's bulletproof vest did not protect him. They shot him in the neck.

"Tamba, take your shirt off and place pressure on the wound," ordered Joseph. "Keep pressure on it. Get him in the car. We need to get him to the hospital immediately."

One man grabbed Bala under the shoulders, and another lifted him from the knees. Tamba kept the pressure on the wound as directed. They placed him in the backseat of the car, which was already running with Joseph in the driver's seat and ready to go.

As the car carrying Joseph, Tamba, Bala, and the treasure sped off, Charles and Mary continued to sit on the hot pavement recovering from their injuries. He asked one of the Gullahs to fetch the pickup truck so they could get out of there.

Minutes later, they sat in the bed of the truck racing from what looked like a mass murder scene. Six men lay dead in the parking lot surrounded by pools of blood, while their boss, Ron 'The Hangman' Martin, did the same inside his warehouse.

When the police arrived at the scene soon thereafter, they found the symbolism quite ironic. Ron Martin was lying on the ground with a noose around his neck that Mary placed on him before Joseph carried her to safety.

55

The hospital in Pooler was a twenty-minute drive from Ron Martin's warehouse. Bala was losing lots of blood. Joseph's white leather seats were now mostly red. Time was running out. Joseph was driving as fast as he could it might be too late by the time they arrived.

The hospital was a three-story brick building. It was big, given the size of the town. He double parked at the building's front door and ran in, asking for an orderly. A handful of hospital staff rushed outside with a stretcher at his request. When they opened the door to the car, they took a step back when they saw Tamba and Bala.

"What are you waiting for?" urged Joseph impatiently.

One of the staff walked over to him and whispered, "I am sorry, sir, but we do not accept Negros at this hospital."

Joseph was stunned. He'd grown up in the south, so he knew segregation existed, but a man's life was at stake. "You must be kidding me. This man just saved my son's life. He's in the back seat dying, for Christ's sake. Save him!"

Tamba sat in the car, listening to the conversation with tears streaming down his cheeks while his blood-soaked hands pushed down on his friend's neck to slow the bleeding.

"Please," he begged the orderlies. "My friend is dying. He needs your help."

"I will pay for my friend's stay in the hospital if that is the issue. I am a wealthy man. Money is no object in this case," pleaded Joseph.

The orderly stood firm. "I am sorry, sir. Money is not an issue on our end. It is hospital policy. If we admit him, we will lose our jobs. Again, I am sorry." A doctor then raised his hand with his index finger sticking up and rotated it in a circular motion. "Back inside, everyone. There is nothing we can do here."

"I will see you all in hell!" screamed Joseph as they walked away.

Some had their heads down to hide their shame for not helping Bala. "How can you sleep at night?" he continued to berate them. "If he dies, it will be on your conscience. I hope you remember his face forever. By the way, his name is Bala, and he has a family."

The hospital staff was already inside the building before Joseph could finish his rant. He was furious that the color of one's skin could dictate whether one lived or died. It was one thing to have separate bathrooms and water fountains, but this was someone's life with which they were dealing. Shouldn't there be an exception?

"Let's try to find another hospital, Tamba. We don't have much time," he said while getting in the driver's seat.

Tamba was now holding this friend's head in his lap while crying. "No need, Mr. Gramer. Bala has died. He does not have a pulse," whimpered Tamba.

"Are you sure?" asked Joseph.

Tamba said nothing. He simply nodded.

Joseph wept for his friend. He felt immense guilt for recruiting the Gullah men to help him with Charles' adventure. Never did he think it would cause one's death. He dropped his head on the steering wheel and cried for his lost friend. How would he and Charles would ever forgive themselves for Bala's death? He prayed for forgiveness and for God to welcome his friend into heaven with open arms.

After sitting in the car for what felt like hours, the pickup truck arrived carrying the rest of the Gullah men along with Charles and Mary. They pulled up beside Joseph's car. They didn't need to ask what had happened. It was clear to all of them that Bala had not made it.

The men sat in the bed of the trunk with their heads lowered. Some were praying aloud, masking the sound of Mary's weeping. Charles sat in shock, overwhelmed with guilt. The treasure hunt that started with a Cotton Mather book had taken the life of one of his friends. At that moment, how could he ever forgive himself?

He jumped off the back of the truck and crouched down at the open door to the back seat of Joseph's car. There he looked Tamba in the eyes with complete sorrow. "Tamba, my friend. I promise you that Bala's death will not be in vain. I will provide for his family, and when Hilton Head Island becomes the mecca for southern travelers, we will erect a statue in his honor. Without his help and the help of you and the other Gullah men, I would never have succeeded in my quest. For that, I will always be indebted to the Gullah community. You will always have a home on my island."

Tamba forced a grin in reaction to Charles' kind words and generosity. It helped a bit but couldn't remove the pain he felt holding his lifeless friend in his arms.

While they continued to sit in silence to honor their fallen friend, the wailing sound of an approaching siren shattered the calm. An ambulance was racing towards them and pulled up just a few feet from where they'd parked. Behind the ambulance were two Cadillac LaSalle sedans. The back door of the ambulance abruptly opened with two EMTs taking out a stretcher with a man on it. They quickly wheeled the man into the hospital while four men from the Cadillacs following close behind. One man threatened as they entered the hospital, "There is going to be hell to pay for whoever did this to Mr. Martin and his men."

Charles and Mary looked at each other in wonder and shock.

Shit. The Hangman survived.

56

Tamba and the Gullah men covered Bala's dead body in a tarp and placed it in the back of the pickup. There would be a large Saraka for his heroics in the coming days. Saraka was a ceremony the Gullah derived during slavery. Once placed in the grave, friends and family would dance to the beat of a drum while breaking plates and glasses around it. They did this to 'break the chain' so that no one related to the deceased would suffer the same fate. After the ceremony, they returned to town to share in a feast where one plate was always left for the deceased.

The Gramer's ride back to Hinesville was filled with silence. Mary sat in the front seat with Joseph while Charles sat in the blood-soaked back seat. The collective feeling in the car was one of sadness for losing Bala and one of fear because Ron Martin survived the gunshot wound.

Joseph dropped Charles and Mary off at his apartment in the middle of the sweltering summer day and brought the treasure back to the bank. Sweat poured down Charles' blood-soaked body as they walked up the stairs to his place. He was thrilled to be home safe with Mary but was exhausted from everything that had happened.

They both entered his apartment and went straight to the couch, where they plopped down next to each other. Charles felt Mary's tears begin to fall as she snuggled in closer to him. He could feel her trembling body quivering against him, so gently wrapped an arm around her shoulders, pulling her nearer. He could see the tears streaming down her face as they both looked up at the ceiling together.

He brushed away a few stray strands of red hair from her face and said, "It's over. It's over. The Hangman can never hurt you again."

Mary sobbed uncontrollably in response. All Charles could do was hold her tightly. He felt her heart racing through her chest as she began to calm down and eventually stopped crying. He kissed the top of her head, and for a moment they just sat there together in silence.

He could feel the weight of everything that had happened begin to fade away. He looked over at Mary and wiped the remaining tears off her face with a gentle touch.

"It's okay," he said. "You're safe now. Everything is going to be alright."

The two sat together on the couch in silence, contemplating what their lives had become. Soon they both fell asleep. The much-needed naps were welcoming to their physically and mentally drained bodies. Both had dreams of wedding bells and honeymoons, which blended with nightmares of The Hangman's revenge.

After a couple of hours of rest, they woke suddenly to the sound of shattering glass. Each jumped from the couch and instinctively fell to the ground for safety. Charles looked at the bay windows facing the street. One of them had a large hole in it. A brick wrapped in white paper was on the floor next to the window, held together by an elastic band.

Charles crawled over the broken glass to retrieve the brick when suddenly a round of gunfire erupted. Glass was strewn all over the living room from dozens of bullets flying above them.

"Stay down!" yelled Charles. "Crawl to the bedroom. We will be safe in there."

Mary and Charles crawled as fast as they could to the bedroom in the back of his apartment, away from the street. The broken glass punctured their hands and knees with each movement. The apartment continued to be riddled with bullets for another thirty seconds. By the time they reached the bedroom, the gunfire had stopped. The sound of shattered glass and bullets hitting the walls was now replaced with an eerie silence, except for the chirping birds in the nearby trees who did not seem to be bothered by the murder attempt.

Charles reached into a dresser drawer and pulled out a pistol. He confirmed it was loaded and aimed it at the door.

"Stay down, Mary. This might not be over. I need to get to the phone to call the police. Stay in the bedroom and lock the door."

Charles crawled into the kitchen and grabbed the phone. After the call, he inched back to the bedroom door and knocked so Mary could let him in. Ten minutes later, several police cars swarmed the street. They broke down the front door and announced themselves.

"We're in the bedroom!" screamed Charles.

One officer heard his cry and replied, "You can come out now, Mr. Gramer. The coast is clear."

They reluctantly came out of the bedroom to see his apartment riddled with bullet holes and several police officers re-holstering their guns. The officer in charge was the father of one of Charles' friends growing up, so he did not need to introduce himself.

He asked him what had happened, and Charles explained that they'd been taking a nap on the couch when suddenly they were awakened by a brick thrown through the window. Then gunfire followed. Another officer picked up the brick and handed it to the officer in charge. He removed the rubber band and paper to see if there was writing on it. There was. He handed it to Charles, who read it out loud. "The treasure is mine."

"Treasure?" asked the officer. "What is this about, Charles? Who'd do such a thing in broad daylight?"

Charles was hesitant to tell anyone other than Mary about the treasure and his newfound wealth, so he was vague with the officer. "It's a long story, sir. I recently bought a lot of land on Hilton Head Island. It appears that someone is not happy that I did so."

"Do you know who did this, Charles?" he continued interrogating while taking notes.

Charles contemplated the answer, then Mary spoke up, "It is one of two people. It is a man named Samuel Goldsmith, or it was Ron 'The Hangman' Martin."

The apartment got eerily quiet when the officers heard Martin's name. They quivered at the thought of The Hangman being in Hinesville. "You think Ron Martin was behind this?"

Charles interjected, "Remember the two dead men found in my father's office at the lumber yard the other day? Those were Martin's men. I bought the Hilton Head land from Martin. Apparently, he has buyer's remorse."

One officer chimed in, "I'll bet he does. Why do you think he wants you dead?"

"Why does The Hangman want anybody dead?" questioned Charles. "Money."

Then another officer walked up to the sergeant and said, "I don't think it was Ron Martin who did this, Sarge. I just heard over the radio that The Hangman was shot, and so were a bunch of his other men. It sounds like it was an ambush of some sort. The scene looks like a massacre."

Charles and Mary both breathed a sigh of relief. The Hangman was gone, and most of his crime syndicate was dead as well. They shook their heads in disbelief at the thought that they had dismantled one of the most powerful mafia families in the past couple of days. This was sure not how they envisioned their treasure hunt going.

The officer gave Charles and Mary a suspicious look and asked, "Do you know anything about what happened to Martin and his men? You didn't have anything to do with it, did you?"

Charles nervously cleared his throat and replied, "No, no. This is the first I've heard of it." He looked away, avoiding the sergeant's eyes, not wanting to incriminate himself.

The officer nodded and said, "Are you sure?"

"Yes. We didn't have anything to do with it. Although it sounds like karma may have finally caught up to him."

The officer seemed satisfied with his answer and replied, "Alright then. I'm sure you'll be hearing from us once we start the investigation. We're bound to have more questions."

Charles nodded in his willingness to cooperate, yet he was unlikely to tell them what exactly happened.

The officers stayed in the apartment for over an hour to finish their investigation. Charles knew they could not stay there for the night, so he went to stay with his parents until he could think of another solution. He invited Mary since she was in just as much danger as he was.

After the officers left, Charles gathered a few things in an overnight bag and drove Mary to her apartment to do the same. On the way out the door, Mary asked Charles, "Do you think Martin was responsible for this, or do you think it was Goldsmith?"

"It must be Goldsmith," he replied. "It was too soon after Martin's death for someone in his organization to take leadership and plan the attack. My guess is they will blame the death on another crime family. They wouldn't believe a father and son from Hinesville could survive such an encounter with Martin and his crew."

Mary replied, "So if it is Goldsmith, how do we stop him? Do you even know where he lives or where he is from?"

"I'm afraid I don't, but I may know someone who does. I think I can end this once and for all."

57

Charles and Mary struggled to escape the memories of their traumatic experiences, but even after a long night at Joseph and Pearl's home, they awoke in an unsettled state. Unforgettable images haunted them. For Mary especially, her conscience was weighed down with guilt from taking two lives while Ron Martin's cruelty still lingered in her veins.

Charles could not continue to live like this. He didn't want to look over his shoulder for the rest of his life. He needed to end this now. Despite their worries, they had a busy day ahead of them. To help ease their minds, Pearl made some of her famous pancakes for breakfast and packed them a picnic lunch for their drive to Bluffton.

The ride to Bluffton went quicker than usual for Charles. In the past week, he had taken the trip so many times that he felt like he could do it blindfolded. Mary enjoyed the scenery. She had never been to Beaufort County, so she was excited to experience its unpretentious surroundings and the beautiful gateway for her fiancée's one-million-dollar investment.

Charles parked his car in the parking lot of the Beaufort County Sheriff's Office. There were a few patrol cars in front of the building, so he hoped the sheriff would be on duty. He entered the office to find

Sheriff Randall at his desk with a couple of officers he recognized roaming about. Randall was on the phone but waved Charles over when he saw him enter. They sat in front of his desk and waited for him to complete his call. When he was done, he got up from his seat and shook their hands.

"Sheriff Randal, I would like to introduce you to my fiancée, Mary Wheaten." Charles beamed.

The sheriff gracefully shook her hand and replied, "It is a pleasure to meet you, Ms. Wheaten. I didn't know you were engaged, Charles. Congratulations."

"Actually, sheriff, we got engaged two days ago, so it is very new to us. We are thrilled."

After a bit of small talk, Charles explained to the sheriff what had happened the day before in Hinesville and that he suspected Goldsmith was behind the attack.

"I would not put it past him," said the sheriff. "I didn't like that guy from the start. The other day, I arrested him and his men but could not keep him locked up. The prosecutor told me I did not have enough evidence to convict him of murdering Deputy Lisenby."

Charles and Mary took in the frustration on his face from his inability to avenge his friend and colleague, so Mary chimed into the conversation, "That's why we're here, Sheriff. Charles may have a way to get Goldsmith once and for all."

"I am all ears," Randall said while sitting in his chair.

Charles agreed that the sheriff would need more evidence to convict Goldsmith on the murder charge. He offered the testimony of he and the Gullah men who were present when Deputy Lisenby was shot but also pointed out that none of them could identify Goldsmith as the shooter. They needed more evidence.

When Sheriff Randall finished listening to Charles' plan, he was optimistic that they could get enough on Goldsmith to put him away for a long time.

The first thing they needed to do was have the sheriff reach out to Goldsmith. This part was integral because Charles did not know how to get in touch with his nemesis. The sheriff knew how to reach him, however. He simply picked up the phone and called the prosecutor. He asked him to contact Goldsmith's attorney and arrange a meeting at the Gramer Lumber Yard the following day. He explained that his attorney could be present if he wanted. It was staged to look like a meeting between Charles and Goldsmith about resolving the rights to the treasure.

After the phone call, Charles and Mary thanked the sheriff for his help and asked him if there was a pleasant picnic spot where they could enjoy the lunch that Pearl had packed for them. Randall suggested a waterfront park a mile down the road. Low country oaks shaded the picnic area, where the water provided a much-needed breeze on hot, humid summer days like today.

The couple sat by the edge of the river on a blanket, gazing into each other's eyes trying to forget the horror of the past few days. What helped most, was feasting on Pearl's fried chicken and sipping cold sweet tea. She also packed a piece of her famous peach cobbler they shared for dessert.

Although recent events had been tumultuous and uncertain at best, the conversation between them was a momentary respite from it all. Amongst tears from fear, they found glimmers of joy in each other's company and thoughts of their future together. It was a temporary escape from the fright that haunted their every thought.

Mary shared her desire for a large wedding in the backyard of her parent's home. She described how they could say their vows under a large Georgia pine with Spanish moss dangling from its branches. They could have white chairs lined up with guests dressed in seersucker suits and floral dresses, making for the perfect low country wedding.

Charles shared how he wanted to build them the biggest house in all of Hinesville. He would find a piece of land with a pond out back and with enough acreage on which their children could play all day before the dinner bell rang.

However, before any of that could take place, they needed to finish their business with Samuel Goldsmith.

****

Charles had requested that Goldsmith meet him at the lumber yard the next day at 10 a.m. He chose the time and place so it would be busy with workers, preventing Goldsmith from trying anything funny. Joseph and Charles arrived for work at 8, as they usually did. Mary visited her parents, but before that, she went to the bank to give them her two-week notice.

After all, she was now engaged to one of the wealthiest men in Georgia, so she found no need to work forty hours a week behind a desk anymore. She could do much more with her life than that. It didn't matter anyway. When she got to the bank, her manager had told her she was fired since she had missed so much time the past month. The dismissal was no surprise to her.

Goldsmith arrived promptly at ten as scheduled alongside his attorney. They both entered the main building, introduced themselves to the receptionist, and asked to meet with Charles. Charles left his office and walked down the metal stairs to meet the gentlemen. They shook hands while never taking their eyes off each other. Charles asked them to follow him to his office.

When they were all in the room, Charles closed the door behind them and asked them to sit on the leather chairs in front of his desk. The attorney was the first to speak, "Mr. Gramer, my name is Anthony Balmer. I am Mr. Goldsmith's attorney. We are eager to hear why you asked us here today."

"Well, Mr. Balmer. Someone tried to kill my fiancée and me two days ago, and I have a gut feeling that your client may be the one behind it," explained Charles in a matter-of-fact tone.

The allegation startled attorney Balmer. "That is quite an accusation. What makes you think my client had anything to do with such a heinous act? He is simply in the low country for vacation. He does not have the time or means to do anything like that."

"Maybe Mr. Goldsmith can shed some light on why he wants me dead," replied Charles while leaning his head to the side, trying to provoke him.

Goldsmith erupted into the conversation. He stood up and pointed his index finger at Charles from across the desk. "You stole my treasure, you asshole! Give it back to me, and you will never hear from me again. Got it?"

His attorney grabbed Goldsmith and told him to sit back down and cool off. "My client has shared with me that you may have come across a significant fortune buried on Hilton Head Island. Is that correct, Mr. Gramer?"

Charles contemplated the question. He had yet to admit to anyone that he'd found the treasure and was reluctant to do so now. As a result, he played it cool. "I am not sure what you are talking about, Mr. Balmer. I purchased a lot of land on the island earlier this week but know nothing about a treasure. Besides, if there were some buried treasure on MY land, it has nothing to do with your client. It's MY land."

"Fuck you, Gramer!" yelled Goldsmith. "You are fucking lying!"

Charles continued coyly, "As I am sure you are aware, your client and I had an encounter earlier this week where I had him rightfully removed from my land. From what you are implying, I guess he was there searching for some sort of buried treasure."

"You know full well why I was there, asshole," quipped Goldsmith.

Everything was going just the way Charles wanted. The last thing he needed now was to get Goldsmith riled up. He was now definitely agitated. Now it was time for the kill.

"It seems this treasure is very important to you, Goldsmith," supposed Charles.

"It is so important that you attacked me and left me for dead in Boston. Do you want it that bad that it's worth threatening my life on the beach earlier this week? Is it so important that you tried to kill my fiancée and me last night… Worst of all, you killed a Beaufort County deputy earlier this week for the treasure. Isn't that correct?"

Attorney Balmer answered before the red-faced Goldsmith could, "Now look here, Mr. Gramer. You cannot just go about accusing my client of murder and attempted murder. You have crossed the line."

SECRETS OF SEA PINES

"It's true, isn't it, Sammy?" uttered Charles with a smirk. "I am willing to negotiate with you about the supposed treasure, Sammy, but I need to know that these attempts on my life will stop."

Goldsmith was now intrigued. The idea of some sort of negotiation about the treasure was, at a minimum, what he'd hoped to get out of this meeting.

"Mr. Goldsmith is this true?" asked his attorney. "Did you do the things that Mr. Gramer has accused you of?"

"You're damn right I did, you motherfucker. My only regret is that I put a bullet in the head of that fucking deputy instead of you. If so, I'd be back in Manhattan right now with what is rightfully mine."

Just then, the closet door of Charles' office burst open. Out popped Sheriff Randall holding a large tape recorder with two wheels spinning.

"Samuel Goldsmith, you are under arrest for the murder of Deputy Jim Lisenby and the attempted murder of Charles Gramer, Joseph Gramer, and Mary Wheaten."

Attorney Balmer dropped his head in his lap in disgust. His client had just admitted to murdering a police officer in a taped confession. There was no way he would get his client off on these charges now. Goldsmith reeled with anger when he realized what Charles had done. He jumped over the table to release his frustration on Charles. Before he could do so, he received a few solid right hands to the jaw, thanks to Charles, who was waiting for him.

While Sheriff Randall handcuffed Goldsmith, Charles wanted to give his nemesis one last thing to consider. "You know your life has been one big lie, don't you?"

"What are you talking about, Gramer?" begged a dejected Goldsmith.

"The treasure was never yours or your family's. Your namesake was a traitor who betrayed his friend and denied William Hilton's family the life he provided them. Instead, he selfishly stole his will so he could claim the treasure as his own. Nice bloodline you have there, Sammy."

Charles laughed at him one last time, continuing to provoke the man who almost killed him and Mary. He finally got his revenge. "Have a nice life, Sammy. I'll see you at your sentencing, you rotten son of a bitch."

58

Samuel Goldsmith's trial was one of the most prominent and notorious in South Carolina's history. The newspapers could not get enough of the drama related to a wealthy Manhattanite killing a police officer. As suspected, Goldsmith was found guilty of murder and sentenced to life in prison. As promised, Charles and Mary attended the sentencing phase of the trial. They sat with Sheriff Randall and the other officers, who celebrated with a collective cheer when the judge issued the sentence.

Ron Martin somehow survived the gunshot wound but could not escape a life sentence for the kidnapping of Mary, all thanks to the testimony of she and Charles. His trial was a spectacle just like Goldsmith's. The press huddled on the steps of the court as Savannah's most notorious mob boss was guided to the prison truck. Just like at the trial, he never showed any sign of emotion.

Finally, their lives were back to 'normal'.

The following year was mainly composed of the Gramer Lumber Company diligently logging on Hilton Head Island. Charles made a point not to clear all the land, however. He'd already started arranging the land's real estate development and even got Beaufort County's approval to commission a new bridge, creating a road between Bluffton and Hilton Head. The bridge was a big step toward his goals.

Not long after that, Charles and Mary were married in her parent's backyard, and a family quickly followed. Over the next few years, they had two daughters who were raised in a house that Charles built in Hinesville. Joseph and Pearl enjoyed watching their granddaughters grow up for almost ten years before they each died from natural causes.

Charles rewarded Tamba handsomely for his efforts in finding the treasure and helping ward off Ron Martin and his men. Bala's family was equally rewarded for giving his life for the mission.

Tamba never had to work another day in his life with the riches he'd received from Charles but continued to work with the Gramers regardless. He also gathered dozens of Gullah men at the request of Joseph to help with the logging. As a result, each one of them led a very prosperous life. Tamba and Charles' friendship continued to grow, so much so that Tamba and his family became frequent guests at the Gramer house for holidays and parties.

Charles created a corporation called Sea Pines Development, and by the 1980s, he had broken ground on one of the country's most significant real estate developments. He called it 'Sea Pines.' It comprised over two thousand homes, four top-level PGA golf courses, two high-end beachfront hotels, and several restaurants. Some of the wealthiest people from South Carolina and Georgia soon made it their home. It even had its own high school.

One of Mary's passions became opening the Hilton Head Montessori School in Sea Pines. They used the funds from a foundation they founded to pay for its construction. They believed it was essential to share the values and teachings of their faith with others in the community they were building.

They also built a hospital in honor of Bala. A sign was place above the entrance door that read 'All patients are welcome regardless of the color of their skin'.

The Gramers lived a humble life building other real estate developments in Charlestown, South Carolina, and Bermuda. Their philanthropic endeavors were far more impactful to the world than the beautiful homes and golf courses they built. They became one of the most beloved and respected couples in South Carolina.

Today, visitors driving to Hilton Head Island go over a bridge named after them. Not far away is a statue of Bala that Charles had built in honor of the Gullah men who'd helped with the development.

As they grew older. Charles and Mary often looked back at their treasure hunt and prayed that they used their fortune to serve their community and make the world better.

EPILOGUE

1992

"**M**ary! Come see this," Charles yelled as he stood at the bow of a one-hundred-foot yacht cruising at a low speed in the Caribbean just north of the Turks and Caicos.

Mary came to his side just in time to see the sun rise over the endless blue horizon. "It's beautiful, honey. It's one of the greatest sunrises I have ever seen in our fifty years together. I'm so happy you sat next to me on that train to Boston and so happy that you surprised us with this trip."

Charles was traveling to Turks and Caicos to inspect a potential hotel development he was contemplating. He'd decided that he and Mary would charter a yacht from Georgia rather than fly. They had been at sea for five days with their daughter Laura. Over the years, Charles had become a skilled captain, so they did not require a crew for the trip.

As they approached Turks and Caicos, Charles turned the engines off and coasted for the day. They did not expect him on the island until the following evening, so they spent the day basking in the Caribbean sun and swimming in the crystal blue water. The mainland, with its vast mountainside, lay in the distance with dolphins jumping through the air as if they were showing off. It was a day they would never forget.

After a nice dinner comprised of fresh Mahi Mahi that Charles had caught earlier in the day, they all went to bed early in anticipation of a long next day. In the dark of the night, the Gramer family slept soundly in their staterooms. They slept so well that they did not hear a small boat approaching the yacht. Nor did they hear a man board the ship.

The tall, slender man wore a black trench coat and held a .32 caliber pistol in his right hand. He entered the ship's main compartment and walked through the kitchen, where he stared at the master bedroom suite. He quietly opened the door, then closed it behind him. Charles and Mary were still deep asleep until he flicked the light switch on to reveal himself.

Charles and Mary awoke to see the man standing at the foot of their bed. "Hello, Charles. Remember me?"

Charles rubbed his eyes and shook his head to clear the cobwebs. At first, he did not recognize the man. He seemed to be his age and had a familiar face. Then it hit him. "Samuel Goldsmith."

"That is right, Gramer. It is Samuel Goldsmith in the flesh," he said.

Charles was awake and clear-headed now. "Shouldn't you be rotting away in some small prison cell?"

"I got parole for good behavior after forty glorious years in a tiny, smelly cell. I never got to enjoy the treasure you stole from me, but the thought of one day possibly putting a bullet in your head kept me going all those years."

Charles pleaded with him for mercy. "You can kill me, Goldsmith, but spare my wife and daughter. They did nothing to you."

Mary interjected, "In fact, I have several pieces of jewelry in my nightstand right here. The value would be enough to spend the rest of your life in luxury. Just please spare my husband." She opened the drawer slowly, reached in, and said, "See, they are right here."

Instead of the jewels Goldsmith hoped to see, he was staring at a .45 caliber pistol pointed at him. Mary pulled the trigger, hitting Goldsmith in the chest. The next two shots found his throat and stomach. He fell to the ground, gasping for air as his hands tried to stop the blood flowing from an enormous hole where his Adam's apple used to be.

Charles turned his head to look at his wife. "Good shot."

"I am glad my father taught me how to shoot a gun so many years ago, and your father told me to always have one in my nightstand. Joseph always feared Goldsmith or Martin's men would come for us one day. It turns out he was right."

The invasion put quite a scare into the Gramers. They stayed up all night trying to figure out what to do with the body. Charles finally came up with an idea of how to dispose of the body and live a safe and peaceful life together.

"We have spent a lifetime looking over our shoulders. We will continue to do so if we continue to do the same old thing," he said. "Tonight, I am going to die on this boat."

Mary and Laura looked at him with puzzled looks. "Die?" they asked in unison.

"There will be a tragic 'accident' tonight. Our yacht will catch fire, and I will perish. You and Laura will somehow escape the fiery wreck," he continued to explain.

Mary had heard enough. "You are speaking nonsense, Charles. Stop this jabbering immediately."

321

"You do not understand, Mary. They will continue to come after me if I am alive. I will not die tonight... not really. I will simply remain in seclusion on the island while you return home with the tragic news of my death. Arrange my funeral and attend the services, pretending to cope with my loss. You shall only tell the true story to the rest of our family. No one else. When the dust settles, return to me here on Turks and Caicos, where we will sip rum drinks and dance to calypso music until our dying days."

Mary stood up and walked over to her husband. She gave him a big hug and said in a bad English accent, "That sounds like a brilliant plan, young chap. So long as my grandkids can visit, count me in."

THANK YOU FOR READING

Thank you for dedicating some of your reading time to *Secrets of Sea Pines*. I hope you enjoyed the adventures of Charles and Mary and that you are looking forward to their next story (Don't forget... Ron Martin is still alive!) This book is the first in a series of several Charles and Mary Gramer Adventures. The next two books in the series are called *Robbers Row* and *Spanish Wells*.

If you would like to be notified by email when I release a new book, you can sign up for my monthly newsletter at www. robthenovel.myshopify.com. The signup form is right at the top of the home page.

In addition to getting updates about another low country thriller, you will also be the first to read my next series featuring FBI Agent Lacie Webb. The first book is *The Disney Riddles*. Visit the website to see its trailer. It's another page turner.

I know not everyone likes to write book reviews, but if you are willing to spare the time to write a sentence or two about your thoughts on *Secrets of Sea Pines*, I encourage you to post a review at your favorite book vendor site or share a message with your social networking friends.

PLEASE POST A REVIEW ON AMAZON!
(It's so important for indie authors like me!)

Liked this one? There are more in the series!
Get your signed copy now!

ROBERT J. PERREAULT

ROBBER'S ROW

A CHARLES AND MARY **GRAMER THRILLER**

SPANISH
WELLS

A CHARLES AND MARY GRAMER THRILLER

ROBERT J. PERREAULT

Made in the USA
Middletown, DE
18 September 2023

38656201R00186